## BLOOD IS THICKER

"Fans of Elizabeth George, P.D. James, Martha Grimes, Caroline Graham . . . should rejoice at this new entry. . . ."
—*Mystery News*

"Some mystery novels begin with such character, such eccentricity and promise that the reader's response is childish glee. Such is the case with Ann C. Fallon's *Blood Is Thicker*. . . . There's humor along with pathos in this charmingly written story."
—*Toronto Sunday Sun*

## WHERE DEATH LIES

"As provocative as any murder you'll find in Agatha Christie or P.D. James . . . Fallon's Mr. Fleming will be welcome with mystery readers for a long, long time."
—*Irish Voice*

## DEAD ENDS

"Ann C. Fallon's Ireland comes alive in haunting and sometimes gritty reality. Brilliant writing and a joy to read!"
—*Audrey Peterson*

"With its prevailing aura of menace and rich Irish lore, *Dead Ends* establishes Ann Fallon in the forefront of today's young mystery writers."
—*Dorothy Salisbury Davis*

**AVAILABLE FROM POCKET BOOKS**

**Books by Ann C. Fallon**

Blood Is Thicker
Dead Ends
Potter's Field
Where Death Lies

Published by POCKET BOOKS

# POTTER'S FIELD

## ANN C. FALLON

**POCKET BOOKS**

New York   London   Toronto   Sydney   Tokyo   Singapore

This book is a work of fiction. Names, characters, places, and
incidents are either products of the author's imagination or are
used fictitiously. Any resemblance to actual events or locales or
persons, living or dead, is entirely coincidental.

An *Original* Publication of POCKET BOOKS

POCKET BOOKS, a division of Simon & Schuster Inc.
1230 Avenue of the Americas, New York, NY 10020

ISBN: 0-671-75136-0

First Pocket Books printing July 1993

10  9  8  7  6  5  4  3  2  1

Pocket and colophon are registered trademarks of
Simon & Schuster Inc.

Cover art by Richard Ross

Printed in the U.S.A.

*For my darling girl,*
*Eleanor*

JAMES FLEMING OPENED HIS EYES, GLANCED AROUND the small empty train station twenty miles outside Lima, and smiled a slow smile of anticipation.

He leaned back on the stone-hard little bench and stretched his long legs, studying for the moment the scuffed toes and scarred sides of his recently new, heavy leather boots. He shifted the rucksack he'd been using to pillow his head and placed it on his lap. Still no activity on the platform and yet still he smiled. Finally he stood up, shrugging into a heavy jersey. Despite the brilliant May morning sunshine, he felt slightly chilly. He walked to the end of the rustic platform that was level with the tracks and peered down the steep grade, squinting against the sun.

He first felt the tremor through the soles of his shoes, and sensed the slight change in the stillness of the air. A low throbbing and a movement so small as to be almost imperceptible, yet he knew he was right. Years of pursuing his avocation of riding trains on three continents had taught him this and much more. He didn't check his watch. No, better to leave that kind of satisfying timekeeping to the more regimented lines of Switzerland, Germany, even England. Here the weather, or terrorists, held more sway over scheduled departures and arrivals.

James watched as a local entrepreneur arrived on the scene. A small, wizened, burnished man pushed

1

a wicker trolley onto the platform from the shack-like station house. Balancing on it precariously were cracked mugs, most without handles, and a large urn. The heady aroma of very strong coffee wafted over to James and led him by the nose to purchase a steaming mug of nearly black liquid. The intense flavour shot through him as he gulped it down. He nodded to the old man as he handed back the mug, watching with interest as the Peruvian rinsed it in a bucket beside him on the floor.

Gradually a sense of anticipation stirred the air and the station master roused himself from his sleep in the booth and marched with some purpose onto the platform. Peering down the line he looked for the train that was expected from Lima and was ongoing to the high Andean terminus of Huancayo, on the roof of Peru.

"Five minutes," James heard him say in Spanish, the language still new to his unpracticed ear.

Anxious now, James waited to see this train of which he'd read so much, the train that plied the hardest and highest railway route in the world, the train that travelled through three vertical miles, sixteen thousand feet up into the magnificent Andes. It had been, in the days of steam, a train enthusiast's Nirvana. He sighed as he imagined what it would have been like to have seen, instead of the modern diesel that now came into view, the wonderful Andes 2-8-0 No. 206. The classic engine was now preserved in the Lima railway station, which he'd visited, as if at a shrine, on his arrival almost three weeks before.

But history still surrounded the line itself, and the arrival of the diesel engine created an excitement of its own as it moved heavily through the station and beyond, allowing only the passenger cars access to the platform. Quickly those aboard threw open the heavy doors. The men, for there were no women passengers, eagerly grabbed and drained the bottles of water they bought.

James moved along the line of cars, finding at last a compartment that was empty both of passengers and belongings. It was a small box with two slatted wooden benches and a window, which, he was glad to discover, both opened and closed. Pillowing his head again on his rucksack, he scrunched his long frame onto the bench, pulled his knitted cap down over his eyes, and fell into a light doze, expecting the jolt of the train's departure would waken him.

Why were Irish people in his bedroom, he wondered sleepily. He opened his eyes just a slit, peering through what he now realized was the stretched fabric of his hat. He saw two men hazily, as he slowly came awake, knowing now he was not in bed but on a train slowly negotiating an incline.

Irish voices though? Was he still dreaming? He listened intently, catching a phrase here and there, playing at still being asleep.

Snatches . . . stolen phrases.

The red-haired man murmured, ". . . it mightn't be so, Tom."

". . . don't be daft."

Had he said daft or deaf? James strained to hear.

"Why was he in Dublin . . ."

". . . an argument . . ." More mumbled words.

James ears pricked up.

"Drugs . . . I don't believe it . . ." The darker man's voice rose to a loud whisper.

"I agree. From what you say about Duggan . . ."

More lost phrases . . . and then some words, clear, startling . . .

". . . murder . . . never. I don't believe it, Tom," the voice trembled with intensity. ". . . surely to God he wasn't murdered in his own home!"

# 2

"THEN WHAT?" THE QUESTION HUNG IN THE AIR.

Somehow, suddenly, both men became aware of James's disguised attention. They looked quickly in his direction and then resumed their conversation in louder tones, speaking of a conference of some kind. He closed his eyes, feigning sleep, and after a suitable amount of time, moved as if he'd jolted himself awake by falling off the bench. He pushed up his hat and blinked into the shaded light of the compartment.

He smiled silently at the two men opposite him. He had been right, for he recognized in both the features of his countrymen: the reddish hair and freckles of the one slighter man, and the dark hair and ivory skin of his bigger, raw-boned companion. He glanced at their clothes: ordinary white shirts, inexpensive black pants, battered vinyl luggage at their feet. Too old to be students, surely. And they were hardly kitted out with the latest gear and camera that identified the tourist.

An almighty screech split the air, startling all three men into alertness. Like a high-pitched scream, the train's whistle sent some ominous signal. James glanced out the small grimy window and caught his breath: the train was passing over a deep craggy ravine in which swirled a turbulent green mist. He swallowed hard as the train seemed to rock against the narrow metal bridge. "Please God," he said softly, hoping that there was not, nor ever would be, a train coming in the opposite direction.

"Not to worry," said a pleasant voice, as though reading his mind. "We've travelled this line many times."

James grunted in response but could not yet draw his eyes from the perilous view. He opened the window, straining to see to the other side of the ravine, willing the train onwards to reach solid ground.

At last he let out the breath he'd been unconsciously holding and he sagged back against the seat. He closed the window and turned then to address his companions, amazed to see now it was they who had both fallen asleep.

Thirsty from the dryness of the increased altitude, he foraged in his rucksack for a bottle of water. Uncapping it, he glanced up to see the red-headed man watching him with a twinkle in his eye. James proffered the bottle and then withdrew it and reached for the packet of sterilizing tablets, one of which he prepared to drop in the bottle.

"Not to worry," said the man. "I've been here long enough so that the water doesn't trouble me. Keep your bottle for yourself. We have our own."

His companion stirred but remained fast asleep.

James drank a few sips and capped the bottle. "Do I detect an Irish accent then?" he said at last.

"Indeed and you do."

"Can a man go nowhere . . . ?" exclaimed James only half in jest.

"You know the old saying, I'm sure," replied the red-headed man. "There's no place you can go in this world an' there's not been an Irishman there before you."

James laughed. The man was pleasant and discerning and after all, it was mere vanity to wish to be the only Irishman to be travelling the trains of Peru. His curiosity overcame him. "Well, I must say it's a surprise nonetheless. Are you tourists?"

"Hardly." The man laughed again. "My name is John, Father John if you like, and this is Father Tom asleep at me elbow. And we're nearly native Peruvians, we're here so long. We don't get many tourists up this far. But you strike me as a tourist now."

James described briefly his long-standing love affair with trains, and the circumstances of his trip. He spoke of the world renown, in train circles, of the Lima–Huancayo line as the world's highest and hardest route. And he explained that once, instead of a diesel engine belching out a clingy black oily exhaust into the pure air, a great Andes-type 2-8-0 steam engine would have performed the task with a far greater dignity. John nodded, indicating that he understood the source of James's enthusiasm.

"They've a good few trains here in Peru and I feel I've been on nearly all of them. But it's hard travellin', with the crowds on some of them."

He and Tom, John explained, were missionary priests who ministered to two neighbouring parishes high in the mountains. They were returning from a retreat held in Lima for their religious order. Tom, now awake, joined their conversation, and for some time their talk ranged far and wide. But as the train ground to a halt, the three men stood up, eager to stretch their legs. They stepped from the train, expecting to find refreshments. And a toilet. But instead of a way station all that greeted them was a flat, arid clearing, rimmed by forest.

James sensed immediately the tension in the two men. Glancing around they quickly stepped back on board. None of the other passengers alighted either. But they watched as the armed guards stepped out onto the rocky ground and walked cautiously the length of the train.

"Something's the matter . . ." James thought aloud.

"Surely, but what it is, we've no make nor model on it," said Tom nervously. "This is no stop. There's no halt, not even a crossing. . . ." He peered across into the trees. "Guerrillas?" Tom looked questioningly at John.

"The Shining Path?" James whispered, but a dour look from Tom silenced him instantly.

They watched as the guards returned to their cars and breathed a sigh of relief as the train began to roll again with a healthy clickety-clack of steel on steel.

They had travelled just a few miles when there was another grinding stop, but this time the engineer came to each car to report the news. As Tom translated, James learned that the train would rest while goods were unloaded, and that there was ample time for the passengers to refresh themselves, particularly at the cafe run by the engineer's sister near the station house.

Amused and undaunted, the three men and a number of their fellow passengers disembarked and made their way towards the wonderful smells of coffee and fresh bread. Over their simple meal John and Tom regaled James with stories of difficult travel on horseback through the harsh local topography as they ministered to the needs of their Indian parishioners.

"Still you must be glad to get back to Ireland," said James.

"Oh, it's two worlds, let's face it," said Tom, his own face white and drawn despite the overlying tan. "There's the world and there's the Third World. The other life loses its flavour when you've been out here . . ." His voice was sombre. "There's those of us who can never really go back . . ."

They finished their coffee and bread in silence and returned to the train, settling in as it slowly moved on. And, as is the way with travellers, it was now James's turn to tell them something of himself. Feeling slightly embarrassed, he handed each of them his business card. His own career as a solicitor specializing in wills and estates appeared, he now felt, relatively dull. And so enthusiastically, eloquently, he described to them the thrill of his journey from Cuzco, the old capital city, to Machu Picchu and its Incan fortress.

But the two priests were clearly less interested in James's train travels than they were in his career. In response to their questions, and with an eye to the conversation he'd overheard earlier, he made mention of the cases he had solved in recent years in Dublin.

"You don't say? A latter-day Sherlock Holmes," exclaimed Tom genuinely when James paused.

"Impressive," said John, glancing up at Tom's enthusiastic tone.

The train was slowing, nearing the terminus at Huancayo.

John and Tom suddenly excused themselves to walk the short corridor outside the compartment. James, curious, observed them closely but this time overheard nothing.

On their return Tom began abruptly.

"Listen, James, I've a favour to ask of you."

"Yes?"

Tom looked at John who shrugged.

"Go on," said James kindly. "Whatever you say to me won't go any further. Us Protestants are very trustworthy, you know." His banter lessened the tension and Tom resumed.

"In a nutshell, a friend of mine, Patrick Duggan, recently died. Back home in Ireland . . ."

"Yes?" said James neutrally.

8

"They say he was murdered," continued Tom, watching James intently.

"What!" James was surprised, not expecting this information despite his earlier eavesdropping. "When was this?"

"Some weeks ago, in April. But I just learned of it this weekend, at the retreat. Some of the priests had Irish papers. I was just reading them, to catch up with the news. I could hardly believe it when I saw the reports . . . Duggan!"

"I must have seen mention of it," said James, scratching his chin. "Give me some details . . ."

"That's just it. I only know what I read." He reached in the bag at his feet, producing a tattered *Evening Press,* folded to the small article about Duggan.

James quickly scanned it. "Yes," he said sighing. "I recall it now. But I know no more than you. I think the news was in the papers and on the television, briefly. As it says here, the police felt it was a robbery gone wrong. I'm very sorry," he added, as he handed the paper back to Tom.

John nodded sympathetically and took up the thread. "When you spoke just now of your various cases, your investigations, it occurred to Tom that perhaps, well," he hesitated, "perhaps you could look into it for him?"

Tom broke in. He opened his big calloused hands wide. "I knew Patrick Duggan very well, Fleming, when we were just lads down the country. Soul mates, I guess you'd say. It grieves me, I can tell you, it grieves me to think of his life taken away in such a terrible manner. He lived in Wicklow. I don't know what he was doing in Dublin, or why someone would think to murder him. He had nothing of value, I mean that in the material sense. A poor young lad." He shook his head angrily, impatiently. "I've no way of finding out more about his death. Time has already passed. Perhaps the police have solved the case by now. If you'd just let me know that? Or anything else that you might find out? It would just be between you and me. But I tell you this, James, there'll be no money in it for you."

James shook his head.

"You won't do it?" John blurted out, clearly pained.

"I won't do it for money. I've never taken any of these kinds of cases for money, although money has come my way. Yes, I'll look into it for you, but I can't promise you anything."

As the train slowly pulled into the substantial station at Huancayo, chugging with exhaustion of iron and steel after eleven difficult hours, Tom scribbled his local mailing address on a bit of paper. James put it in his notebook.

"What did he do?" he thought to ask before they parted, the priests hustling, pushing their way through the crowds to catch their bus.

"He was an artist, worked in pottery. And I know he lived in Wicklow. The papers got *that* wrong. . . . It's bitter I tell you!"

The men were running now, and James fell back, watching as they gained the bus as it was pulling away. And as he waved to them, a sudden loneliness, a sense of finality washed over him. He saw John looking back, raising his right hand in a formal blessing.

"God keep you safe on your journey through life," he called and then they were gone, swallowed up in the crowds of Peruvians pressing onto the bus, swallowed up as the bus departed into the ever-present green mist that enveloped station and people, that swirled around them all, as it rose from its source in the tropical vegetation in the deep valleys far below.

# 3

IN OTHER CIRCUMSTANCES JAMES WOULD HAVE BEEN incensed at the notion that a scheduled train, which he'd travelled thousands of miles to meet, was in fact not about to come in until the following morning. But because he was in Peru for the express purpose of riding this particular line, James was patience itself.

He habitually endowed the trains he encountered with animal qualities. He admired these trains as a horse lover might admire a variety of horse breeds. One might be a high-strung Thoroughbred, necessitating endless care and concern but, in return, filling its world with the beauty of line and proportion, energy and speed. Yet another might resemble a farm horse, a workhorse broad in the shoulder, a model of strength in its every sinew and muscle, its very bones heavy with endurance. The absent train James viewed as a rare species, worthy of patience and devotion, such as that due a breed which, because of the forces of modern life, might one day no longer be needed and, no longer sustained, would in the end become extinct.

So instead of feeling irritation he was able to keep his delicious anticipation intact. And his apprehension. For not until tomorrow would he finally know if he could see and touch and, at last, ride on one of the most outstanding steam trains in the history of the railway.

He booked himself a room at the railway hotel and, without stowing his bag, he set off for a walk through the town of Huancayo. Within minutes he found himself in a bustling market area open even at this, the shag end of the day. After much indecision at the various stalls, James purchased a tightly woven striped rug wrought in deep earth tones. He bought it for his mother as a trophy to prove that he'd fulfilled at least one of his dreams. And because he had no one else to buy it for, he admitted ruefully. Another rug, this one in soft pastels, immediately brought to mind Sarah. And in the hope that he would see her again soon, he bought it.

From an unsmiling woman, garbed traditionally in round brimmed hat, colorful skirts, and heavy woollen shawl, he purchased a coarse alpaca-wool sweater and hesitantly put it on. He looked at the woman and received a small nod, as good as a smile of approval he hoped. Lumbered with the two rolls of carpet that were heavier than he anticipated, he returned to his hotel as night fell suddenly and totally.

In his small third-floor room he looked out at the sky; not one star penetrated the light fog that surrounded him and the town. Beneath him he spotted an inviting orange light, cast from the frosted window of what seemed to be an eatery. Having washed and shaved he ambled down to fill his belly. And over a jug of local beer he reflected on the beautiful elusive Sarah.

Tall, slim, with deep blue eyes and an inner serenity, a composure he had never encountered in anyone except the old nuns of his acquaintance, she had intrigued him from the moment they'd met. A musical prodigy as a child, she was now in the blooming years of her career as a concert violinist, with fame and renown surrounding her. Her career and her wealth, which he'd had a hand in establishing for her, made her seem to him at times unreachable. Yet still he harboured hopes, dreams of marriage with her, of a home and family with her. If only. . . . He shook himself and stood up, suddenly weary. Returning to his hotel, he pondered on his meeting with the two priests that day and on their shared confidences. How odd to be thrown together with strangers and, for a few hours or a day, become so close and then be parted, divided by circumstance, just as circumstance had brought you together. Was it so in general? he wondered, not for the first time. Were all meetings merely random chance or the product of some larger design?

He stretched out on the narrow hard bed and threw a woven blanket over his body. Had meeting Sarah also been part of some only vaguely understood plan? His heart sought an answer, but sleep came quickly, obscuring for now the solution to this question.

The morning broke clear, and with it his own sombre mood of the night before. After quickly packing, he settled his bill with the railway hotel's proprietor.

His heart raced with a keen mixture of anticipation and dread as he literally ran to the station. Yes! It was there! And at last James beheld the object of his immediate desires.

The trains that usually ran this three-foot, zero-inch–gauge line from Huancayo to Huancavelica had for years been pulled by diesel engines. But James had hoped against hope that he would have the good fortune and timing to be present when one of the steam engines, which were still kept in reserve for emergency situations, might be in use. And now here it was—a dream in steam come true!

Unself-consciously, he stood in awe, gazing open-mouthed at the Hunslet 2-8-2, No. 107, as the locomotive stood like some great mythical beast taking on water for the journey. Finally, drawing breath, he took out his camera and scrupulously recorded every feature, large and small, of the rare locomotive that would inevitably pass into history.

As he photographed, a man whom he determined to be the engineer approached him, waving and hurling what James assumed rightly to be questions, unfriendly ones. The man pointed to the two armed guards standing on the platform, staring in his direction.

James stopped snapping the pictures and reached into his bag. The man drew back, suddenly fearful, but James pulled out a small leather folder. He opened it and gesturing in a friendly manner, called the man's attention to the photos within.

As he turned over the pages of pictures of other trains, steam engines, and coal tenders, the man's face relaxed and he looked into James's eyes, trying to read the answers there. He pointed at one or two engines in the folder, smiling in recognition. James pointed to pictures of himself standing on the platform, and in one case shovelling coal with a fireman. His interlocutor pointed from the pictures to James and back, nodding at last.

James took out his phonetic phrasebook and struggled to ask in the simplest terms possible if he could ride in the cab with the engineer. He showed his ticket purchased the evening before and was rewarded with a slap on the back. He assumed this meant the engineer consented to his request. And, after an introduction of sorts to another man, apparently the fireman, the three climbed aboard. James stowed his bag and camera in an insulated box which held the oxygen bottles kept on hand for any passenger who experienced the *soroche*, mountain sickness from the thin air. And when the ten or so guards positioned themselves in the cars, James was given

14

the privilege of letting off the whistle to signal their departure. The train began to move slowly at first, summoning its resources like a panther preparing to pounce.

James joyfully hung out the open cab window, looking down the line, watching the tracks ahead as they bent zig-zag fashion to accommodate the steep grade, listening to the unique throb of the steam engine and the hypnotic clackety-clack of the wheels.

If he'd been asked, which he never was, what it was he loved about trains, he couldn't have said. It was an amalgam of many things: his imaginings of the men who had hacked out a path from the forest and the stone of the mountain, of the navvies who laid the tracks, of the minds that had designed the incredible bridges that hung over bottomless ravines, of all the planning that had gone on so many years before. Or was it that the steam engine connected the modern era to an era long past, where man and machine had had to work in actual physical harmony to succeed? Or that each engine had a history of its own, from the yard where it was built to the lines it rode, living for decades a full and useful life. Or perhaps it was the idea of the service the trains rendered hauling needed goods, reuniting families, bringing someone to a new life, or bringing someone back to a home long missed and yearned for. Maybe the answer lay in the travelling itself, the metaphor for life's long journey and its vicissitudes? There was a word that said it all, a word that made such a passion clear to any other like-minded soul: romance.

This love affair with the Hunslet 2-8-2, No. 107 filled James's last week in Peru. By the end of it he was fitter than he'd been in two years and nearly sated with the detailed information he'd recorded about the engine. Many happy hours lay ahead when, back in Dublin, he would reread his notes and compare his experience and knowledge with others, both in books and in person. And so it was that he consoled himself, as the wonderful Hunslet steamed back into its station at Huancayo.

The next day was spent travelling on the diesel back via Huancavelica to Lima—his last journey on the hardest and highest route in the world. And as he passed through the station where he'd first encountered Tom and John, he was reminded again of their shared stories. And in his heart he bid them and the mountains a sad farewell.

He rose early on his last day in Lima. The elegance of his hotel, its heavy Spanish opulence and decor, the rich varied food and international wines, were jarring to him. He had a late-morning flight and was soon packed, his mood glum and irritable. In the crowded lobby he stopped for some chewing gum and some reading material. Scanning the many Peruvian papers on the racks, his eye caught one photo, which seemed common to all, a small grainy picture of a priest with a Roman collar. He picked up a paper, ignoring the man demanding payment. Sick at heart, he studied the benign face of a younger Father John. The vendor fell silent as James turned to him.

"Do you speak English?"

"Yes."

"What does it say about this priest?" James demanded.

"What they all say."

"I don't read Spanish," James shouted.

"It says, señor, that the padre was murdered, tortured with some peasants by . . ." the man shrugged expressively.

"The *Sendero Luminosa?*"

"Who can say, señor," said the man, uneasily

glancing around them, cautious even in this urban setting. He put out his hand and James gave him the money.

Too stunned to think, James moved automatically towards the street. He was assailed with questions. He was filled with a desire to go back to the mountainous villages, to seek out Father Tom.

He raced to the taxi rank and jumped in one of the cars, directing the driver to take him to the train station. He would go back. He would find Father Tom. And then what? As the taxi stalled in heavy Lima traffic, he realized how impractical his thoughts were.

And, full of anger, he realized that he could do little to combat events. Father John, who'd given him his blessing as the bus had pulled away, had himself been swallowed up in a conflict of terrible dimensions. Sobered, sombre, James redirected the taxi driver to take him to the airport, and home.

# 4

As James parked his car in one of the spaces reserved for him and his employees in the carpark near his Merrion Square premises, he took a deep breath. It was going to be hard to return, to set aside his adventures in Peru. He thought again of John, and of Tom and his promise to him. The link with Peru was not yet broken. But focussing his mind on the present, he ran up the steps of the pale granite Georgian four-storey building and threw open the door.

"Honey, I'm baaack!" he called in an American twang.

"So soon?" Maggie, his red-headed office manager, said dryly as she came from the reception area, glancing archly at her watch.

"Very funny, Maggie," he said and, in seeing her and the comfortable old office, he felt a sudden sense of homecoming.

He settled into his old leather chair, the one that had stood in his father's office and served him well. He pulled it up to his desk, happily tackling the three weeks' accumulation of correspondence, briefs, and updates on the work of the other two solicitors and the four clerks in his firm. His staff had done well in his absence, and James was proud of them and proud of his own judgment in hiring them. He felt comfortable with the responsibility he had taken on when he'd bought out the small firm from Fitzgerald, his previous employer. His staff could now run things quite well without him. But the idea startled him. Perhaps that wasn't so good, he thought ruefully.

At a three o'clock conference he and the staff bent their heads over the government's new inheritance tax law and again he felt all was well in hand. But at five, as his staff drifted away, another mood fell. He walked restlessly through the offices, arriving eventually at Maggie's desk. As she completed her work for the day he twiddled the decorations that adorned her desk.

She looked up finally, her wide, frank blue eyes smiling. "It'll pass, James."

"What?" he said, jumping as her words cut into his thoughts.

"We all do feel it, the first-day-back blues. You need to find someone to go out and play." Maggie's sarcasm was ever to the fore.

"That's ridiculous," James bristled.

"I know, but there it is. As I've told you before, for an eligible handsome bachelor you have the dullest social life I've ever encountered."

"Is this supposed to make me feel better?"

"Not at all. It's merely an observation. Here, these are your phone messages, judge for yourself."

While he'd been in conference Maggie had taken his calls. He looked with happy anticipation at the blue slips of paper.

"This is it?"

"Afraid so," she said as she covered her word processor with its fitted plastic shield.

"Two calls from my mother?" His voice rose.

"Yes. Now you have someone to go out and play with."

"Jaysus, Maggie, you're worse than any relative I could name."

Maggie laughed loud and, throwing on her purple

coat that somehow blended beautifully with her wild mane of red hair, she was gone, leaving James feeling sorry for himself.

As he glanced at his diary for the week, he noted again that he had a lunchtime engagement the next day with Mr. O'Connor, a man he'd met at the Dublin Horse Show the previous year. O'Connor had phoned recently to discuss the writing of his will. And James was delighted since the issue promised to be a complicated one, involving sons of two marriages, and two wives.

"I can't even get one wife, never mind two," he said forlornly to his desk. And against his better judgment he locked the office and turned his car towards his childhood home.

It was still daylight, the last bright hour of an early summer evening. James found his mother in her garden, which, for the suburbs, was large and wide, a garden where he and his brother Donald had spent many hours in the long summer evenings playing football or bicycle polo. Happy hours, surely. And yet now he and Donald, a successful physician in private practice in a surgery added on to the parental home, barely spoke. Whose fault, James wondered, and then shook his head. Such introspection about his family was no longer in his disciplined nature—it got him nowhere, as he'd learned years before.

"Mum?" he called at last, rousing her from her kneeling position where she was inexpertly bedding out the Michaelmas daisies and struggling with clumps of long straggly weeds.

"James! Why, I didn't hear you. You're just in time. Finish this bit of the border here and I'll wash my hands."

James groaned. The "bit" of border extended a

good six feet and was a tangled mass of bindweed.
"Honestly, Mum . . ."

But she waved his protest away. "Good hard work
in the garden never harmed anyone."

"No, but what about my suit?" He looked ruefully
at his custom-made pants and polished brogues.

"Donald never complains," she said sharply.

"Donald never does the weeding. Is he here then?"
James asked, wondering if his brother kept late hours
at the surgery.

"Don't be ridiculous. What would Donald be doing
here at this hour on a Monday evening? He's very
strict, you know that. He keeps short hours. It's good
for the patients, let's them know he's not at their
every beck and call." She brushed the soil from her
hands and gave James the trowel and small three-
pronged fork.

"I didn't know it was custom for a doctor to keep
banker's hours," James snapped.

"The best ones do, dear, and Donald expects to
be among that elite. You wouldn't believe how his
name has spread. Very trendy clientele he gets here.
A nice class of people . . ."

"No gunshot wounds then, or unwed mothers?"
asked James, but his sarcasm was lost on his mother.

"No, and none of those drug types."

"How fortunate."

"Indeed," said Mrs. Fleming, looking at him
closely. "My goodness, is this what people love to
call a tan?"

James beamed.

"You look as though you have—what is it now—
malaria, something tropical . . ."

"What?" squawked James, ever ready to be
insulted.

"James! Why don't you pop in and see Donald
tomorrow. You probably contracted jarndyce in that

Peruvian place you insisted on seeing. Terrible water, they say."

"It's jaundice, Mother."

"See! I knew it," she said victoriously.

"No, no. Jarndyce is the court case in Dickens's *Bleak House* . . . A story that always reminded me of this mad family," he added pointedly.

"Now you're raving, James. I tell you, it's all from that dreadful hot climate in Peru . . ."

"Mother, I have a tan. Other people perceive this as healthy, even attractive."

"Well, it's not, with your sallow skin. But it will soon fade and you'll look much better. Now if you don't mind . . ."

As his mother wandered off, not, presumably, to put on the kettle for a cup of tea, James knelt gingerly on an old scrap of carpet and proceeded to roll up his sleeves. Actually James enjoyed weeding, finding it therapeutic, unbidden thoughts floating to his mind. This time he found himself longing for a patch of ground to call his own. He dreamed, as he had done in recent months, of what it would be like to have a house of his own, with a garden back and front. But then he thought of all those empty rooms. His flat, although large, would never seem as empty as a house. Typical, he thought, as he extricated one particularly long and lusty vine of bindweed from a despairing rosebush and followed it to its roots: what you gain on the roundabouts, you lose on the swings. Yes, he'd gain the pleasure of a garden, a sense of roots—he laughed aloud at his pun—but he'd lose that same pleasure in the loneliness of a house that was not a home.

As he wandered desultorily back into his mother's house he saw she had changed into one of her summer frocks, one that her nameless "woman" had made up for her.

"You've finished? Good."

"Yes," said James, smiling in spite of himself.

"We can leave then?" she said, bustling around to the front hall to retrieve a matching purse. "It's so mild tonight I imagine they'll have drinks on the terrace."

"Who?" said James, confused.

"The Wilsons, of course."

"When?"

"Now. Tonight, I told you," said his mother, exasperated.

"You said no such thing."

"Well then, I told that girl Martha . . ."

"Maggie. And she's not a girl, she's the office manager."

"Whatever she is, you need a new one, James, if she can't write down a simple message."

James felt an impulse to tell her that he'd only rung her back for lack of something better to do, but he didn't. It was hopeless to protest. In her mind, his mother had firmly decided he knew of this arrangement for the evening. And although he was very dubious indeed, he washed his hands and prepared to spend yet another evening of polite and indescribable boredom with his mother's friends and their unmarriageable daughter, Jean.

# 5

JAMES TOSSED HIS PENCIL IN THE AIR AS MAGGIE ENtered his office the following Friday, her arms laden with manila folders.

"Take me away!" he exclaimed.

"Take you?" replied Maggie archly, panting theatrically.

"Away, Maggie, take me away!"

"Sorry, James. I'm taking myself away to Mayo. The Ma and the Da are having their fortieth anniversary this weekend." Maggie fell into her broad country accent. "And the brothers and sisters are throwing a hooley in their honour."

"A hooley? Sounds great. Dancing, drinking, and great crack altogether, yes?"

"Yes, and family only, James. Which in our case runs to the hundreds. But thanks for letting me take the afternoon." She raised her eyebrows, daring him to contradict her. "Now, what's up with you?"

"Need I say?"

"Sarah?"

"Yes, Sarah, or the lack of Sarah. I'm fed up, Maggie, up to the bloody teeth. You know what?"

"You're entering the monastery?"

"I don't have to. No, listen. I've been thinking about buying a house, seriously. Since a few days now. But really longer than that. I think that's what's been wrong with me, only I've just realized it. I'm longing for a house of my own."

"What about your gorgeous flat?" Maggie had always admired the cool Art Deco interior of James's bachelor flat.

"That's just it, Maggie. It's a flat. I want a solid two-storey house, perhaps with a garden, front and back. . . ." He waved his hands vaguely.

"You're longing to till the soil, is it?" Maggie smiled as she stood up, pulling a hairpin out of her pocket. James watched as she expertly swirled her long thick hair into a loose French twist and secured it with the single pin. She seemed to James suddenly transformed from office colleague to a glamorous free spirit, all in one small movement. Her blue eyes twinkled.

"Perhaps that's just it," he said at last. "I'd like to get my hands dirty, I'd like to build something, I'd like . . ."

". . . to settle down," she finished as she put her hand on the heavy mahogany door. "You're too settled by half, James."

"Thanks for all the encouragement," James said moodily as she shut the door with a satisfying thud. But anxious to keep his lunchtime appointment with Sergeant Moran at the Kevin Street Police Station regarding the more pressing matter of Patrick Duggan, he quickly followed her out the door.

On leaving the station an hour later, James decided to walk rather than drive to the Liberties, a centuries-old section of Dublin sheltering in the long and ancient shadows cast by the great cathedrals of Christchurch and St. Patrick's. It was a mere half-hour's stroll across Dublin and across the history of that city. On this rare and glorious June afternoon, he walked leisurely, reviewing his earlier conversation with Sergeant Moran.

Unfortunately, there hadn't been much to tell. Patrick Duggan, a strong young man in his late twenties, had been found dead in April. Now, more than a month later, the case was still open. The police had been called by a neighbour who'd noticed that Duggan's front door had been standing wide open all the afternoon. This wasn't so unusual, the man had said, but he hadn't seen Duggan passing in and out, as he was wont to do. The house had been still as death.

The neighbour, a retired man in his late sixties, had little else to do that dull April day but watch Duggan's door out of sheer curiosity. Eventually he observed a street cat wander in and not wander out. On this pretext, he had gone to investigate. He was sorry he had, for what he'd found was Duggan dead on the floor of the small sitting room.

According to Sergeant Moran, the police had little to go on. The medical examiner had determined Duggan was killed by a blow to the head by a heavy pottery planter. Pieces of the base, unglazed but fired, apparently in Duggan's own kiln, had been found embedded in his skull. Other fragments were discovered in his hair and surrounding the body.

The police believed it had been a sudden, unpremeditated blow, and yet they'd found no fingerprints. There was a good collection of compact discs on a shelf in the room, and a space where a CD player might have stood. There was no CD player in the flat. As a result they concluded that Duggan had surprised a burglar in the act, that the burglar panicked and hit Duggan, probably not intending to kill him, and that the same burglar had fled with the CD player.

James observed the area as he walked, following the sergeant's directions to Duggan's house. It was a mixed neighbourhood. The houses were all nine-

teenth century artisan dwellings made of brick; one-
and two-storey row houses lining street after small
narrow street, creating a warren that in its day had
been virtually self-contained. The quiet streets were
neat and clean, with only a few cars parked up on
the narrow pavements. There was unemployment in
the area certainly, which led to petty burglaries. And
like any area of the city, it was vulnerable to outsiders, drug addicts looking for ready goods to sell
quickly.

The police had concluded Patrick Duggan was yet
another innocent victim of random urban crime.
James became suddenly bitter that nowadays such
deaths were nearly routine, thus losing their inherent
power to harrow the public soul.

Many young, optimistic artists had been attracted
to the Liberties in recent years as its small houses
became available. The older tenants had died and
their families scattered to the suburbs. Artists, writers, academics, had since bought into the area, lending it a certain cachet in Dublin.

From his pocket James took Duggan's old-
fashioned heavy front-door key with its attached police identity tag. Moran had felt James's request for
the loan of the key acceptable when James casually
placed on his desk two tickets for an upcoming sold-
out football match. Now he placed the key in the
lock of number seven. The door was painted a deep
blue as were the two tiny window frames on either
side. Few people were about and he saw only a yellow dog fast asleep in the sun.

Letting himself into the house, he was suddenly
filled with dread, as if he would see Duggan's body
still sprawled on the floor. But of course the floor
was clear, swept clean by the men of the forensic
team. He shut the door behind him, letting his eyes
grow used to the darkness. He found himself in the

sitting room, about ten feet square. Both windows let in light filtered and diminished by the nylon curtains hanging limp and gray.

The room was covered with a fine film of dust, that was clean and still, like a soft mantle. Shelving had been rigged on each wall from floor to ceiling. The shelves held a vast array of pottery: earthenware bowls and vases of a natural red colouring, some glazed, many still unglazed, perhaps on purpose. On other shelves were neat rows of stoneware, pitchers, jugs, and vases of all sizes. Some of these, too, were unglazed, but most were tinted deep blue. And beneath these were a series of stoneware containers with fitted lids. Many were undecorated, but some bore the indentation of the words flour and sugar. These also were coloured in the same intriguing blue glaze. What James found most appealing lay on the shelves on the north wall. These were shallow bowls, unglazed, and retaining the look and feel of the earth from which their clay was dug. These terra-cotta bowls and rimmed plates felt rough and warm as he touched their surfaces. The design, the texture, the simplicity recalled the native pottery he'd seen on display in the markets of Peru. There were even more pots in their natural clay colouring, others stippled in maroon or in deep blue, and yet more, painted in patterns that brought to mind Native American motifs. James realized that Duggan had stored his finished work in all its variety right in his living area.

The east wall was lined entirely with very appealing and detailed modeled figures, also made from fired clay: small dogs, horses, cats, four-legged farm animals—Duggan's concession to commercialism perhaps, James thought. The deep earth tones and absence of a shiny glazed finish appealed to James's taste. He fingered some, very much taken with one piece that strongly resembled the yellow dog asleep outside. James was struck by the notion that Duggan had truly drawn on his own simple experience of nature, whether that of the country or a Dublin city street.

There were other telling signs of Duggan's life. An old easy chair looked well worn and comfortable. A resplendent peacock fan concealed a small fireplace. A stack of reading material was piled haphazardly by the side of the chair, mostly art magazines and colour supplements from the English Sunday papers. A small table stood at the ready, a bottle of Jameson whiskey and a clean but dusty glass by its side. James wondered how this unstable arrangement had remained intact during the violent confrontation between Duggan and his killer.

James walked through a low doorway into the rear of the house. The minute kitchen was dominated by an old soapstone sink standing on legs. Beside this relic of plumbing history stood a squat-legged gray enamel cooker. There was no fridge. He tried the light but the electricity had been cut off. James was amazed the tiny space could hold so much. Curious, he pushed aside a curtain that hung between the little kitchen and a third room, a bedroom accommodating a bed and dresser. This room was equally spartan. A pair of reading glasses rested on the bed locker, a few well-thumbed paperbacks lay on the shelf beneath, poetry mostly. James opened the locker door, revealing a large stack of papers and letters. Sighing aloud he pulled them out and placed them on the bed and patiently settled to reading them through.

His own impression that all artists led chaotic lives was slowly altered as he perceived that Duggan was orderly in all his habits. First he read through a clipped sheaf of letters, some personal but the majority of which were answers to inquiries to galleries and exhibitions throughout Ireland and Britain. Duggan's address book was thick with hundreds of entries. Again the majority related to his work as a potter. Among the entries were personal friends, he guessed, since some names had lines drawn through, or new addresses or numbers amended. Father Tom's address in Peru, James noted, was neatly pencilled in. James found invoices, neatly done out by hand, records of shipments, payments received. All of these bore Duggan's previous Wicklow address, and James learned that Duggan had supplied many shops throughout Ireland with a line of stoneware pots for flour, tea, sugar, and sundry dry goods. In fact this stoneware seemed to provide the mainstay of his income.

James continued his perusal and found Duggan's passport, a birth certificate, his deed to his house. He found a ledger where Duggan had kept careful track of his relatively small income and outgo, and James, thinking of his own improvidence, was impressed to see how frugally and carefully Duggan had lived.

Stuck in among the ledger's pages was an eight-by-ten–inch black-and-white photograph. It was obviously out of place in this tidy ledger. James studied it curiously. A bit grainy, it showed a rather charming child, perhaps four or five years of age. James recognized the style of the wool coat, the matching cap. He was amused to see scrawny bare legs, crumpled knee socks, feet encased in buckle shoes. It was the garb of a child of a prosperous family of two decades ago. James tried to assess the photograph's impact on him. It was not merely the charm of a curious period piece, but the expression of the child. Behind round, black-rimmed glasses were the startled eyes of a child not quite frightened, but decidedly wary. Startled yet intense. A strong intelligence there, thought James.

The young boy was not smiling. In fact the little

mouth had a slight pull at the corner, not quite a grimace. James wondered if perhaps he were afraid of the camera. He looked again at the thin legs. Perhaps the child had been ill. His build looked frail and he was tightly clasping the hand of a young sturdy woman, dressed as a nurse, whose face was turned, bent towards the child as though speaking to him. In the background was an English saloon car dating from the sixties, an expensive one, perhaps waiting for the boy. It was not a happy picture and its image remained with James, suggesting a past for Duggan that James found curious, and worth looking into. He set the photo aside and continued his study of Duggan's life on paper, but he found nothing else of such compelling interest. James replaced everything as it was, except the single grainy photo.

Returning to the sitting room he rummaged through the only two bottom shelves that held objects other than pots. There he found the neat stack of compact discs that featured largely in the police report. James noted the small space near an electric outlet where a player might have stood. Some expensive art books rested on the shelf above in company with a vinyl album of photographs. James leafed through the album, noting the photos of Duggan as a child and youth. Duggan's passport photo clearly resembled the album pictures of him as a boy. James found several copies and took one. Puzzled, James compared the grainy eight-by-ten photo of the boy with the buckle shoes with the pictures in the album. This frail, be-spectacled child was hardly Duggan.

James's curiosity persisted, but there was no way of ascertaining why Duggan had kept this particular photo in his ledger. He returned the album to its place and, without a twinge of conscience, pocketed the black-and-white photo.

James turned his attention to the exterior buildings

in back of the small house. The yard was paved with ancient cobbles and crowded into it were two low outbuildings whose back walls were formed by the brick walls of the perimeter. Such walls were common to all the yards, resembling little brick pens appended to each house. On quick inspection James found the basic lavatory with its old-style pull chain linked to a cistern above his head. Beside the outhouse was a recently enlarged and remodeled coal house, which now housed a complete studio. James examined the top-loading electric kiln curiously. Nearby stood Duggan's potter's wheel, which, as James discovered on examination, was operated by a foot treadle. On the wall nearest the wheel hung the simple tools of the potter's trade: ribs, prickers, sponges, and sponge-sticks.

In a third building James found plastic-lined boxes of red powdered clay, buckets, more plastic bags, a bag of broken pottery, and a wedging board. Everything was scrupulously clean, neat, and well ordered.

All stood in readiness for the artist to return, thought James. He replaced the padlocks on the sheds and, returning to the kitchen, locked the back door also. Wandering back to the sitting room, he dropped heavily into the upholstered chair and stared at the objects on the shelves.

He tried hard to get a sense of the man who'd lived within these four walls. Part of the problem was that James himself knew very little about the work of a potter. He tried to imagine the man whose livelihood rested in the skill and strength and artistry of his own two hands. Duggan had supported himself with his own work, as James knew from the ledgers. He tried to picture those hands, large, muscular, roughened.

Another part of the problem, James realized, was that Duggan had hardly been settled in this little cozy house when he'd been murdered. Apart from Duggan's pottery, there was little to indicate his personality. He hadn't had even the time to hang a few pictures, to buy a little furniture as he made more money. And yet, there had been a personality at work here: James imagined it to be trusting, simple, secure, hardworking, orderly, and finally—as James studied the clean lines of the pottery—honest.

Gentle too, perhaps? James stood up. Perhaps too gentle to strike out at a youthful robber, a scrawny teenager, frightened in the act of stealing something Duggan perhaps did not value beyond its price? He hadn't defended himself, the medical examiner had concluded. He'd been struck from behind, yet he had been standing dead centre in the room. Had he turned his back? Had the killer emerged from the kitchen, grabbing a heavy pot, to knock out Duggan, but not to kill him? Had it really been an accident? He needed to learn a lot more about this man than these small rooms and their contents could tell him. He locked the front door securely, whispering a prayer for its departed owner, and turned to scrutinize the short street.

Joe Finn, the neighbour who'd found Duggan's body, was only too willing to talk to James. He'd been waiting at his open door in anticipation of just such an occurrence. As James crossed the street so narrow any boy worth his salt could spit across it, he stuck out his hand.

"Finn I am," he said cheerily. "I'm the one who did find poor Duggan's body."

"Mr. Finn," smiled James, grasping the thin bony hand of the older man. "James Fleming. I'm a solicitor looking into Duggan's murder."

"Is that so? I would have guessed that, you know. Come in, come in and sit yerself down. You'll have a cup of tea, or something a bit stronger?" Finn waited expectantly.

"Whatever you're having yourself," said James diplomatically.

"Indeed, a drop of whiskey now that the sun is droppin'. The end of the day, you see, that's my rule. Don't like to take too much hard stuff during the daylight hours. Stout now, that's a different matter altogether. Hardly the same thing. A pint of stout can do a man good in the course of his labours."

The thin man, dressed in a worn gray and red pin-striped suit shuffled off in his slippers to the kitchen where James could hear the clink of glasses and the splash of running water. He observed the room, an image of Duggan's in its dimensions but, unlike Duggan's, jammed to capacity with heavy wooden furniture upholstered in a faded navy floral pattern. Chairs, sofa, standing lamp, tiny tables, a breakfront filled with knickknacks, reprints of country scenes lined the walls. Suddenly James felt as though he couldn't breathe in the crowded room and gratefully accepted the full glass of whiskey from Finn's trembling hand.

"Your health," he said to Finn as he took a large satisfying drink and caught his breath. The whiskey was neat, nothing added, and he had at least a half a tumbler left.

"Very kind of you," James said, nodding at the glass, acknowledging the man's generosity.

"No trouble, thought you looked a little peaked there. Not an easy thing going in where a man's lost his life. Terrible thing, to die in your own house. . . . No, not that . . . to die of violence within your own walls." He shook his head sadly and took a large gulp himself.

Before the whiskey caught hold of Finn's grasp of the facts, James gently led him through the statement he'd given to the police.

"You know, people think you lose your wits when

you get on in years, but I'm the same as I was, just a bit slower. And I tell you, I am used to watching things. I had a good job across in town, in a fine new building. I was the guard, even had a uniform, and six floors of businesses to mind. Had a big new aluminum desk and a chair. I took in parcels and answered questions. Worked there near on fifteen years. It pleased the missus too. We did good out of that job." He shook his head sadly and James concluded that Mrs. Finn must have passed away.

"So you're sort of a trained observer, am I right?" James said smiling.

"That I am. An observer. You have it exactly."

"Did you make any observations of Mr. Duggan that might be a help to me?"

"Aye, Patrick I called him and he called me Joe. Yes, I took great interest in him when he moved here. Never had the likes of it on this road, I can tell you. There's a good few widows on this block, and still some families left, the O'Hares across there now, and there's a few like meself, widowers they call us. But we've had none of his kind, although there's a scattering of them around the neighbourhood."

"Them?"

"These new types, you know: artists. There's a good few of them here now. But I'll tell you—" Finn took a big swig of his drink. "We prefer them now to these young couples who come in with their big cars and their money and make the place over into something it's not."

"And Duggan was not like that?"

"You've seen his house," Finn said simply.

"So you were on friendly terms?"

"We'd share a word or two if we met, but that was enough. Yes, we were on friendly terms." Finn obviously had liked the phrase. "You see, on a good day, like today, I'll sit out here on a small stool, get the sun and the like. I'd pass the time of day with the road, and Patrick was the same. He was a quiet sort. He worked hard on his pots. He had me in once to look at them. And I'd see him sometimes, bringing in the clay he used, big sacks of stuff. And he'd bring in his food and drink."

"That's all?" James was disappointed.

"Sure he was only here six months. That's not a long time on a street like this."

"How about friends, entertaining, that sort of thing?"

"Well, he had an old car when he came here, but he sold that. Didn't seem to mind. He needed the money at the time. So he shopped down the corner. I never did see any callers to the house, but you know I'm not in the window day and night." Finn's eyes twinkled at his own admission. James smiled in acknowledgement.

"I'd see him down the pub, sometimes. Sullivan's pub on the corner. He'd be there with mates much like himself, and he'd nod over."

"Mates?"

"You might know the like, longish hair for these days, work clothes. I just always thought they were potters or artistic types like himself."

"I imagine you're right. But do you remember if he'd ever had a woman with him, a girlfriend perhaps?"

"Not that I can remember . . . but he was young. There must have been one or two," he winked broadly at James.

James smiled a knowing look but kept to his main inquiry. "I know you said there'd been nothing like this here before. But what about petty crime, robberies perhaps?"

"Oh, I admit there's been some of that. Not on this road, thank God. But the house just behind this one now, robbed blind when the family was at a funeral in Rathmines. Dirty bastards, stealing when there's been a death in the family. They tell me the thievin' bastards check the death notices. Would you credit it!''

"They're making sure the house is empty. But tell me, the day Duggan died, it seems to me the robber would have been watching to see if his house was empty?" He led Finn skillfully.

"That day? That day I remember mainly the sorrow of it. To see a fine young man like that, stretched. I touched nothin', saw nothin', I'll admit to you, except him on the floor dead still. I knew he was dead he was so still.''

"Did you look around the house?"

"No, I just closed over the door to keep out any animals. I went next door to Mrs. Farley and rang on her phone. Some of us still haven't bothered to get in the phone. No need . . .''

James could see that the whiskey was dulling the old man into a sort of melancholy and made haste to take his leave. "Perhaps I could speak to Mrs. Farley, if she's in," he said as he stood, draining his own glass.

"Aye, she's on her own too, like so many of us."

Finn accompanied him next door and was pleased to introduce the solicitor in his fine clothes to the plump woman who answered the door.

But Mrs. Farley was as deaf as a post, which Finn mouthed to James, and it was a while before she grasped the meaning of his visit. In the end she only confirmed Finn's assessment.

"He was a dear young man," shouted Mrs. Farley. "Quiet as a mouse. I'll tell you this, Mr. Flame, I don't see that a robber broke in there. There was nothin' to draw anyone's attention to that young fella.

No car, no loud music . . . I saw no one suspicious that day,'' Mrs. Farley added finally.

"No, nor I,'' confirmed Finn, "but you remember, Mrs. F.?'' He mouthed the words. "You and I were down at the bookies.''

She looked blank as Finn explained he'd walked with her to the local turf accountants for a flutter on the races at Naas, horse racing being a shared interest.

James cursed to himself. The two people most likely to have seen something, were in fact not even home at the critical time. This had not, he noted to himself, been featured on the police report. At a loss to continue, James smiled weakly at Mrs. Farley who, still a bit befuddled, closed her door.

"Listen, Mr. Finn, just one more thing. The police say that no one on this road saw anyone visiting at Duggan's house that day. And no one has come forward since then. Now I realize that people aren't always comfortable about talking to the police, but perhaps amongst yourselves something might have been said?''

"I take your meaning,'' said the old man, stroking his grizzled chin. "And I can tell you, we've jawed about the murder for weeks. We did think that the robber might have staked out Duggan's house, and knew when he'd gone out that day. But we saw no one and that's the strange part of it. The only person we saw who didn't live on the road itself was an old woman collecting tins of food for the poor, said she was from Adam and Eve's on the Quays . . .''

Finn noted James's blank look. "The big church, R.C., the one near the big new development. It's an old church and they've worked with the poor around here for near on sixty years, and that's only according to me! Sorry, Mr. Fleming, that's all I can tell you.''

"That's quite a lot, quite helpful, actually, Mr. Finn," said James, wishing it were true. He gave Finn one of his business cards. "If you think of anything else, or if any of your neighbours think of anything, please let me know."

They shook hands warmly, and James turned his steps towards Kevin Street where he would return the key to Moran. Sullivan's pub he would save for later.

**6**

JAMES'S PRELIMINARY INVESTIGATIONS INTO PATRICK Duggan's death had yielded little and he felt dissatisfied as he dictated his report to be sent to Father Tom in Peru. It wasn't much to report to a man who'd lost two close friends inside of three months. He switched off the recorder and gazed out the high window overlooking Merrion Square. Eye level with the sparrows twittering in a mass of deep green leaves, he let his attention wander.

He'd chatted with the patrons of Sullivan's and learned nothing of value. A few of the artists knew Duggan but only as a local who drank with them on occasion. None was a potter or sculptor, so he'd learned little of Duggan's working or social life. Two of the men were session musicians who played traditional music on the fiddle. They had lots to say about music, but about Duggan only that he was quiet and pleasant enough. The publican agreed with the patrons' recollections. It was not very much to tell Father Tom—that his childhood friend had been liked by his neighbours and acquaintances.

James was stymied. He was not inclined to agree with the police, for something about the manner of Duggan's death did not ring true for him. He again tried to reconstruct the final confrontation between Duggan and the robber. Assuming Duggan had entered the house through his front door, he would have come face to face with the intruder. What did not make sense to James was that Duggan had turned his back on his assailant and in that brief span of time allowed the intruder to clobber him from behind.

James had seen the room where Duggan was killed. Small as it was and sparsely furnished, there was no place the assailant could have hidden and snuck up from behind. So they must have been face to face, must have had words. Why had Duggan turned away? This was surely significant. James turned as he heard Maggie's efficient rap at his door.

"Mail call!"

"Something interesting, I hope."

"All routine," she said as she dropped the stack of legal-size documents on what she deemed to be James's pretentious In Tray, causing it to collapse. "Mr. O'Connor has sent some amendments to add to the previous thirty or forty he's already sent you. That might give you a laugh. And you do have one personal note, from Peru, I see by the stamp."

James sat upright in his creaky swivel chair, catching the mail as it tumbled. "That is a surprise!" He stood up to restack the mail on his desk. "By the way, have you grown?"

"Mmm, temporarily." She flicked her three-inch high heels as she trod across the thick oriental carpet. "My lunch date is six foot three . . ."

James smiled at her back and turned his attention to the letter in his hand. He eagerly read Tom's short note, surprised that the priest only briefly mentioned John's tragic death. He got straight to the point that he was enclosing a letter from Duggan which he'd received posthumously. It had been delayed in the post. Duggan's letter was dated in February of that year, two months before his death.

Dear Tom,

Thanks for your Christmas card. Sorry I didn't get around to sending you one, but you'll see from my return address that I've moved! I've a great little house in the Liberties. Do you know the area at all? It's snug and peaceful and I'm finally feeling I can work again. There was a lot of stress for me in Carrigbawn. It got to the point where I couldn't concentrate on my pottery. There are things I miss of course—the peace, the beauty of the country around there. I've gone from the green of the fields to a little gray city street. But it was worth it, Tom. I'm alone here and at peace. I haven't made many friends as yet and that's the way I want it. The world is too much with us late and soon, as the poet said so much better than I. Too many people, too many complexities. In Carrigbawn, I was in close relation to too much pain.

All this must seem strange to you, Tom, out there where you are working so hard with people who barely have the necessities of life. How petty and trivial my problems must seem to you. If I were free to tell you, though, I know you of all people would understand my recent moral dilemma. It was a situation where, if I acted I caused pain, and if I didn't act, I caused pain. A no win situation, I say. A thorny spiritual problem, you'd say. If you had been here I would have asked your advice. However that may be, I've put it all behind me. I'm snug as a bug in a rug, here in the wee house. Rain is belting down the tiny windows and soon I'll make a fry (can't you just taste that Irish bacon!) and later I'll go for a quiet jar at the corner pub. Now, does all that make you homesick in your mountain eyrie?

Write when you can. Be safe, be well.

Duggan's signature was a scrawl across the page with a tiny sketch of the yellow dog placed in the corner. James smiled at the verve and the warmth of the man as he appeared in his words.

James reread the letter until he'd nearly memorized it, seeking some sense of what Duggan was trying to tell Tom between the lines.

Perhaps Duggan had given his word to someone to keep a confidence, and he could not break that word even in a letter. But James could make no sense of his veiled references, nor could Tom, as he stated succinctly in his accompanying note. Tom explained that he'd always thought Duggan had been happy in Carrigbawn, living there for many years and speaking well of its artistic colony. He had no insight to offer into the pressures Duggan had referred to, pressures that had obviously driven him away from Carrigbawn. Tom averred that Duggan had not been a temperamental artist.

James was no wiser. Like Tom he was inclined to think that Duggan had not left his former home lightly. Yet unlike the priest, James was inclined to think that the moody temperament of the artistic type was indeed a reality. He'd certainly encountered it in other cases he'd investigated and, more to the point, in Sarah.

She was scheduled to arrive that morning and it had slipped his mind. He snatched up the phone and called the Berkeley Court Hotel, where she always stayed when in Dublin. Although she was registered, her extension rang without answer. Reluctantly he dialed the number of Sarah's parents in Monkstown. He pictured the tall, narrow, four-storey townhouse, which he thought of as an impregnable fortress. He anticipated a maid coolly lifting the phone to answer. Instead he heard the unmistakable low and sultry voice of Sarah herself.

"Sarah?" he blurted.

"Is it . . . James?"

"Yes. Look, I'm sorry," he rushed on, "I meant to call two days ago but this case . . ."

"It's always the same, James. Always another case . . ."

"Sarah, I want to see you . . ."

"That's not going to be possible, James."

"Oh, Sarah, come on."

"No, I . . . I have some things to resolve here at home. Look, I really don't want to get into this right now."

"Why the hell not? How else am I supposed to know what's going on in your life. Tell me, is it your career? Your reviews in the London papers last week said your playing was superb, better than ever. And I'm sure it is."

"Thank you. And no, it's nothing about my career, as you term it." She hesitated. "Except in an indirect way. It's family. A family problem, James. And because of that you should know your calls are not welcome in this house. Do you take my meaning?" The tension mounted in her voice.

"Great, just great. The sooner you resolve that one particular 'family' issue the better then, Sarah! It's more than a year since that, that . . ."

"That other case you worked on? You're right, James. Only a year, and no one in this family has recovered from your so-called help, I tell you . . ." She paused, then resumed in a calmer tone, "I do want to see you, James, but not this weekend . . ."

"Right, right. I'll get back to you. At your hotel then. When you've got away from your family problem. Cheers." He rang off without giving her time to reply.

He jumped from his chair and slammed the desk with his fists.

"That's it, that's bloody it! I'm not hanging about in Dublin playing bloody cat and mouse games with you, Sarah Gallagher."

And with that, James made a decision to visit Carrigbawn, a decision which would irrevocably change a number of people's lives, including his own.

THE PICTURESQUE VILLAGE OF CARRIGBAWN WAS A mere hour's drive south from Dublin; even less in James's recently delivered silver-gray Citroën CX. Escaping the congestion of Friday night rush hour in Dublin on a clear and calm evening, James quickly felt refreshed. As each mile passed, he shed some of the frustration and anger of the previous few days.

Although seldom self-analytical, he now speculated about why he was feeling so content. Perhaps it was that whenever he took action in his life, he felt decidedly better about the world in general. In this case, Duggan's letter had given him the lead he'd needed.

For how else could he learn about a man who barely unpacked his bags in the Liberties? It made perfect sense to visit the place where Duggan had previously lived for nearly six years, a place he had loved.

Something in Carrigbawn had driven Duggan to make his sudden move to the city. *Cherchez la femme*, conventional wisdom would say. But James had discovered that conventional wisdom had served him poorly in his other investigations.

This time, his mind was open to suggestion, open to all possibilities. And the bonus was that, for at least this weekend, his days and nights would not seem so empty.

Maggie had made his reservation in a well known

local hotel, the Carrigbawn Inn, and was pining to know the purpose of his weekend in the country. Eager to pin him down, she'd inquired if he would need a double room, and mischievously James had said he did. He smiled to himself as he recalled Maggie's frustrated curiosity. But the road ahead was narrowing suddenly and for the next twenty miles or so, his concentration was taken up by negotiating with minimum loss of speed the tight turns on the winding roads that threaded through Wicklow and led on to his destination of Carrigbawn, the whitened rock.

James had only recently acknowledged to himself that his role of sleuth, as opposed to his role of sober solicitor at law, brought out most clearly his native sense of irony. And so it was in this case, that almost without thinking he had decided on a cover story for his first visit to Carrigbawn, a story that would hold up even if he were required to return to the village. As he signed the register that lay open on the reception desk he chatted freely to the proprietor, Mr. Cadogan.

"Been here to Carrigbawn before, then?" inquired the genial man.

"Not often enough," James expanded as he took his key. "In fact, that's why I'm here this weekend. Had enough of Dublin. I'm thinking of buying in this area."

"Indeed, and would that be to settle down?" Cadogan looked for a wedding ring but, this being Ireland, he knew that its absence was not always indicative.

"Well," faltered James. "Perhaps marriage and children in good time." He tried to sound heartier than he suddenly felt.

"Ah, sure, there's time for that. None of this biological clock for the menfolk, now, is there?"

James cringed. Quickly changing the subject he inquired of the man if he himself knew of any properties in the area.

"I've found word of mouth often more helpful than the estate agents," he added conspiratorially.

"Don't we all, sir. Let me say, if I hear of anything, I'll let you know." He offered to see James to his room, but James declined.

Carrying his own battered Vuitton leather bag, James climbed the old creaking stairs and eventually found his room on the second floor. On opening the door he felt his spirits soar.

A perfect room, he thought. If only Sarah were with him! He would make her forget their troubled past in the passionate embrace of the present, here, in this cozy room tucked under the old inn's gables. The roomy old-fashioned feather bed, covered with a slightly faded eiderdown, was pushed under the eave so that only one side of it could be approached. "The better to keep you there," he murmured, smiling at his fantasy. Ducking his head, James stretched his long frame out on the soft goosedown, and he felt every muscle go limp. From this vantage point he studied the flocked wallpaper, the antique washstand and its porcelain basin and ewer. Pure white towels waited neatly beneath. The wardrobe with its narrow mirror reflected half of the room: the large easy chair, the plain mahogany writing table, the window that let in the soft air of a summer evening that rustled the white curtains. Reluctantly he got off the bed as he felt slumber and warm imaginings of Sarah drawing him in. Too early to let the room work its magic, he decided. Work to be done.

After a quick shave and wash in the bathroom down the hall, he followed the narrow dark blue carpet down the stairs, across the lobby, to the door of the comfortable darkened lounge bar.

Here, he was glad to see, no musicians plied their

trade, as they did so commonly in country hotels. This bar was pleasantly full and the murmur of voices, not piped or live music, filled the air. Taking a table, he made himself as prominent as possible and within minutes had a beer in his hand and a plate of ham sandwiches before him. Friday night, and the whole pleasant weekend still ahead. He munched on his food and took in the surrounding crowd at a glance. Well dressed, trendy, most in their thirties and forties. A few in their twenties who looked suddenly much younger. God, he wondered, was Sarah really that young? He seldom thought of her as in her twenties; he didn't feel much beyond his twenties himself. But, perhaps, five years, ten years, made a difference after all. Did she think of him as being in his late thirties, and did that somehow make some subtle difference? He shook away such thoughts to be dealt with some other day.

As he leaned back to sip his beer he watched Cadogan walk from one table to another. No matter how sophisticated, no matter how surreptitious, James caught the glances of the other guests, and in each case he nodded ever so slightly, acknowledging the curiosity he had provoked. Within a short time, a slender man, youthful despite his graying hair, detached himself from a table of four and lounged towards James.

Thrusting forward a surprisingly strong, veined hand, he introduced himself.

"Eustace, Malachy Eustace. Local inhabitant of this fair village."

"James Fleming," said James simply, repressing the desire to announce himself as solicitor, visitor to this fair village. Overlooking the man's style for the sake of his own mission, James smiled warmly.

"Mine host here has mentioned in passing that you're visiting for the weekend?"

"Yes, indeed. On a bit of a scouting mission."

"It's too late to chat now," intoned Eustace, his slightly bloodshot eyes giving away either fatigue or alcohol consumption. "But let me recommend to you the art exhibit tomorrow at the gallery here. Very fine."

"I hadn't known of a gallery," replied James honestly.

"Mmm, as I say, very fine. It's by invitation only. Pen?"

Startled, James took a pen from his tweed jacket as the man withdrew a rather grubby card from his wallet. With the pen, he scribbled something on the card.

"Just hand this in at the door. It's my card. I'm not exhibiting, but it's still worth your while." He arched his brow slightly at James. "Starts at two but come nearer to four. Drinks, you know."

"Look forward to it," said James as the man moved away and then departed with his companions.

James examined the small white business card. It was adorned with a tiny pallette in one corner, and bore the printed name of Malachy Eustace with the legend, portrait artist, beneath.

James sighed. No wonder Duggan had fled, if this were any indication of the so-called bohemian life of Carrigbawn. He pocketed the card and, bringing with him a large whiskey, returned to his room, well satisfied with his progress. He fell asleep almost immediately on the downy old bed, and long-forgotten boyhood toys and a yellow dog filled his dreams.

James slept much later than he had intended. He jumped into his clothes and hurriedly grabbed a hasty breakfast. And yet, why the haste, he reprimanded himself. This was a holiday of sorts. And as he stepped from the inn he resolved to slow down and absorb whatever ambience and information was available.

A quick survey of the village from the steps of the inn revealed a square of sorts, dominated in the middle by a statue of a rebel of the Rising of 1798. This statue served as the informal terminus of the Dublin bus route and around it were parked higgledy-piggledy the cars of shoppers in the town.

It was a layout common to many Irish towns. On one side of the square stood a newsagent's, already a hive of activity since, in the usual Irish way, it provided most of life's immediate needs. Papers were to be had from Dublin and all the southern counties, along with sweets, bottled mineral waters, sandwiches in cellophane, potatoes by the sackful, and, round the back, bales of turf. A telephone kiosk stood at the front, and a small caged counter in the corner served as the sub–post office for the area. This most essential shop was frequented by travellers on the buses, both coming and going, and locals alike. Abutting it was another essential building, a small ancient pub, Molloy's by name, which James studiously avoided, knowing if he entered he might never leave its wooden, worn, womb-like interior. But as he walked by, he noted it for future reference.

On the opposite side of the square stood a modern mini-market, challenging the traditional bakery and butcher shops close by. Here, James noted as he strolled around, was clear evidence of the suburban rather than rural nature of Carrigbawn. Expensive fresh fruits and vegetables, free-range eggs, fresh baguettes, a cheese counter with a vast choice, a stall of imported delicacies, were witness to the kind of urban taste, leisure, and money available in the village. Even a basket of bagels stood on the low counter, adorned with a sign announcing that a New

Yorker who'd emigrated to Carrigbawn was supplying them daily.

James moved on, gleaning a sense of the surrounding community as he passed a number of boutiques. Fine woollen hand-knit Irish sweaters filled one tastefully decorated window; in another were woven belts, bags, and wonderfully light pastel lap rugs. One small cobbler's shop held magnificent leather handbags, even saddle bags, made on the premises and costing the earth.

Another little shop was jammed with earthenware pottery of all designs and colours, items both useful and decorative. He noted on the display shelves the small hand-lettered cards announcing the name of the artist and the names of the lines. James entered and spoke to the shopkeepers, a young married couple, both anxious and pleasant. He asked if they had any pottery by Patrick Duggan but they shook their heads in unison, steering him to a table of lidded jars which they claimed resembled the type of work Duggan did. They acknowledged they'd known him and had carried his work, but neither referred, naturally enough thought James, to his death. With his new-found interest in pottery he purchased a small deep dish suitable for nuts or sweets, yet another knickknack his mother didn't need.

James soon realized that what he had viewed at first as merely trendy or faddish stores were in fact essential in their own way. It was a necessity to the livelihood of the artisans in the area to have outlets to display their work. For Carrigbawn had over recent years acquired a reputation as a vital and viable artists' colony.

Two coffee shops sat on either side of the road. One displayed wonderful French pastries; the other, more conventional, offered equally wonderful Irish breads and pastries. Both were full at this mid point of Saturday. The crowds were, as at the inn, casually well dressed young people. James caught the strains of taped classical music coming from the open doors. Indeed, he concluded, this was not your typical Irish country town.

Having sampled a pastry in the French shop, he took his bag of goodies and strolled back towards the inn. There he climbed into his car and with no particular plan he began to drive slowly. His tour gave him a general picture of the beauty of the surrounding green-backed Wicklow mountains. Long winding lanes lined with burgeoning hedgerows dipped and meandered and revealed here and there a few sprawling modern homes, bungalows for the most part, beautifully kept, with one or two cars in each driveway. Some older, more substantial Georgian homes, set back from the roadways, had been refurbished. Here and there were restored cottages, whitewashed in the old way, some with newly woven thatch. Discreet signs on some of the lawns or gates of the houses bespoke their owners' occupations. One indicated, surprisingly for Ireland, a local winery, with free tasting sessions on Sunday afternoons. Another spoke of homemade preserves and jams. Another cluster of cottages comprised a small mill where, he speculated, the rugs displayed in the shops in town were woven. Yet another sign announced the owner was a painter, a further sign that the owner worked in pastels. Another more aggressively proclaimed in bold lettering that the artist within would paint an accurate picture of your house and grounds, or your horses and stable.

James was intrigued, for here was a version of work as old as Ireland itself—the cottage industry. And the sense of it somehow thrilled him. This was industry of the best sort: creative, independent, individualistic. He imagined the houses and cottages as bursting with energy and activity and his heart warmed to them.

He envied the carpenter, the woodworker, the artisan of any kind, supporting himself in one of these houses, labouring side by side with his neighbours who were engaged in like concerns, meeting for drinks at the end of a hard, satisfying day. He possessed none of these skills, but he did like to work on the land. The longing to have his own house and garden possessed him again and he drove now with more purpose. Perhaps his cover story had held the kernel of truth. He would actively house-hunt here in Carrigbawn, giving way to what appeared to be an impulse. But James was not an impulsive man.

In his meandering drive of nearly two hours he did not spot a single FOR SALE sign and, mildly discouraged, he returned to the town. Rifling through his car for Friday's *Irish Times,* he pulled out the property section, but there were no listings in Carrigbawn. Of course, it couldn't be that easy, he mused, and he returned to his hotel.

Lingering at the desk, he asked Cadogan if he'd heard of any properties, mentioning his drive and his lack of success.

"Ah, now, I'd be surprised if you came upon a house hereabouts in that fashion, Mr. Fleming."

"Why is that?"

"I'll tell you, now you've got a feeling for the neighbourhood, as they call it. Nearly all the houses in this area when they do come up for sale—which is seldom, mind you—are sold by word of mouth. They're a very tightly knit bunch here, I can tell you. Don't get me wrong, though. I think that's all to the good. I might add, Mr. Fleming, it's not everyone I'd take under my wing. But I've put the word in the right ear. I think Mr. Eustace spoke with you already?"

James was startled. "Yes, he gave me his card . . ."

"A good omen, then, Mr. Fleming. Privately I call him the social director. Very 'in' with the right people. My advice is to get to know him. If he likes you, you'll be in good hands."

Walking briskly down one side of the square, following Cadogan's detailed directions, James passed over a narrow stone bridge and turned right into a yellow, gorse-lined lane. At last he came to the gallery, tucked away on a level piece of land, screened by chestnut trees. As he joined the loose queue of people, he wondered if in fact he would like being taken into "good hands."

A fair number of cars were already parked on the short grass that served as a car park. More were arriving. The gallery itself was a pleasing modern single-storey building of simple lines that blended, as the architect clearly intended, into its sylvan setting. Again James was impressed with the sophistication and prosperity that surprised him at every turn and he found himself looking forward to this departure into the world of art.

On entering the small glassed-in entrance hall filled with Queen Anne's Lace, gorse, and other wild flowers from the hedgerows, he was asked for his invitation by a thin young man in a black polo-neck jersey. Surprised by such formality, he handed him Eustace's card and was waved on with a silent smile.

Inside, he moved slowly through the display of paintings. As the sign had announced, this was a showing by two local female artists who worked exclusively in watercolours. Although pleasing to the eye, the paintings, perhaps a hundred in number, had a numbing effect on James. Picture after picture of fields, streams, cottages, all afloat in some mystical sea of pale blues and greens, somehow did not capture for him the quintessential Irish landscape. Nor did they offer any fresh interpretation of it. He looked in vain for a portrayal of the loneliness, the barrenness, the isolating nature that represented the Irish landscape of his inward eye. But these pictures seemed to have been influenced only by the lush pastoral and prosperous scenery of Carrigbawn. Perhaps such blandness would please the tourists, he opined silently, for he couldn't imagine an Irish person worth his or her salt hanging one of these above their hearths. Of course, he had seen the likes of these in foyers everywhere in Ireland, in lobbies of new buildings, in waiting rooms of all kinds, in banks and insurance companies.

"What do you think?" It was a soft voice that murmured at his side and he jumped, seeing suddenly the anxious face of a woman in her twenties.

"I think . . . I think . . . these paintings will definitely find a deserving home. And you?"

"Well, since I painted a lot of them I hope you are right."

Relieved that he had not offended the young artist he tried to dredge up something more substantive to add but nothing came to mind.

"May I give you my card?" she said at last, hopelessly.

As insight struck, he accepted her card graciously, and in his most charming manner explained he was a mere guest of Mr. Eustace and not in the trade. Her expression relaxed.

"Oh, I see. I thought perhaps you were a gallery owner from Dublin. This is a closed showing you see. You were so quiet and I . . . Excuse me," she said hurriedly, moving on to make more fruitful contacts.

It was just gone four when James noted that the outer door was closed and curtained off, and from a side door, which apparently led to a kitchen area, young men dressed in chef's whites appeared carrying trays of champagne and hors d'oeuvres. Deftly arming himself with a plate of salmon and a glass of surprisingly good champagne, James searched the now more animated crowd for Eustace. He spotted him in the far right corner in the middle of a lively group. Moving to its fringe, he caught Eustace's eye.

Eustace was nattily dressed, a rakish kerchief at his neck. More animated than the night before, he drew James into the crowd, making swift introductions of the group, by avocation rather than by name. In the space of seconds James met a novelist, an aspiring film producer and his wife, a market gardener, and three art dealers from Dublin. However, his years of training at his mother's many social affairs stood him in good stead and he rose to the occasion with suitable small talk and attentive silences. No one as yet, he noted, had asked his occupation.

Having, James assumed, made sufficient effort to impress this newcomer, the group soon broke into smaller clusters and Eustace pointedly took James aside.

"Now that you've run the first gauntlet," he intoned, "let's talk about you. What is it you do, exactly?"

"My profession is the law and I specialize in wills and estate planning. My avocation is travel by steam train. My hobby is train trekking as we call it. And I have other related interests." James was stiff and formal, disliking being put on the spot.

"Yes, yes, yes . . ." Eustace repeated rapidly. "What I need to know is what brings you here, just now, here." He fixed a wild eye on James.

"Your invitation, I would have to say," replied James dryly.

"Of course, ha ha." Eustace glittered still. "But here to our Carrigbawn. Our little bijou, hhmmm? If

I am not misled in my inebriation of last night, Cadogan at the inn said you were house-hunting?"

"Yes, in a diffident way . . ."

"Ah, but not indifferent, yes?"

James persevered, conscious of his original quest. "Hardly. I feel ready now. No, I feel prepared now to buy a substantial property, one which I might call home for many years to come. Carrigbawn is convenient to Dublin, less rural than many other villages, let me say, and yet still a part of the country. If not the heart of the country."

"But we are, as we like to think it, an artists' colony. And by your description you are not an artist."

James bristled at last. "No I am not. But I hardly think that should be an obstacle."

Eustace responded to the edge on James's voice. "No, no, no. I am, please, I am, Fleming, only concerned that you are aware of your . . . your surroundings here."

"Well, I doubt I would wish to live in a village comprised solely of solicitors at law! No more, would I think, than you and your neighbours associate exclusively with artists, as you term them."

"Of course, variety is the spice, et cetera. I probe merely to ascertain whether you would not be lonely?"

"Surely you mean out of place?" James's reply was crisp.

"It's early days yet, Fleming." Eustace's voice was soothing. "To that end I want you to accompany me to dinner tonight. Friends are having me over and I can bring a companion. Come. Talk. I'll collect you at seven at your hotel." James nodded and Eustace moved on to join his associates.

James himself approached the young artist he'd met earlier. She was clutching a glass of champagne by the stem, self-consciousness apparent in her very stance. Kindly he chatted a bit about the soft colours of the various paintings on show and vainly tried to lead the conversation, stiff as it was, around to pottery. However, Miss Conly knew little of pottery and could only suggest the shop James had already visited. Then she introduced him to Miss Rattigan, the other artist whose work was on display.

Miss Rattigan was more lively, self-deprecating rather than stiff. At last James began to realize that far from being the stars of the gathering, both young women were unsure of themselves, anxious that the viewers of their first showing think well of their work. For them, small talk was difficult when the desire to study the people who were studying their pictures was irresistible. The pair of artists were very vulnerable and, as an outsider, he provided a brief respite from local judgement. Mercifully, they were all three saved from becoming part of the furniture by an animated female dealer from Dublin who approached Miss Conly with enthusiasm and a promise to hang four of her watercolours in a small show in a bistro in Dublin in October. James sighed, as the conversation turned to which four would be most suitable. Poor Miss Rattigan's eyes were wide with strained disappointment and envy.

He took a circuitous route back to the hotel and wondered at his change in mood. The houses on this route were equally attractive, bathed now in the softer sunlight of a clear June evening. The place held promise of all kinds, he mused, but Eustace was a different story altogether. Eustace's attitude had had a souring effect. James disliked the idea that he was being vetted, that he had to pass some imaginary muster. Perhaps this whole notion was only in Eustace's rather eccentric mind? Perhaps not. Cadogan had referred to Eustace as the "social director" and James's first encounter with the locals at the art gallery had been clearly intended to be off-putting. Maybe Eustace was right after all. If his neighbours were such that they made newcomers run the gauntlet, as Eustace had put it, then James might prefer not to live among such a self-appointed elite.

James purchased a bottle of wine for his unknown host and returned to the inn to change for dinner. Having no idea what was expected of him, and being in a vengeful frame of mind, he attired himself in his dinner jacket and black tie. It would be fun to upstage the pompous Eustace.

Eustace arrived in the lobby at the stroke of seven, similarly dressed. James, catching his inadvertent but smug smile, was irritated that Eustace perceived him to be trying to live up to Carrigbawn's supposed standards, and not his own.

Not far down a lane that led off from the main road, Eustace pulled his car into a drive obscured by rhododendron bushes just passing out of flower. Although they hadn't driven far from the village, James would never have spotted this drive or the house, secluded as it was. James liked the place at first glance. The structure showed an amalgam of styles—the main body was Tudor—and it sat at an angle to the drive, with a deep overhanging roof. Two obvious additions had been built on either side but in different styles and obviously at different periods. The main door was tucked under the roof and was fronted by a porch made of a simple single granite step with two narrow benches on either side. A trellis sheltered the doorway and was covered with a Russian vine, heavy and lush, its fragrant pale purple flowers only now closing in the falling darkness. The drive was gravelled and short but provided for a U-turn at the front of the house. Large hedges abutted the house and prevented any view to the grounds at the back. And roses and honeysuckle rambled everywhere in lush profusion. The air was perfumed with their scents, the aroma of new-mown hay somewhere near, and of peat smoke. A heady mix, thought James, breathing deep.

A bell rang in the interior and the door soon opened. They were greeted by a short, balding man in his mid fifties, with a shiny forehead that a few strands of hair could not hope to conceal. His face was shiny, too, and he beamed at his guests.

"Welcome, welcome. Elsie, dear heart, come greet Eusty and his friend."

And Elsie bustled into view, also short in stature and round with it, her figure lost in a magenta dress that fell in multitudinous folds to her sandalled feet, a dress that had seen its heyday twenty years before.

The evening began pleasantly enough as Elsie and Fred poured out a very fine red wine. The crudités were crisp, the dips generous and caloric. But as time passed James suspected no dinner in the usual sense was forthcoming. As pangs of hunger set in, he made do with additional florets of cauliflower and drank more red wine than he'd intended.

As Elsie and Fred, an English couple for each of whom this was a second marriage, talked at length about their children, all in England leading their own lives, James felt his attention wander. If he was to be scrutinized by this couple he didn't notice it. They asked him very little and he had ample time to study the dimensions of the gracious, irregularly shaped room, the marble mantle in the Adams style, the green Connemara marble surround that supported it. The room's furnishings were relatively new and characterless but the room itself was of interest. Deep mullioned bay windows were set into two walls and wide mahogany window seats stood waiting, inviting. The low, open-beam ceiling made for a sense of coziness and warmth that was not diminished by the blandness of the furniture.

As the threesome chatted on, James let his mind roam further. This house reminded him of an aunt's house he'd visited often in childhood, a sprawling cozy home that he'd loved for its narrow hidden passages, for the steps that had led up into one wing and down into another. This house had a similar effect on him and he longed to explore. Eventually he realized the conversation was petering out. Eustace, catching James's attention, suggested indifferently that perhaps Fred and Elsie might show James their house. And so it was with delicious anticipation that James followed Fred and Eustace into the front hall.

# 8

UNLIKE ITS OWNERS, THE HOUSE ITSELF HAD A strong personality, emanating individuality in its every angle, experience in its time-worn woodwork, and comfort in its solid stone and wooden structure. James, once he'd learned that Fred had opted for an early retirement and had lived in the house for just a year, felt free to dissociate him and the unlovely Elsie from the house itself.

Together all three climbed the old intricately carved central wooden staircase to an unusual gallery that looked over the front entrance hall. Off this open corridor were four heavy oak doors, also carved, leading to the four main bedrooms. Only two of these were furnished and in those that remained empty, James had a clear view of the dark wooden wainscotting and the large windows that looked out onto the rear gardens. Like those in the sitting room, each of these windows was fitted with the original folding interior shutters, and with window seats. With a boyish sense of mystery James lifted the seats, looking for hidden treasures of any kind.

At either end of the corridor stood a bathroom, another unusual feature in an Irish house of this age. They were spacious and tiled in dark Italian ceramic. The ceiling which overhung both the gallery and the entrance hall was centered by a wood and iron chandelier.

Retracing their steps downstairs, they toured the other two enormous reception rooms, which stood on either side of the hall. In both were large fireplaces, similar in design to the one in the smaller sitting room he'd seen first. A panelled room, lined with empty shelves, appeared to be a study. This unused room, in an architectural quirk, physically joined the original house to its nineteenth-century addition on the eastern side of the house. Although dark, it was beautifully proportioned and its arched mullioned windows looked out on the gardens to the rear. A perfect room to work in, dreamed James, to read and to write. And by the time they returned to the sitting room James had decided this house was truly going to waste.

"We saw it as a honeymoon house, Elsie and I . . ." Fred commented as if in answer to his unspoken and derogatory thought. He asked about the house itself and learned that the central structure was a hundred and fifty years old; that one wing, which they'd closed off as unnecessary, was added in the late nineteenth century, the second wing in the thirties. Both wings, he was told, were in disrepair, a do-it-yourselfer's dream, according to Fred, who felt his interests lay elsewhere. However there was no dry rot, no rising damp. The plumbing was sound, what there was of it. The wiring too. James asked in vain about the history of the previous owners, but the past didn't interest the robust Fred, who'd come for the fishing, as he insisted on repeating.

"So it's back to Britain for Elsie and me, Eustace. A fine snug bungalow for us, with all mod cons."

"For the best, for the best, Fred," Eustace was encouraging. "Elsie will like to see her children, I imagine?"

"Oh my, yes!" Fred babbled out a list of her children and his children but James had already been distracted by the fact that Fred and Elsie would be leaving Carrigbawn, leaving this wonderful house. He smiled benignly at Eustace for the first time. And held his enthusiasm to his chest like a royal flush.

Elsie reappeared with a tray of sandwiches and a pot of weak tea. Choking down dry bread with potted meat spread on it was effortless for James now, as he suddenly saw the house in an entirely different light, and its occupants as mere tenants passing through. His mood was so enlivened that he managed an anecdote about a recent train enthusiasts' meeting, which ended the evening on a lighthearted note.

But James's silence was cunning as he and Eustace strolled to the car and waved yet again to Elsie in her magenta dress standing incongruously in the picturesque doorway of Oakdale Lodge, as their old house was called.

James, suddenly aware of the incongruity of Eustace's and his own evening dress, in view of the evening just passed, laughed out loud.

"Enjoy your evening?" asked Eustace, smiling.

"Yes, most interesting. You've known them long?"

"Since they came, a year ago. Fish out of water, as you might imagine. Thought they'd like country life—fishing, as Fred said. Mistake obviously. They're dying to get back. I tell you, Fleming, it pays to do a little research, mmm?"

"Always," James replied neutrally.

"You liked the house?"

"Very much."

"You didn't show it."

James remained silent.

Eustace let out a sharp laugh. "Not a lawyer for nothing then, am I right?"

"Who's handling the sale?"

"Dunno. I'm the yentl, but I don't know that they

even have a solicitor or agent yet." They'd arrived at the inn.

"Come in for a drink then, Eustace?"

"Not tonight, Fleming. Other fish to fry. But listen, from your name I assume you're Church of Ireland like myself. We'll see you at St. Killian's in the A.M." As Eustace sped off James realized it wasn't a question.

Tired of the evening's fishing metaphors, James was only too glad to sip his whiskey alone. And as he ordered a generous basket of tasty ham and cheese sandwiches to quell his residual hunger, he allowed himself to speculate on the interesting possibility of buying Oakdale Lodge.

Sunday morning broke dark and windy. The glorious June weather had disappeared overnight, replaced by driving rain and scudding clouds.

As James ran across the empty cobbled square and down the narrow road that led to the Church of Ireland, he regretted not driving the short distance in his car. That is, until he saw the numerous cars already parked on the verge and along the gravelled drive leading to the small granite church. Its sturdy spire rose in the air above the wind-blown trees.

James shook the rain from his light summer trench coat and patted his damp hair into place. Having expected a sparse summer congregation made smaller by the inclement weather, he was amazed to see nearly every pew packed.

Taking a seat in the right transept, vacant because a pillar obscured a clear view of the altar, he recognized a number of the guests from the inn's lounge. He spotted the back of Eustace's head and observed him as he, in similar fashion, glanced around, nodding to his friends. Fred and Elsie were seated stolidly near the front. She was unmistakable in a colourful woven poncho, while Fred's bald head seemed to reflect the gently wavering light of the altar candles. Above, rough stone pillars supported an oak-beamed peaked roof, the wood of the beams engraved with golden lettering, displaying the legend: Build not thine house upon sand.

The altar itself was simple, covered with white linen bordered with lace and displaying two ornate candlesticks holding thick beeswax candles. The modest stained-glass window behind the altar depicted St. George slaying the dragon. As the congregation settled into silence, James became aware of the fine organ music filling the church. He stood with the others to join in the opening hymn as the rector emerged.

At the first prayer, James's attention was drawn immediately to the minister's voice, rich and gentle and pleasing to the ear. He studied the young man at the front of the church. Almost six feet tall, the Reverend Desmond had black hair that fell over his forehead, nearly brushing the rim of his bottle-thick eyeglasses. His height and thin build gave him an awkwardness that was intensified because he had to hold the text so close to his face. The effect was almost comical and James suppressed a smile. But that first lighthearted impression was erased twenty minutes later when Reverend Michael Desmond began his sermon.

"I have taken my text today from the great mystical poet and scholar, John Donne, who wrote in his Meditation Seventeen: 'Therefore never send to know for whom the bell tolls; it tolls for thee.' "

The rector continued, mentioning that the famous phrase had become timeworn, that to fully understand the poet's meaning, his congregation must refer to the longer text.

" 'No man is an island, entire of itself; every man is a piece of the continent, a part of the main . . . any man's death diminishes me.' " Here Desmond paused dramatically, allowing his listeners time to consider.

James's attention drifted as Desmond began to relate his text to the recent death of an elderly and well-respected man, a well-known member of the congregation. But Desmond's novel twist on the words called him back.

"In sending to find out who has died, we send to know if we also have died." His voice was raised.

"Indeed, part of us died with him. Therefore, perhaps we might speculate that that same part of us that died with him has also passed into God, passed beyond this present life and is now part of the eternal . . ."

James suddenly thought of Father John's death, and of his own promise to Tom: his reason for being in Carrigbawn. He wondered, as his attention was distracted, if anyone here in this prosperous group would have known the Catholic potter.

". . . one who went to meet his God, we hope as well prepared. Although Patrick Duggan . . ."

James was riveted to Desmond's words, words that seemed to have miraculously meshed with his own thoughts.

". . . had left this community to move on to Dublin to further his career, he is still, I hope, well remembered. We as a community were diminished by his leaving. And, as the poet has it, diminished by his death. Although he worshipped at a different altar, he worshipped the same God."

James wondered if he had missed something earlier in the sermon, some clue about Duggan. As Desmond spoke of the community of faith, James stirred restlessly, but he listened intently.

". . . we are blessed to have living among us artists of every kind who value life in just such a way, whose very work is intended either to enhance our understanding or our appreciation of that abundant life. We must live as the artist does, and we must see the world as the artist sees it, as new and fresh. And so although Mr. Duggan was cut down tragically in his relative youth, living out only half the allotted span, he too, I know, had lived each day to the full.''

As the Reverend Desmond continued the service James was encouraged in his quest. Surely Desmond's mention of Duggan, who was neither a member of the congregation nor just recently dead, indicated that he had known him personally.

Here, he thought, was an unusual clergyman, unusual in his sensitivity, in his knowledge and rhetorical skills, and in his extreme youth. For as James knew, it was not common for a man so young to be made rector of his own church, even less so in a parish as prosperous and sophisticated as this one at St. Killian's.

At the conclusion of the service, James joined the file of his fellow worshippers and, like them, shook hands with Reverend Desmond. He was struck by a sense of familiarity as they spoke face to face. Just before turning to go, he expressed this feeling.

"No, Mr. Fleming, I don't remember that we ever met," Desmond said softly, peering intently into James's face not six inches away, "but I'm glad to have had you in our congregation today. Please attend again. We welcome all newcomers to our village."

"Yes, indeed, we will meet again," said James sincerely, knowing now there was at least one person in Carrigbawn whom he would question.

James rushed from the porch into the continuing downpour, racing down the gravelled path past open car doors and people shouting out hurried greetings. Hearing his own name called by Eustace he waved and sped on, only to be followed out the drive by Eustace's car, passenger door swinging wide.

"Hop in, for God's sake," cried the damp-haired Eustace.

James did as he was bid.

"We were all glad to see you here this morning."

"Mmm," murmured James, wondering just who "all" were, and knowing that it wasn't on account of their keen religiosity that "they" were glad to see him.

"I had a quick word with Lamia earlier this morning and she said to bring you along."

"Pardon?" James was irritated by Eustace's paternal airs.

"Sorry, I should have said Mrs. Desmond, the rector's wife. She holds a coffee morning of sorts, you know, after the service."

James groaned inwardly, familiar as he was with this kind of quasi-social occasion where certain members of the congregation, generally in their nineties at least, or else parents of young noisy children, stood about in the church hall drinking weak coffee from urns and munching the inevitable dry fruit cake. Trapped in Eustace's car he couldn't see how to extricate himself gracefully.

"You attend these, ah, get-togethers?" He couldn't keep the surprise from his voice.

"Mmm, religiously, Fleming." Eustace was laughing now. And although feeling the butt of a silent joke, James laughed too, liking Eustace's humour for the first time.

"I'll introduce you to the rector."

"We've met."

"How interesting," said Eustace, taking a hairpin turn down a narrow lane.

"No, no, I mean just now, at the church door. I was impressed by his sermon," he added.

"I daresay. Today it was short. He seemed a bit preoccupied. His health is poor, you know. But he seemed moved as well, I thought."

"When speaking about Duggan? I noticed that too. He seems a compassionate man."

"Yes he is, and he also knew Duggan personally. Perhaps you heard of him?"

"Duggan? I don't know anyone from Carrigbawn." James was cool but privately startled at Eustace's question.

"It was in the papers some time ago. He was murdered, you see. In Dublin."

James felt as though the last phrase had been weighted and attempted to deflect the question in Eustace's voice: "Did you know—"

"Here we are then," Eustace cut in.

James was greatly surprised as Eustace drove the car through a set of imposing pillars, the wrought-iron gates thrown wide. As they drove down the tree-lined driveway, the chestnuts' branches, heavy with rain, nearly touched the roof of the car. James was further surprised to see many other cars pulled up to the front of a substantial granite-fronted house dating perhaps from the mid eighteen hundreds.

"This is the rectory?" James's voice was heavy with sarcasm that was quickly erased by Eustace's answer.

"Yes and no. This is Monks Hall, Reverend and Mrs. Desmond's home."

"You might have warned me," said James, emerging from the car.

"Un-huh, it was worth it just to see your face. You're not the first that I've fooled. Come on then, people want to meet you."

"Me?"

"Mm, of course. You don't think we'll allow just anyone to buy Fred's house, do you?" He raised an eyebrow at James and let the door knocker fall once. "Chin up, Fleming."

James didn't know whether to be outraged or amused. He hovered between the two emotions as the large front door opened on the instant. In front of him stood a plain young girl in a plain dress.

"Please go on in," she said, taking their wet coats without looking them in the face.

Eustace swept in, more animated than James had yet seen him. James followed slowly in his wake, observing the quiet good taste and elegance of his surroundings and the evidence everywhere of what his mother would have called, old, very old, money.

He glanced around the large sitting room, recognizing again the faces from the hotel lounge, the gallery, and the service that morning. Quite a little clique, he thought. But trays of tiny delectable sausage rolls beckoned. As he munched, he studied the many framed photographs displayed on the grand piano.

But such an occupation was no defence against the voluble Fred who planted his solid body beside James and scoffed down three rolls in three seconds. "We meet again."

"Yes, and let me thank you for your hospitality last evening," responded James amiably, speculating as to how Fred and Elsie had earned the blessing of the clique to purchase Oakdale.

"No problem, as the Yanks say. Self-serving, you see."

"Say no more, Fred," Eustace's voice bore in on them. "Fleming, this way." Arms waving, he ushered James to the side of the most striking woman in the room, in perhaps any room. James waited patiently as she finished talking to her companion and then turned to him with a brilliant smile. A wealthy member of St. Killian's, guessed James.

"Lamia," said Eustace, beaming at her, "let me

present to you Mr. James Fleming, solicitor, from Dublin. James, this is Mrs. Desmond, Reverend Desmond's wife."

James recovered quickly, he hoped.

"How do you do," he said meekly, feeling like a schoolboy.

"Actually, just slightly under the weather. I was telling Constance here how sorry I was to miss dear Michael's sermon today. I couldn't possibly risk going out in that dismal rain." She offered a cool, slim, beautifully manicured hand to James. He felt the pressure of her strength however, and the warmth of the heavy gold wedding band. She placed her other hand over his with a gentle pat. "James, I feel I already know you, since Malachy has been filling me in."

James was mesmerized by the mellifluous quality of her voice and by the clarity and shade of her blue eyes. Silently he let her lead him to a brocade sofa that stood on the far side of the room in a narrow alcove that gave onto the main part of the room. She was tall, nearly as tall as James in her black suede heels. Her shimmering blue and green jersey dress shaped itself sinuously against her long slim figure, the cowl neck falling in graceful folds around her neck and shoulders. Her chestnut coloured hair was in a French twist and it framed her face: pale, oval, and serene. She was speaking.

"Sorry?" said James as he sat down.

"I repeat," she said soothingly yet infinitely formally, "have you been to Carrigbawn before?"

"Oh, yes, over the years, day trips. More often when I was young—when I was in college." Stupid, he thought. She's older than I am, why speak of age. Judging from his brief observation of Reverend Desmond, James would have said he was much younger than his wife.

He wanted to test his observation. "Is your husband here?" he asked, apropos his thought but not the conversation.

James thought he saw Lamia's eyes narrow ever so slightly. Or perhaps he was mistaken.

"He'll be here shortly. He is inclined to pray after the service. He is, as you no doubt saw for yourself, a truly holy man."

"Certainly I was struck by his sermon. I thought I was immune to sermons, allergic in fact. I seem to fall deaf as soon as one begins."

Did her eyes narrow again?

"Yes, well, tell me, are you staying with us long?"

"Sadly no, I leave today. It was a brief holiday, a respite, and I admit, I am toying with the idea of buying in the area . . ."

"Toying?" Her beautiful voice punched the word ever so slightly. "Surely buying what might be one's home for the rest of one's life is not to be viewed so lightly?"

He was duly admonished.

"Poor choice of words, I suppose."

"It's just that . . ." she continued, crossing her legs, the silk of her hose catching the light from the fire. "It's just that one can make a mistake, as was the case with Mr. White."

"Mr. White? Fred, of course, Fred. Yes, Eustace said much the same."

"They made a mistake, you see, and now they must rectify it. Buying, selling, moving one's goods. James, perhaps you might tell me what it is you hope to find. I was born in Carrigbawn. Perhaps I may be able to tell you if you will find what you're seeking here . . ." She smiled for a second time, showing perfectly even, small, white teeth. For James it was the only unattractive feature in an otherwise stunningly beautiful woman. He was thinking about teeth instead of formulating his answer. Why, he wondered rather desperately, did he want to compose what he had to say? Why did he want to convince this particular woman that Carrigbawn was right for him?

"You cause me to focus a bit more than I had," he said.

"Ah . . . the solicitor's trick of buying time," she laughed again in such a soothing way. "Just let your thoughts tumble out uncensored, the kernel of truth will be there."

Uncensored thoughts would tumble out, thought James, and tell you that I wish you weren't married, that I want to take you on a long cruise. I want to drink rough red wine with you on a beach in Crete. I want to see you naked in the dawn.

"Uncensored now," she said again.

"I think I want a large house, with many rooms. I want land, an orchard, I want to plant potatoes, I want to sit at my own fireplace with two large dogs . . ."

"What breed then?" she said seriously.

"Ah, well, big dogs, amiable dogs. Perhaps golden retrievers."

"Two. You see two. And what else? What would you do in this house?"

"Do? I would live in it. I mean really live. I would paint . . ."

"You paint, I see." She smiled again, those small even teeth.

"No, I meant to say, I would paint the house, inside, and wallpaper. Put up shelves, tear down walls, renovate. Make it mine," he finished almost wearily.

"James, you have so much energy. I take it you are not married?"

James shook his head, wondering at the connection between the two thoughts.

"You want to make a home?"

"That's it exactly." James shook away the feeling

she was some sophisticated version of a palm reader, reading his future in his fretful words instead of from cards.

"Making a home for more than just yourself, but the wife and family you see in your future?"

"Now that you express it that way, yes. Far away as that eventuality may be." He suppressed a sigh, not liking any more to be closely questioned, by Lamia or Eustace or Cadogan at the inn or anyone else for that matter.

She read his expression and changed the topic.

"Carrigbawn is a closeknit community. Although, as you see, our homes are rather far flung, there are shared goals, mutual tastes, common bonds that tie us together. I am pleased to say that the church is one of those bonds. A centre, a hub if you will. My husband is an extraordinary man . . . and I see he's returned at last."

Lamia stood as Desmond approached. She extended her hands to him. He took them in his own, with what James thought was a wan smile.

"Tired?" she said simply, softly.

"Just a bit," he said, barely shaking his head and glancing at James, not wanting to be observed in an intimate exchange.

"Michael, this is Mr. Fleming, a weekend visitor."

James, already standing, shook hands again. "I was moved by your sermon, Reverend Desmond," he said, "and saddened to hear of that young man's death."

"Tragic," Desmond replied, leaving James no further opening.

"Coffee?" Lamia intervened. They moved towards the large coffee pot and she poured out three cups. Nodding graciously and dismissively to James she walked off with Desmond towards her other guests. Bereft, James stood at the window watching as the rain beat against its panes. He feigned drinking his coffee, but was instead wishing he could escape the intensity of this atmosphere, willing his Citroën to appear in the drive. Sensing this, it seemed, Eustace materialized at his elbow, damp coats in hand.

"Had enough then?"

"Ready when you are."

On the drive back, Eustace was silent for once and only at the hotel did he speak in response to James's farewell courtesies.

"Think nothing of it, Fleming. Just thought you'd like to meet some of the gang."

James cringed at the characterization.

"You still have my card? No? Here's another." He proffered a fresh white one.

James duly returned the courtesy and removed one of his own from the neat leather case he carried.

After a slight hesitation Eustace spoke again. "Listen, Fleming, I was just chatting with Fred. They're away this afternoon but they said if you'd like to walk around the property"—he glanced at the now lessening downpour and smiled—"you are perfectly welcome. This is not a commitment, you understand."

"Nor on my part," said James briskly. "But I will take advantage of the offer on my way back to Dublin. Thanks for the lift."

Secretly very pleased, James bounded into the inn, settled his bill, and within the hour was walking the land in the perversely brilliant sunshine of an Irish summer afternoon.

# 9

"IT'S EVERYTHING YOU COULD WANT!" EXCLAIMED James to his oldest friend, Matt, as they stood pressed to the bar at Doheny and Nesbitt's, their favourite Dublin pub. "Over five acres. God, it even has a well-established orchard. And wait, wait for it, not only a small stream but good land, land that was tilled obviously before the Fred Whites took over."

"Sounds great, Fleming, but a little rural, no? Not to mention the distance from Dublin," said Matt dubiously. He drew circles in the small puddles of stout on the worn bar counter.

"An hour! What's an hour?" James drained his pint of Guinness, and waved for another.

"It might be only an hour the way you drive in that car of yours. If Dorothy and I come to visit, you'll need to put us up for the night."

"Any time, seriously. You, Dorothy, the kids . . . long weekends. Listen, there's . . . I dunno . . . ten bedrooms! Not furnished of course." He paused briefly. "But look, I'm going to do a lot of the renovations myself, and I'll need help, your help I might add."

"You're talking as though you've bought the place!"

"I know this is a bit premature. I've barely got to the stage of chatting with the owners. But I have a good feeling about this place. I can't explain it. I feel this house has my name on it."

"There's something more, something you're not telling me."

James laughed and raised his pint to meet Matt's own. "You're right, as usual. Remember the fellow Eustace I mentioned? He phoned me at work on Wednesday. He's asked me down for the weekend. Seems he has a wife I've never met and they are having a bit of a get-together, as they call it. He told me to bring a guest as well."

"And you're bringing me?"

James was startled into silence until he saw Matt's expression.

"No," he laughed heartily, buoyed along by a raging enthusiasm. "I've spoken to Sarah! You remember I told you she's at home in Monkstown after that continental tour with the Vienna Symphony? She's agreed to come," James added with a flourish.

Matt pondered this new information before dismissing it. He was well used to the trials and tribulations of James's involvement with Sarah. "I'm happy that your personal life seems to be taking off. But what about your investigation? My curiosity is getting the better of me, not to mention Dorothy's. You said earlier it was the reason you went to Carrigbawn in the first place."

James sighed. "Oh, Lord, my conscience speaks?"

"No, your superego. Now, what's the scoop here?" Matt sipped his pint, prepared to hear the full details of what he hoped would prove to be a tangled web of intrigue.

"I've learned very little. But what I've learned is extremely useful. The Reverend Desmond knew Duggan."

"That's it?"

"In real terms, yes, but I'm establishing myself in

Carrigbawn. My cover story is better than I'd imagined. My questions about Duggan will be entirely natural. Perhaps, Matt, after this weekend, I'll have some answers.''

"Separate bedrooms," James murmured to Sarah as they followed Mrs. Eustace up the curved and balustraded staircase.

"Shussh," whispered Sarah.

"This is the blue room," said Mrs. Eustace, a tall, painfully thin, aloof woman in her forties. "Miss Gallagher, I think you'll be comfortable here."

James shrugged as Sarah disappeared into the room to find blue towels and blue accessories arranged for her convenience.

"And Mr. Fleming," said Mrs. Eustace in her flat voice, "you'll be sleeping in our second guest room." James wondered if she had stressed the word sleeping as he looked at the small comfortable room. It was decorated in tones of brown and sported nineteenth-century Irish prints of various racehorses and race meetings.

"Please come down for drinks as soon as you've changed."

Changed to what? A monk? wondered James irritably. He washed his hands at the small basin and threw his few clothes into the chest of drawers. Within seconds he was tapping at Sarah's door.

She admitted him reluctantly.

"What do you think? Is this all right?" she asked, stepping back.

James admired her slim, brown cord trousers, thick white shirt, and tweed hacking jacket. She exhibited a dainty foot clad in butter-soft leather boots.

"It's more than all right, Sarah," he said, moving to hug her.

She responded stiffly.

"We'd better go down," she said.

They descended the stairs, carefully observing the portraits by Eustace that hung on the curved wall. Two, they guessed, were of Mrs. Eustace, at different ages. Another was a portrait of an elderly man bearing a striking resemblance to Eustace.

"His father?" guessed James. He asked Eustace himself as he approached them on the stairs.

"That's my Dorian Gray . . ." he said mockingly.

"Meaning that you've painted yourself as you will look in the future, I suppose," said Sarah. "Keeping age at bay?"

James was surprised at her tone, slightly critical he thought, for a guest.

"How perspicacious of you . . ."

"Sorry, I didn't introduce you," said James hastily, "Sarah, this is our host, Malachy Eustace. Malachy, this is my good friend, Miss Sarah Gallagher."

Eustace's prominent eyebrows shot up as he looked quickly from James to Sarah and again to James.

"I had no idea," he smiled, graciously clasping her hand and leading her gently down the stairs, leaving James in oblivion.

Drinks awaited them in a startling room, less a sitting room than a spacious furnished gallery. The rest of the house, although large, was nothing out of the ordinary. This room, however, was painted a soft white with a hint of green, infinitely soothing. Low white sofas and green chairs were scattered around the room. Eustace explained it had originally been three ground-floor sitting rooms. A free-standing fireplace, with a black hood and chimney rising to the ceiling, centered the room. A low glass table and two others formed from slabs of green Connemara marble, rough hewn on the edges and polished on the surfaces, stood waiting with little bowls of nuts and crisps. A large, high bar, also free standing, stood at an angle to one of the corners and it was here the three of them gathered as Eustace mixed martinis in a tall, curiously shaped glass pitcher. "From Sweden," he duly informed them. The room's various elegant appointments were outshone, however, by the nearly fifty portraits hanging on the walls. The initial effect was breathtaking, thought James, but it felt rather more like an art gallery than a home.

And so it was in part, as Eustace explained, his eyes continuously on Sarah, his very voice modulated in a mixture of homage and braggadocio. He took her hand again, leading her to the centre of the room. Ignoring James, he spoke as though they were alone.

"I change the arrangement of the works fairly frequently. It's like having a permanent exhibition. My studio is out back you see, off limits except to my sitters."

"Your privacy when you work must be quite important to you," Sarah responded.

"Oh my yes, and to my subjects."

"I never see him when he's working," said the dry Mrs. Eustace who had entered silently.

"Margaret, Margaret, I didn't see you there. Do you realize whom Fleming has brought to grace our home these few days? Ms. Gallagher is *the* Sarah Gallagher, the concert violinist!" Eustace was flustered and voluble.

Mrs. Eustace blushed quite suddenly, an unpleasant red flush rising to her face.

"I had no idea," she said. "Please, feel at home. My husband's work may interest you," she finished lamely, obviously intimidated by the fame and reputation of the guest she had not recognized.

Husband and wife chatted together as James and Sarah moved slowly around the room, studying the pictures. James looked in vain to recognize even one of the subjects of these numerous portraits. Privately he thought the works too florid, too rich in colouring, the oil too thick. Sarah on the other hand seemed to him unduly impressed. He held his tongue.

"Tell me," said Sarah, rejoining the couple sitting on one of the low sofas, "surely you paint portraits on commission. So why is it that your subjects have left their pictures with you?"

James cringed at the unexpected bluntness from Sarah. This was a side of her he'd not seen before and he began to wonder if this was Sarah when she was amongst her peers in the music world, a world to which he'd had no entry.

Eustace's confidence was unshaken, however. "It's simply that these were not commissioned portraits. They were people I chose and who agreed to let me do them, as we say. It's one way of displaying my work to prospective clients. But the real reason is that often my paying clients bore me to tears— visually, I mean. Bland, prosperous faces. I'm happy for their prosperity—it means I can charge a great deal for my work. But I earn it, you see, in the excruciating boredom of painting faces with no character whatsoever. My subjects are inevitably in their sixties, and there's a sameness about them."

"Surely by that age, their life experience, wisdom, perhaps even pain is showing in their features," queried Sarah, handing over her empty glass.

"There speaks an artist, James," said Eustace as he lounged over to the bar and began concocting another drink. "And Sarah, I would have agreed with you before I got into this game. No, I have found more character in the faces of my other subjects." He waved his elaborate glass swizzle stick at the walls. "This man here is a barman in Dublin. This woman here I met in the casualty ward one summer when I'd sliced my hand stretching a canvas. And this dear soul! She used to run a little local library here, now defunct. Look, look," he grew animated. "Look at her eyes. There you see pain, as you say, and the wisdom that grows from pain . . ."

Margaret's flat voice interrupted him. "Sorry, Malachy, but I see only an embittered spinster, too thin for her own good. She never got over the fact that Brendan Boyle, our butcher, didn't see fit to marry her."

Malachy said nothing at first and merely looked at her. "Another country heard from then."

A slight tension filled the room. James had wanted to agree with Margaret. He himself could not see this so-called pain.

"Surely that was enough," said Sarah. "The disappointment of a life unfulfilled. I think that may be a subject worthy of being captured on canvas, and not many artists would see its embodiment in someone who appears to be what we may call ordinary."

She turned. "James, what do you think?"

James had never experienced an out-of-body event, but he did so now. It was as though he saw himself open and shut his mouth, with no words coming out. With whom should he agree, of the three opinions just offered? To speak his own feelings would, he sensed, disappoint Sarah most of all.

"I think your analyses are very interesting," he said at last, resuming his body once again. Did Sarah look away? He gulped his drink.

"Since you are obviously intrigued by how character is formed by its environment and by its life experience," Sarah addressed Eustace, "I am surprised that you did not undertake photographic portraits?"

"Or perhaps sculpture?" James said suddenly, not merely attempting to redeem himself. "I find heads, or rather busts, rather fascinating. Did you ever turn your hand to that?"

"No," said Eustace, handing him his drink and smiling smarmily.

"Or pottery?"

"Dear me, no. That's an entirely different matter. In fact potters see themselves in a different way again, even from sculptors. As sculptors do from portrait artists, and portrait artists do from photographers. It's the difference in the actual medium one uses. There are reasons why one works with one's hands. Or why one chooses oil paints and a brush. Much as one is gifted on one instrument rather than another." He smiled intimately at Sarah.

"This Duggan whom the Reverend Desmond mentioned, what was his field then?" James persisted.

Did James imagine that Mr. and Mrs. Eustace exchanged glances before he answered?

"Duggan was a potter. I think someone once mentioned he'd an interest in sculpting, did a few heads. Not on a commission of course."

"Why of course?"

"Perhaps I shouldn't have said that. Perhaps it's snobbery on my part. I believe you are either one or the other. If you're interested in shaping little bowls . . . it's just that I don't think you have the heart or the spirit or the . . ."

"Gift?" supplied Sarah.

"Indeed, the artistic gift to also sculpt. Two different art forms altogether," he concluded pompously and James felt his anger simmering, remembering as he did Duggan's beautiful terra-cotta, remembering the little yellow dog.

"Is this a bit of a class thing?"

Eustace was frank. "Possibly. You no doubt have hacks in your profession."

"I hardly think a man or woman who attempts to make a life by making beautiful and useful things can be termed a hack. And I don't think there are hacks in my profession either."

"My mistake," Eustace said, "I should have said artisan. You put it well. Artisans make useful items that may or may not possess a beauty of their own." Eustace spoke dismissively.

"And did you know this Duggan?" James pressed.

"Very slightly. We'd meet at showings." Eustace glanced pointedly at his watch. "I see time is passing. This is our game plan," he said with a return to his energetic wry manner. "I have a sitter coming at four. Why don't you two explore and we'll all meet here again at seven." He paused. "Actually if you don't mind, I'd like you to pick up one of our guests. He is, aptly enough, a sculptor. Doesn't drive." He shrugged and then quickly sketched out a small map. "My advice is to call on him early—he loves to show off his stuff." Eustace laughed loud. "I'll let him know you're coming. Margaret . . ." He nodded and was gone.

Margaret excused herself to prepare dinner and James and Sarah were left alone. Taking her hand, James let his enthusiasm show.

"Come, come with me, Sarah. There's something I want to show you."

Malachy Eustace left his house from the back door and walked diagonally across his garden to a narrow but well worn path. This path led to the rear of a small cottage set in a sylvan grove. Perhaps it had once been a gardener's cottage or a gate lodge, but now it had been transformed into a complete art studio.

Eustace went around to the front of the house which gave onto the side road. He began to run lightly as he saw the silver Mercedes parked ahead. He unlocked the low front door and held it ajar as Mrs. Desmond emerged from her car.

"I'm so sorry, Lamia, I have house guests and couldn't break away."

Lamia Desmond didn't respond. Eustace breathed quickly as he held the door wide, allowing her to enter ahead of him.

"Every moment is precious, Malachy," she said in a low, forceful voice.

"I know, I know. Please, make yourself ready." He walked quickly to the easel that stood in the centre of the room and threw off its covering. Working in silence he prepared his palette and his tubes of oil paint, checked his brushes, and then began switching on photographer's lamps, focusing their light on the chair, which was covered with a throw of thick red velvet.

Mrs. Desmond adjusted the low neck of her black velvet dress and the single emerald suspended from a thick gold chain. The jewel rested in the hollow of her throat. Perfectly composed, she sat in the chair.

"Nearly ready," said Eustace breathlessly. "Just let me adjust the lighting."

The shaded lights threw her face into shadows that defined the line of her jaw, and the prominence of her cheekbones.

"Just turn slightly," he said as he stood back at the easel. "Nearly there . . ." He moved towards Mrs. Desmond, lifting her chin and turning it gently. He let his fingers drop lightly, touching her breast bone with a single thin fingertip. He traced the jewel and the chain at her throat. Lamia shivered almost imperceptibly.

"There are other artists, Malachy."

"No, no, not for you. Hush," he said as he quickly turned back to his paints. "Only I can entertain you. I have gossip, you see, about our Mr. Fleming." Malachy, the sometime court jester, was, after all, no fool.

JAMES PULLED THE CITROËN INTO THE DRIVE OF OAK-dale Lodge, throwing up the gravel in his haste.

Leaping from the car he shouted to Sarah, "Wait, wait here."

He ran to the sheltered porch and rang the door-bell, once, twice, three times, in vain. Glancing over at the ancient garage he noticed the old green wooden doors thrown wide. Disappointed at first, he then smiled and dashed back to the car.

"It's all right. I didn't phone ahead. They're not here, but I'm sure they won't mind."

"What are you babbling about, James?" she said, laughing at last at his gazelle-like bounding and his animated nonsense.

"I'm thinking of buying this house, Sarah. The own-ers aren't here. I want you to see it. But they're not here."

"You said that."

"But it doesn't matter. We can walk over the grounds. Acres of land, acres I tell you, of beautiful land."

He grabbed her hand and they passed along the side of the house and the outhouses and into the back garden proper. At the rear of what had been a squared off third of an acre, they climbed over a dry-stone wall and into the field beyond. He threw his arms wide.

"Look, Sarah, just look!"

And together they gazed over the field knee deep in waving grass, with buttercups on long fragile stalks lifting their yellow bowls to the sun. A gentle breeze moved the grasses, swaying and shimmering in the sunlight. On the far right lay a grove of ancient, low gnarled fruit trees and at their feet a thick carpet of bluebells, sheltering in the darkness. In the distance was a stand of trees, sycamore and hawthorn and some beech, a nook of cool shade. Walking hand in hand downhill through the grass they came to the small stream meandering lazily, its pure water almost white in the sunlight. Together they cupped the water and let it flow through their fingers. Going farther than he had explored before, James linked her arm in his, saying nothing, letting the place work its magic. They walked uphill again as if headed toward the horizon of low mountains, dark blue and gray against the azure sky. At last they came in silence to a low dry-stone wall on which they sat.

From this vantage point they could see the patchwork of far-flung farms, the land spreading across the horizon at the foot of the mountains.

"My neighbours," he said, laughing like a boy.

"Not yet," said Sarah dryly.

"Shussh," James said suddenly. "What's that? Lord, wait . . . wait . . . It is!"

Sarah, listening intently, first heard a hum, then a rhythmic thud.

"What is it?" she whispered.

"It's a train, bejaysus! It's a train." Within minutes, a short goods train rattled past them on tracks that had been hidden by the slope of the dell through which it passed.

James jumped to his feet waving wildly at the passengerless train. He spun around, grabbing Sarah's hands.

"Sarah, if that wasn't a sign from the gods, or the fates, then I never hope to see one." And in his enthusiasm he hugged her with all his strength and she returned his embrace.

Gently James steered them back towards the knoll of sycamore. Did the stream flow through there? he wondered aloud. And was there a pool to bathe in afterwards!

"I had no idea you were house hunting," Sarah said at last.

"I wasn't." He squeezed her around the waist. "You see, I'd used this house-hunting ruse as a cover story. I'm here investigating a case . . ." He hesitated.

Sarah removed his arm as though it burned her.

"A legal case?" Her tone was bitter.

"No. I'm checking into a matter for a friend I met in Peru."

"You know my feelings about this sort of thing, James," she said sternly. "Obviously you do, since you neglected to tell me what it was you were really doing down here this weekend. And I, foolishly, thought it was a bit of a holiday, for you—and for me."

"But it is," James interjected. "I'm not on the case now, for God's sake. I'm showing you this house, this land!"

Sarah went on as if he had not spoken, walking quickly ahead, away from the little wood and back towards the house. "I can't understand why your life as a lawyer is not enough for you. You chose your profession, you trained for it, why can't that be enough for you? Why must you insist on dirtying your hands in other people's troubled lives? It's morbid. Get above it, James. Look beyond all that . . . look for what is beautiful and whole in this life."

"Sarah, painful as it is to remind you, I must. If it

hadn't been for my so-called sleuthing, then I would not have met you."

"I would think, James, you'd have the sense not to open that matter with me. I told you on the phone . . ."

"Right, right . . . enough said." He had blown it. There was no going back. Not today at any rate.

They reached the car in silence, both attempting to shake off the mood that had intruded so abruptly.

"Well, anyway," said James resignedly, "let's pick up this sculptor fellow . . . what's his name?"

"Garreth O'Brien. Yes, yes, I'm looking forward to meeting him. You've seen one of his statues in Stephen's Green."

"Have I?" James was startled.

"Can't miss it, James. The one of the fallen soldier . . ."

"Of course, very moving. I never made the connection."

O'Brien's house was set back on one of the side roads near the centre of town. The front garden was filled with children's toys: broken bikes, bent wheels, hurley sticks. More toys were rusting where they were left abandoned; others were still new and whole. Grass grew everywhere, as did low vines and pachysandra, leafless from being continually underfoot. The house was a rambling cottage, behind which could be seen the much higher roof of a barn.

James and Sarah stepped over the debris and banged on the open front door. Screams of shrieking children could be heard from deep within the house.

"Hallo. Hallo! Anybody home?" yelled James.

No one replied.

The shrieks and laughter continued. James took the initiative and led Sarah around the sprawling cottage to the back. Here was the source of the merriment. O'Brien, as they assumed, was armed with a broom and leading a team of three children armed with sticks, broken bats, and mops. An opposing team, equally incongruously armed with branches and rakes, was also battling to hit a child's bright red ball towards an empty laundry basket, apparently the goal. O'Brien had scored, and lifting up two tiny children, one clinging to each muscular arm, he waved them in the air like dolls.

"Victory is ours!" he roared, his long red hair clinging to his massive head, wet with sweat.

"Da, look there, Da." One of the older children pointed to the interlopers.

O'Brien turned and, bearing his tiny children aloft, came to greet them. Dropping them to the ground in a gentle sweeping motion, he rubbed his huge hands on grubby corduroy trousers and patted his flowing beard into place.

"And who might ye be?" His eyes glinted hard and clear.

"Fleming, James Fleming?" He assumed they were expected.

"Either you know who you are or you don't!" laughed O'Brien.

"Malachy Eustace phoned you, yes?" said James, bristling.

"Dunno if he did. Been out here for a good while. Never hear the phone out here. That is, if it's still on the hook!" He glared at his brood now clustered around his massive legs. Six children from four to twelve, thin as waifs, all topped with the same golden red hair of their father.

"Did he send you?"

Sarah intervened and O'Brien looked at her appraisingly as she explained who they were and why they had come.

"Jaysus, I forgot all about it. It is seven already? No . . . no . . ." He stooped to pick up the youngest child, who was playing in a muddy puddle. "I lost my watch. Where's my watch?" he bellowed, and an older boy appeared by his side, sporting it on his thin wrist.

"For Chrissakes!" O'Brien looked at them balefully. "It's only six now."

"Eustace thought you'd like to . . . well . . . we were interested to see . . ."

"Malachy said we might see some of your work," Sarah finished.

"Eustace, that horse's arse! Maria," he roared suddenly.

A slim young woman appeared at the back door.

"Take this flock o' geese in and give them their supper. Is there food in the house?"

"Yes, Mr. O'Brien," called out Maria. "Rashers and sausages and eggs. I got them in this morning."

"Right. In with you then," he said kindly, pushing his flock towards the door, peeling off bike helmets and collecting sticks and stones from their hands.

"Listen, O'Brien, we can call back for you at seven . . ." said James, warming to the gentleness of the man with his children.

"Not at all, my boy, you're here, aren't you? I'm used to bloody Eustace." He led them towards the barn. "Skinny bone and a hank of hair, he is. He's no idea, you see, none at all. Hasn't produced any little bastards to clutter up his studio now, has he!" he roared, laughing again. "He actually thinks the rest of this world works according to the clock."

He threw wide the doors of the barn.

They stepped into a shadowed room of huge dimensions; the slanting evening light was pouring through four skylights built into the original roof. Along the sides, now filled with shadows, stood benches with sculpting tools and barrels, which they learned held the powdered form of the clay O'Brien favoured.

Rolls of copper wire stood ready, and a hoist was rigged to a block and tackle fitted on a huge beam running across the top beneath the skylights.

In the centre of the room stood a statue of a woman raising a flag on a pole. Its size, even in this huge room, was overpowering.

"It's wonderful," whistled James.

"Thank you very much," beamed O'Brien, slapping him on the back. "It's early days yet. It's going to be cast in bronze, a long, long process. But this is the germ, the kernel. The Galway County Council have commissioned it, thank God, or they'd be no rashers on the table tonight." He laughed again but more ruefully.

"Do you ever do pottery?" James asked mildly.

"I have in my day. Loved it. Led me on to doing bigger things." He looked up at his statue with beaming affection, rubbing its muscled leg. "Do you have an interest in pottery?" Not waiting for an answer, O'Brien led them towards the rear of the barn.

"I haven't thrown pots for some years now, but I've kept everything at the ready. As the childer grow in wisdom and age, if not in grace," he roared at his wit, "I'd like to start them off with the pots." He waved his hand expansively at the equipment. James recognized a large kiln in the corner and a much older style potter's wheel than what Duggan had possessed. Arrayed on one wall were simple tools, wooden bats, scrapers, as well as fitted shelves, mostly empty. A large wedging board lay covered with gritty dust.

"The usual way is to start with earthenware, get a feel for the clay and how it responds in your hands, the give and take between it and your own personality. Just the feel of a ball of it between your hands, and feeling your own strength, ah . . ." His voice throbbed with enthusiasm. "Making your own little bowls or jugs, I tell you, molding them . . . it gives you a great feeling of getting back to basics, back to mother earth. It will teach them little brats self-sufficiency, I tell you. Let them know what it was like in the old days, when people grew and raised the food they ate, the wheat, the chickens, the hogs, the eggs. Let them know the feeling of making your own cups and bowls and then to eat from them. That every bloody thing didn't always come from a store. Bejaysus, it'll put them in touch with the beautiful simple life. Ruskin said it better. . . .'' He stared off into middle distance, caught up in his own thoughts.

''What did he say about pottery?'' asked James.

''Oh, it was not just about pottery, but about all the art we create with our own two hands. He tells us to ask the question when we gaze upon a work: 'Was it done with enjoyment? Was the carver happy while he was about it?' Answer that and you'll know something deep, Fleming! Ah, but you don't want my lectures. Just facts, am I right?'' Before James could answer, he barged on.

''After earthenware, a potter can move on to stoneware. That's when you can get into the glazing. Now that would be tricky for the kids, and I've not kept up with my supplies for making the glazes. But that's the stage where you can experiment with colour! Great fun altogether. The little gobshites don't know what awaits them!'' He led them back to the more brightly lit work area.

''And the other stages?'' asked Sarah. ''Porcelain, for example?''

''Well, you can move on from stoneware into china. China making is more costly, very time consuming. Usually you'd see that done in a larger setting, such as the pottery at Belleek. Bisque ware is fragile to work with and you need to be able to absorb the cost.

''And then there's the porcelain, an evolution of

china I suppose you could say. It has a wonderful romantic history, but if you're a collector you know that.''

Sarah shook her head in demurral. "No, it's just that I've seen some great pieces in museums when I travel. I don't collect, but I do have a fondness for sculpture." Sarah was diplomatic.

"Come, then, come into the house, I'll show you more." They followed him out of the wonderful barn and watched as he locked it carefully.

Stepping gingerly, they crossed the yard, which territory had been reclaimed by the hens, clucking and seeking in the rutted ground a few seeds for their evening meal.

"Come on, come on," O'Brien called as they passed through the big kitchen area, where six clean faces looked at them over a scrubbed wooden refectory table. Six pairs of blue eyes stared soberly at the intruders.

"Oh, wait, here we are then. This is Sinead, Caitlinn, Connor, Oisin, Kevin, and Bridget." Six auburn heads nodded politely. "And this is Maria, who saved our lives when she came." Maria laughed gaily as she stood at the range cooking.

"Is Maria your . . . ?" Sarah began as they went through the living area to a rear room.

"My wife? I'd be lucky. No, she's a Mayo girl come here to mind the children, thank God again. My wife, God help her, is in Paris, I think." He paused, squeezing his eyes tight, as if in an effort to recall this detail. "Maybe not. Went off with a student of mine, a painter, for God's sake. Lily-livered spotty youth! She'll have no red-headed children with that no-talent shite!"

Speechless now, Sarah and James followed O'Brien into another, smaller work room.

Here lay the tools of the sculptor as well, more red

clay, red powder covering every surface. On the wheel stood a wonderful head immediately recognizable as the well known face of Eamon De Valera. Sarah and James murmured their appreciation at the liveliness of the face and its expression.

"Glad you like it. Dublin County Council are holding an open competition. I'm up against tough rivals for this particular commission." He touched the bust gently at first, and then pushed at it with his thick strong fingers. Then, to their astonishment, he began to pull the face apart. He worked quickly, reshaping, reforming, but the expression was gone and only featureless clay remained. Somehow his speed and ferocity were frightening, and the demolition of the head unnerving. O'Brien punched it with his huge fist, and then began shaping it in earnest. He looked up as though surprised to see James and Sarah still there.

"No, no, no, no." He waved his arms wide, and answered their unspoken question. "It was too conventional. If I'm going to beat out these cocky young bastards with their art school training, I've got to do better than this." He slapped the lump of clay affectionately. "I'll be back, sir."

He swept them through the house. "Come and let the children stare at you rudely while I change into something more presentable. Wouldn't want to dirty up that thin-cheeked artiste's pristine showroom. I ask you . . ."

James and Sarah laughed at his innocent expression.

"I tell you, it must be like living in a hospital. Pays off though, I can tell you. Eustace makes good money, money for old rope as I say, but then that's only my jealousy talking. I'd give my eye teeth to see into that studio of his. The bloody whore makes more in a month than I make in a year. And with no mouths to feed! I don't think that Margaret of his eats at all!''

They entered the kitchen to see those very mouths shovelling in what looked to be a delicious country supper.

As they stood awkwardly in the warm room, Maria presented them with two huge mugs of tea, ''just to tide them over.'' As they drank, they commented aloud on the design of the mugs, which were as heavy as beer steins.

''Ah sure, they're all we've got at the moment. Can't keep a cup in one piece with this lot.'' Maria nodded with affection at the staring children. ''These here now, Mr. O'Brien made them, but it's years ago. I found them in the barn. He tells me he started off on this lark of sculpturing by being a potter, a trade that makes some sense, at least to me.'' She laughed gaily as she splashed water into the sink and began the dishes. ''Ah, God, he'll kill me now surely.''

Sarah and James looked blank.

''No hot water, you see. I forgot to turn on the immersion heater.''

Roars from somewhere in the house followed this statement. And shortly thereafter O'Brien arrived, changed into a decent pair of jeans and a denim shirt but looking only slightly less grubby.

He shook the red powder from his hair and glared at Maria.

''I know, I know,'' she said, spreading her hands wide.

''Not to worry.'' He smiled at her and sprinkled kisses over the heads of his children and left at last with his exhausted escorts.

''Well, didn't I tell you! Did they speak or were they not struck to stone?'' O'Brien asked, waving his hand towards the house.

" 'Stone' about captures it," said James as he slipped behind the Citroën's wheel.

"Can't understand it," said O'Brien. "People passin' through the house all hours of the day and night, think they'd get used to it, but no." He sighed suddenly, an enormous sigh from his barrel chest. "Suppose it's the Ma goin' off like that, without a word. But they'll have to get over it, won't they . . . ?"

He shifted abruptly. "What line of work are you in then, Fleming? It's not the artist's game payin' for this fine car now?"

James briefly explained his job and the purpose of his visits to Carrigbawn. In describing the house he also alluded to Sarah's career and renown.

"Violin, is it? Can't say I've heard of you. Now the fiddle, that's a different story. Don't suppose you can fiddle worth a damn?"

Sarah shook her head, slightly annoyed.

"No, I thought not. But give me a jig or a reel or even a fine air, that's music I can understand. Don't like this country music crap though. Takin' hold here in Ireland, it's daft to me." He slapped his knee heartily and shifted abruptly again in his conversation. "So you're thinking of settling down here, are ye? Well, be the looks of it you're well in. Staying with the fair-haired Eustace. He's hand in glove with Lamia now. . . . But you know all that. . . ."

"No, tell me," said James carefully.

"You mean to tell me you don't know that she runs the show here in Carrigbawn? And you a lawyer. Man, she makes you or breaks you around here. There's more to that pair than meets the eye. But enough said . . ."

O'Brien remained silent for the rest of the short journey, till James, hoping to learn more, reluctantly pulled the car in front of Eustace's house.

Then O'Brien burst forth yet again.

"Have to mind my p's and q's now, for the uppity Margaret." He placed a large fingertip on the end of his nose, like a schoolboy. "Free meal though, and despite all, she's a marvelous cook. Hope a few more are comin' or it'll be a deadly evening. Oh bejaysus! We're stuck."

James looked in the direction of O'Brien's gaze and thought likewise as he spotted Fred and Elsie. But then he smiled. There was no harm in currying their favour, he thought shamelessly, in his plan to obtain their house.

"I wish you'd let me paint you in the nude," said Eustace as he watched Lamia slide her pale ecru silk slip over her lithe and naked body. He moved to run his hands over the firm line of her hips.

She shrugged away from him. "That's enough. Anyway, you'll be late," she said, kissing him full on the mouth even as she pulled away, taking up her black dress.

"I know. I don't care."

"Don't ever say that to me," she returned sharply. "You can never draw attention to yourself in this matter." She turned and stared at him as she adjusted the fall of her dress. "You understand?" Her eyes were hard and glittering and he watched as she hissed through her teeth, fascinated by the quick shifts in her moods and tones.

"Yes," he said simply, because he did.

"I'll come on Wednesday. Michael's going to Dublin for a clerical conference, an all-day affair at the cathedral. "Two hours, that's all you can have. And one of those is for the portrait."

"Lamia, anything you can give me, anything . . ."

"Good night," she said and was gone.

Eustace hurriedly tidied the room. He covered the raised mattress, which served as a bed of sorts, with its satin sheets and heavy woven spread. Dousing the lights, he locked and secured his studio against all prying eyes.

Many hours later James and Sarah dragged themselves upstairs to their rooms, leaving Margaret and Malachy to clean away the debris of a strenuous evening. Everyone had drunk too much wine and everyone had talked too much nonsense. Margaret and Elsie had kept their heads, talking of gardening and a recent flower show and the merits of cats versus dogs. But the whole of the evening had been dominated by an explosive argument between O'Brien and Eustace over their competing mediums. Sarah and James and the luckless Fred had acted as jury, coming in at last with a hung vote.

"Hope your evening was okay?" James said dubiously as he kissed Sarah at her door.

"Stimulating I guess is the word," she smiled kindly. "Sleep well, James. From what you've told me I'd like to hear the service at your church in the morning." James groaned aloud at the thought of another social encounter with the Carrigbawn crowd, but agreed. Secretly, he was heartened that she had not referred to his hidden agenda, and pleased too that she was willing to go to his church. And so he slept, dreaming restless dreams of Sarah and of talking heads and of Lamia's small even white teeth.

AT ABOUT THE SAME TIME THAT O'BRIEN WAS WOLF-
ing down pork loin and applesauce and attacking Malachy Eustace's chosen profession, the Reverend
Michael Desmond was poring over his scholarly texts
in the small office attached to St. Killian's church.
He sighed as he leaned back in his chair and checked
his watch for the hundredth time. A mere twelve
hours and he would be standing in front of his congregation—with nothing to say.

His eyes were aching and he removed the heavy
glasses. Virtually blind, his vision was immediately
blurred, and he could perceive only light and dark
shapes. Since he had been a boy he had done this
same maneuver. When under stress at the small private school he'd attended, and later at the seminary,
he would remove his glasses and instantly be trans-
ported back to another place and time. During his
childhood his visual impairment had seemed almost
magical, removing him from reality and releasing his
imagination. He could let his mind float, free from its
fetters, drifting as if in cloud, buffering him from his
surroundings. But now his mind returned to the more
immediate past, the early days of his relationship with
his wife. They had been so happy, he believed. He
remembered sailing with Lamia for the first time,
across Dublin Bay. He again felt the exhilaration, the
wind whipping cold, drowning out all but the quick

snap of the sails. They were laughing, carefree, together. He rubbed his eyes and forehead, massaging gently as he'd been taught, releasing the tension and the fatigue. His life had taken on a wholeness when he had met Lamia. He'd never realized that he'd been lonely before he'd come to know her. Not because he'd denied it, but because he'd not even recognized it. He'd always been alone. It had seemed the natural condition of the only child of an older widowed father, despite the friends he'd made, the many colleagues, and despite the spiritual life he'd found.

But when he'd met Lamia, he'd realized that he had indeed been not merely alone but lonely. And when he came to know her, he had felt such a sense of . . . relaxation was the only word he could find to describe it. And then they had married and he experienced for the first time the security of emotional well-being he believed only a sacrament could bestow. But now the psychic pain was excruciating as he felt the familiar loneliness creeping back.

"Patrick," he said half aloud. He'd been able to talk with Duggan about such things, if only in a roundabout way. He missed him. He shook himself. How paltry was his spiritual life that he missed the dead man out of self-interest. He turned his mind to prayer then, in humility acknowledging his selfishness and praying for the soul of his friend and for the eternal rest of that soul.

Yet, he was distracted in his prayer. What was wrong between him and Lamia? Was there something new? There was nothing he could pinpoint except their ongoing problem. He cringed as he termed it that: so "pop" psychological in its vagueness. Lamia had been patient, was still patient. Why did he suddenly feel this angst, this soul searching? Desmond stood up restlessly and paced the room, replacing the glasses on his nose. Another hour lost and no further along. He pushed from his mind yet again the distraction brought on by his uneasiness about Lamia and his grief for Duggan. "Time heals," he said aloud. But when?

He turned to the Gospel reading for the following day, Matthew 10, 28–33. "Are not two sparrows sold for a farthing? And yet not one of them will fall to the ground without your Father's leave. But as for you, the very hairs of your head are all numbered. Therefore do not be afraid; you are of more value than many sparrows."

Desmond felt a weight lift from his chest, his breath came easier and he let his mind dwell on the comfort of the familiar words. If you are loved, he considered, how much easier to love others; not just in reciprocation, but as an ever-widening circle, a love of all life. Yes, the Lord loved him, He numbered the hairs on his head. And yet, what about Duggan? Duggan's death had well and truly rattled him. Not for his own personal loss, which he realized now was greater than he would have credited when Duggan was alive. What disturbed him most was the manner of that death.

Desmond had worked with the poor and the sick in all of his ministry. He'd seen death come in many forms, but he'd never encountered a death by murder. Death inflicted by one man on another. How could that be part of God's plan for Duggan? What emblematic meaning could be drawn from Duggan's death? Why death so young, in an absolutely cruel and useless fashion? He wanted to shout. His concentration broken again. He bowed his head to pray over the words one more time.

Perhaps he should focus on the murderer. The police believed the death was accidental, that a youthful offender had tried to knock Duggan out when he surprised him in the house. But the pottery planter was heavy and the robber's panic powerful: the results more dreadful than the robber had probably intended. Perhaps he should pray for the soul of that unshriven youth who'd taken Duggan's life. But he could not, he found. Not yet.

Desmond turned to the readings for the previous day, June 26, the feasts of Saints John and Paul. The text from Ecclesiastes caught his attention: "These were godly men whose virtues have not been forgotten; their wealth remains in their families, their posterity are a holy inheritance and their seed has stood in the covenants. And their children remain forever . . . there name lives on and on."

Duggan had lived a decent life and yet his name would fade. For that matter his own name too would fade, as would his father's. He, the last of his line, would not have children, he thought sadly, allowing the thought to surface clearly for the first time. Desmond shivered. The solace he sought for so desperately was not forthcoming from the word of the Lord.

He bent his head to the text. It would be a very long night, this Saturday night, as Desmond worked on his sermon and the members of his congregation occupied themselves with matters of the flesh—and of the devil.

"What did you think?" asked James almost anxiously, his proprietary air showing itself.

"It was a fine sermon, James," Sarah answered diplomatically.

"Mmm, well, he seemed tired. And the text was difficult."

"I see you wanted more."

"I don't know what I expected." James's voice fell away. He and Sarah seldom spoke of substantive issues. And he was reluctant to say that, yes, he did want something more, some explication of how God's love showed itself in a world too often filled with violence and sickness and pain. He sensed this young priest was actively seeking the answers. Perhaps that knowledge in itself was enough for today.

"Right," he said energetically, "let's nip over to join in the morning refreshments. Meet the rector's wife and all that . . ."

"You must be joking?" said Sarah, as James, as Eustace had before him, attempted a ruse.

"It's only polite."

"Well, I never had to do this after Mass," she said, stung.

"You didn't need to, did you?" he laughed. "Being in the majority. Wherever you go in Ireland you're going to meet another Catholic."

She smiled at last. "Okay, okay. Let's go."

James had the satisfaction of seeing her face drop as they arrived at Monks Hall, and the further fun of introducing her to Mrs. Desmond. Lamia, however, realizing immediately who she had for a guest in her home, efficiently shed James and drew Sarah away into the alcove. The interview room, thought James ruefully as he scanned the crowd for the Reverend Desmond. Anxious to engage the man in a conversation concerning Duggan, James asked a few of the guests standing near him. No one had seen the minister and James learned that this nonappearance was not in the least unusual. Finding himself standing next to the nervous watercolour artist whom he'd met at the showing the week before, he struggled to recall her name.

"I didn't realize you lived here in Carrigbawn," Miss Conly opened the conversation, tossing her straight blond hair over her shoulder in an habitual gesture.

"Oh, well, I don't. I'm visiting the Eustaces. But I'm seriously considering the idea."

She relaxed. "I'm glad to hear it," she said. "Sometimes it can be very wearing to be surrounded by artists, by your competition, seven days of the week."

"And by large egos," James said, mockingly serious.

She jumped like a cat. "I wouldn't go that far. But the pressure can be intense . . ." She trailed off, as if wondering if she had said too much.

"Surely it can act as a spur though?"

"Oh, yes. A great motivation, keeps you focussed. But, well, I can tell you since you are not a part of the scene here. There are a number of very well-known and successful artists in Carrigbawn—financially successful. They have some fame and recognition. Oh, they've paid their dues, all right. But years ago. For the younger artists it's . . . it's very hard." She closed up like a clam.

"Hard for you?" James persevered.

"Yes, hard at the start, when I left the art school, and believe me, it's still hard. But I'm lucky. My parents live here. Perhaps the environment here led me to painting. No, I'm sure it did. But I live at home. When things are not going well I still can eat! There've been others who . . ."

"Like Duggan, Patrick Duggan?"

Miss Conly jumped again. "Well, yes, I had him in mind. But how did you hear of him?"

"Oh, a number of people have mentioned him."

"I see. Well, yes, it was hard for Patrick . . ."

"Financially?"

"Oh, indeed. He supported himself. I admired that so much. He had no one but himself to rely on. We used to meet for coffee in the town, you know, the French place. I'd treat him to pastry and he let me only because he was teaching me a bit about throwing . . ."

"Throwing?"

"You know, using the clay on the wheel. I was working on some terra-cotta with him."

"He left Carrigbawn, I understand?"

"Yes, I was sorry. I enjoyed our morning coffees." Her strong thick features suddenly softened and James warmed to the young woman.

"Why was it he left?"

"Och, I still don't know and now I never will. He'd got a grant from the EC, on a scheme for young artists. He'd applied for it years ago and then out of the blue it came through. He was very happy about that. But he'd never talked of leaving Carrigbawn, at least not to me. And then I didn't see him for a week or so, but that wasn't unusual. I wanted to do some more work with him and I called round to the little cottage he rented and it was empty. There was no one to ask, well no one I could ask directly." Suddenly she glanced around her, not wanting to be overheard. "He just up and left apparently. I heard later someone had seen him get off the bus one day a month or so afterwards. If so, he never came to call on me . . ."

James heard the lingering anger in her voice. "And then he was killed," he said softly.

"Yes, and I was sorry. For a lot of reasons . . ." Miss Conly suddenly glanced away as she saw Sarah approaching. "See you," she said quickly and as quickly walked off.

Sarah rolled her eyes discreetly as she neared James's side.

"Whew!" she whispered.

"The third degree, I take it?"

"Absolutely, only so subtly done as to be nearly imperceptible. I think I can see what O'Brien meant last night. Mrs. Desmond is the shaker and mover here in Carrigbawn. Much of what you see, the gallery in particular, is due to her largesse. She fancies herself a patron of the arts, all right." Sarah reached for a glass of sherry that stood on a full tray near them. "The thing is, she is very knowledgeable, not only about the art world but about music too. So unusual I think for someone in her line of business. Did you know that she's a stockbroker? An extremely successful one. So much so, she now works from home. She lived in London for years, making her career."

James was surprised. "I see, I see. I had just assumed that all this represented some great family fortune."

"Oh, but it does. She referred to that also. Perhaps to impress me in turn. This is her family home all right. But she's obviously improved on it." Sarah indicated the opulent furnishings.

"But when did she return? She seems so well established here in Carrigbawn."

"I'm not sure. It's a few years though." Sarah sipped her sherry as she glanced around the crowded room. "What is this all about really, James? I feel I was just interviewed, despite the fact she was so candid about her own career. And you are being scrutinized. I'm starting to feel uncomfortable . . ."

"I agree, it's bizarre . . ."

"Do we have to go back to the Eustaces?" she whispered.

"I imagine so," James faltered. "Hush . . ."

Eustace was approaching them, having just completed, as they could plainly see, an intense conversation with Lamia. Or rather, he had bent his head and listened intently to what she had to say. James couldn't shake the impression Eustace was following instructions, bearing some message.

"Fleming! Listen! Fred and Elsie have gone off to a reception up in Dublin. Yet another anniversary of something at the British Legion, if you can believe it?'' He laughed pleasantly at his English neighbours' foibles. ''But Fred kindly gave me the key to their house. Thought you might like to show Sarah, Miss Gallagher, around.'' He turned deliberately to smile at Sarah. ''Just lock up when you leave. Oh, by the way,'' he said as he casually handed James the heavy keyring. ''No need to come back to us for lunch, we'll see you at four for tea. Cheerio . . .'' And with an irritating slap on James's back he herded them to the foyer.

With mutual sighs of relief, James and Sarah headed out through the double doors and ran to his car. Bright drops of summer rain were splashing down around them like tiny water bombs at a children's summer party.

''This is great, really great. Makes up for yesterday!'' said James as he put the car in gear. ''I can't wait to see inside the house again, in daylight! And I can't wait to hear what you think of it!''

Sarah, he thought, was unusually quiet, even for Sarah, but he chose to suppress his anxiety. Nonetheless, it was with trepidation that he let her into the house through the ivy-covered entryway and shut the door carefully behind them.

Mrs. Desmond shut the door behind their last parishioner and instructed her young maid, Goretti, to clear away the remnants of the coffee hour. Silent and severe, she alarmed the girl even more than she did normally. Her face was rigid and her thoughts dark as she sought out her husband in the large comfortable study at the rear of the house.

She observed him silently. Desmond sat lethargically in the desk chair, gazing, hunched and disconsolate, out the French windows to the wide and manicured back gardens. The wind had risen and although the sky remained blue, the sudden shower was developing into heavier rain. He watched as the drops spattered like bullets, pounding the delicate rose petals and the last of the tulips. The gladioli were drooping precariously, their stems ready to snap.

Consciousness of another presence made him turn and he started in his chair to see his wife standing there.

"Lamia, what is it?" he said almost alarmed.

"Nothing, darling. I was just thinking . . ."

"I, too. Thinking I might cut some gladioli before the rain brings them down."

"No, Michael," she said sharply.

"Why ever not?"

"They're too funereal. And I have had enough of such things." A silence came between them. And it lengthened as neither made a move. At last Desmond relented, knowing full well his next question would lead to an unwelcome comment.

"Enough of what, Lamia?"

"You know, I think." Her tone remained level, modulated but firm. The tone, he reflected, that she maintained with her brokerage clients: efficient, impersonal, and confident.

"I'd rather not . . ." He shrugged.

"Oh, I know you'd rather not discuss it. But you must stop these depressing homilies. The parish will notice, if it hasn't already."

"I am working to resolve something, Lamia." His voice was tired and sad. "Something personal . . ."

"You are not here to resolve things, as you say. And certainly not your own personal preoccupations."

"Preoccupations?" He was genuinely surprised. "Lamia, death can hardly be dismissed as a mere

111

preoccupation. And it's a subject of interest to many."

"Michael," Lamia was sharper than before. "You will not mention Mr. Duggan in your sermons again. That's final. Not directly as you did last week, or indirectly as you did today. I'm not interested in why you have felt it necessary to keep his death fresh in all our minds. Suffice it to say, you have done that. Enough is enough. Your congregation needs more from you than elegies. These people are intellectuals, artists. They look to you for inspiration. That's why, if you recall, I brought you here." She watched as the very faintest of blushes crept across her husband's face.

"Michael." She was softer now, as soft as the wind rustling the long curtains at the open windows. "Michael, darling, I am worried about you." She crossed over the chasm that had separated them, however briefly. Standing by his side she placed a slim delicate hand across his forehead as he closed his eyes and leaned back in his chair.

"Lamia?"

"Hush. It's all been too much. I should have been more vigilant. Tell me, did you take your insulin?" She massaged his forehead.

"Of course I did." His tone was weary, almost irritable.

"Your mood of late, so . . . so depressed . . ." She hesitated, picking her way in a minefield she knew well could explode. "I want you to go up to Dublin tomorrow to see Dr. Gregor."

"I don't feel like it." He was petulant now.

"That's just it. Your mood has been black for a good while and you have no energy." She went around and knelt in front of Desmond, her hands on his knees. "I want him to check your hemoglobin. Maybe he could change your insulin."

For an answer, he closed his eyes, silence giving assent. He always agreed with her, as she well knew. Too tired to argue he sat and felt the weight of Lamia's head as she leaned on his knee. They sat for a long time, just that way, until he fell into a deep and exhausted sleep, untroubled for once by dreams of the corruption of the body in the grave, untroubled because dear Lamia was with him.

While Desmond spent the next forty-eight hours ensconced in Blackrock Clinic, where Dr. Gregor adjusted and monitored his insulin and glucose levels, Lamia made herself comfortable at the Shelbourne Hotel. Normally when visiting Dublin overnight she kept to her familiar room at the Gresham. But the Shelbourne this time was more convenient for her purposes.

To James's thundering surprise, she called upon him at work.

Maggie neglected to announce Lamia and as she led her into James's office her eyes danced with mischief and curiosity. It wasn't every day that Maggie had the treat of observing such high couture. And such jewellery, as she exclaimed later, even among James's fairly prosperous clientele.

A flustered James had been engrossed in his notes concerning the fair division of property and the rights of the sons of Mr. O'Connor's two wives. He hurriedly bustled about his office, picking up and putting down ten files in a fast two minutes while trying to mask his initial surprise.

"Please, Mr. Fleming, this is a purely social visit."

Social, my foot, thought James.

"I'm in town on some business and thought I'd look you up."

At least James had the presence of mind not to ask how she had found him, since he knew Eustace had his card. And he suspected that a few discreet calls had been made to colleagues in the small world of law and justice in Dublin. A woman as wealthy as Mrs. Desmond had to be very well connected. His desire to learn more calmed him.

"I'm happy to see you, of course. May I offer you a sherry, or . . ."

"A sherry please, dry."

"Certainly." James went to the drinks cabinet and poured two sherries into the Waterford sherry glasses that stood ready on the tray.

"I understand," Lamia said slowly, "that you deal mostly in wills and estates."

"Yes, for the last ten years now."

James explained how he'd worked for the firm of Fitzgerald's and had eventually been in the position to purchase it. But he realized from her diffident manner that she probably knew all of this already. He paused almost as if she had spoken.

She smiled a benign smile and he relaxed. Too soon.

"I also understand that you have done some, how shall I put it, some detective work?" Her mouth made a small moue of distaste.

"In a manner of speaking," said James, "but as an avocation only. Circumstances led me into some tangled webs." James's manner was smooth.

"In fact, that is how you came to meet Sarah Gallagher?"

"Mrs. Desmond," James was abrupt, amazed at the extent of her knowledge about his so-called private life, "is this relevant to your visit?" He thought back to Sarah's summary of her conversation with Lamia, certain that she of all people would not have mentioned their complicated past.

"Pardon what seems to be my prying. As I explained to you, James, I take a great interest in Carrigbawn. And I believe that you and perhaps Miss Gallagher," her tone was inquiring now, "might be happy in our little community."

So Sarah was the prize to be captured here, it dawned on James. His pride was piqued.

"I'll be the judge of that. I do happen to control my own destiny." He tapped a pencil on his desk in irritation.

"I doubt that, Mr. Fleming."

"How can . . . ?"

She lifted her pale hand imperiously, as if to silence him. "I only mean that in the largest of contexts. You see, living with as spiritual a man as my husband, I am influenced by his thinking. But I digress. I want to ascertain that you . . . no . . ." She paused to light a cigarette and began again. "We've never had a scandal in our small community."

"I hope I don't see what you're driving at," said James, fed up to the teeth with her constant references to her "community."

"I refer to your avocation, your detective work. I'd rather not think about the kinds of scandal that may follow you."

"Mrs. Desmond," riposted James. "This is unacceptable. I'm not sure with whom you have been speaking about my career. But I am sure that you would have to do a bit of digging to discover my role in any of my recent cases. I admit that they may have been, on occasion, *causes célèbres*, but my part in them was played out behind the scenes. Deliberately so." He modified his tone. "Really. Perhaps your concern is kindly meant"—of this he was none too sure—"but my life is my own." He now took his best shot. "And on the other issue you raised—I understand, for example, that Mr. Duggan, who was from Carrigbawn and with whom your own husband was acquainted, was murdered!"

But Mrs. Desmond didn't miss a beat. Standing, she stubbed out her cigarette. "Mr. Duggan, if you'll recall, was killed in Dublin, Mr. Fleming. But enough of this. I see by your demeanor that you are very determined in this matter—of settling in Carrigbawn, I mean. Such vigour, such commitment pleases me. And so it also pleases me to tell you that Mr. White would consider an offer from you on his house." With a flourish she handed him an envelope. "The details, you'll find, are all in this letter."

James was taken off guard, as she'd intended.

"We'll meet again . . . I have no doubt. My regards to Miss Gallagher," she said pleasantly as she left the office.

Where armies clash by night, thought James, both provoked and intrigued by the formidable and beautiful Mrs. Desmond.

Wondering just how much he'd allowed himself to be manipulated in this matter, he sat heavily in his chair to study Fred's letter. The price mentioned was better than he'd dared hope. James buzzed Maggie to get his banker on the line.

# 12

"HE CALLED FROM LIMA. COLLECT." MAGGIE'S news was startling and she knew it.

It was Friday morning and James had arrived late to his office after an interview with the mortgage department at his bank. The news had been good.

"Did he say when he's arriving?" asked James, a little tense.

"His flight leaves from London today. He thinks he'll make a connecting flight sometime over the weekend. He said he'd ring you when he was finished in Carlow."

"I see, I see." James ran his fingers through his thick black hair, as he habitually did when worried.

"I can't understand it. I was certain Father Tom had said he wasn't due any leave for some time."

"Oh, sorry, sorry. He did say something. Look, James, the line was atrocious. But I think he said he was bringing Father John home. Does that make sense?"

"Oh my God." He stared blankly at Maggie for a second. "Father John!"

"Yes, I'm sure he said that. What's the matter?"

"Father John was . . . Father John died weeks ago. In fact just before I left Peru. Tom must be accompanying the body home . . . God!" Suddenly Peru seemed very close indeed. He saw again John's jovial ruddy face before his eyes. And Tom's more serious

117

expression. With some guilt, he realized that recent events, especially his excitement over the house and his dreams of living there with Sarah, had obscured his Peruvian experience. He sat heavily in his chair as Maggie left him to his uncharacteristic silence. Granted, he'd only gone to Carrigbawn to pursue Father Tom's wish to establish the cause of Duggan's death, but he'd lost sight of his mission. He glanced at his watch, willing time to stand still until he could assemble his forces. He could not face Tom with the little information he'd collected.

He drummed his fingers on the desk in front of him. Allowing that Tom was probably airborne, allowing for some delay coming through London, allowing time for him to journey to Carlow—perhaps he had until Monday before the priest contacted him again. Three days!

Putting his pride in his pocket he snatched up the phone and called Eustace, hoping for an invitation.

"Sorry, Fleming, almost any other weekend would have done. But we've got a full house this weekend because of the gallery showing. And I just heard today that the inn is booked up. Great for us, bad for you. Glad to hear, however, that you're so anxious to see us all here in Carrigbawn." His tone was wry, thought James, but then it always was. He couldn't tell if he was laughing at him or not.

"It's just that the bank's surveyor is travelling down today." Was this true, he wondered, realizing that now he'd have to call the bank to arrange it. "He's checking out the house preliminary to mortgage approval."

"Great, great! Sorry we can't accommodate you."

"Not to worry," said James. "I just thought . . ."

"Listen, why don't I ring O'Brien? Now *that* would be a bit of fun. And you can come to the showing of twentieth-century Irish book illustration at the gallery. Lamia's contributed some of her collection to beef it up. And she's got some London people coming over. But I tell you, if you can stand it, if you stay with O'Brien you'd at least be part of the scene. Let me get back to you . . ."

"Well, if you think . . ." said James, embarrassed to be seen to be pandering to the Carrigbawn "crowd" as Eustace insisted on referring to it.

"Let me get back to you," Eustace repeated and rang off, leaving James to wonder what he'd gotten himself into.

Reflecting on his impulsive phone call, he sighed. Eustace would see him as playing his own game and be delighted. James could hear it in his voice. He wondered why he consistently viewed Eustace as game-playing and could not shake the feeling that Eustace had some hidden agenda. But, he cheered himself up, this time that agenda might meld with his own.

Eustace's return call came that afternoon when he was in conference with Mr. O'Connor of the two wives. And James eagerly got back to him.

"It's all set. O'Brien expects you when he sees you, as he said himself." Eustace laughed.

"I'll ring him then. Can I have his . . ."

"No, no. No need. He doesn't stand on ceremony, as you no doubt saw for yourself. His message to you was, and I quote, 'It'll do that lonely Dublin bastard some good to kip in with a real family.' "

James was silent.

"Don't take him seriously," said Eustace, suspecting he needn't have quoted O'Brien exactly.

"Maybe I shouldn't impose," said James stiffly.

"Too late now, Fleming. He'd take great offense." Eustace let the sentence hang but James didn't answer.

James realized he'd put Eustace in the middle and

that he had no choice. "Thanks for making the arrangement," he said at last.

"Good man, good man. The showing is Saturday and Sunday afternoon. Come late on Saturday. Everyone will be there. Drinks, the usual. See you."

James's embarrassment was intense as he put down the phone. He had liked O'Brien. He shook himself. What did it matter what strangers thought of him? He had a larger goal, and if truth be told, he was using O'Brien, just as he was using Eustace.

He reflected on this observation. Since the beginning of his first visit to Carrigbawn, he'd viewed the village inhabitants as characters, with himself acting out a role. Perhaps this was because he had come to Carrigbawn under false pretenses. Only his adopted role had now taken on a reality and momentum of its own. He recalled his first meeting with O'Brien. He had met James as himself. Surely he was a man who was exactly what he seemed, and if he had made an observation about James's life, he'd no ulterior motive. And so James resigned himself to the fact that O'Brien must have observed a truth about his loneliness that James would rather have kept hidden.

It was lunch time. James took advantage of the break to stroll to the Powerscourt Centre off Grafton Street. Unconsciously feeling he'd something to prove to O'Brien, he spent a considerable time choosing what he decided were six perfect toys for the six red-headed children. Not too expensive so as not to offend O'Brien, and yet thoughtful, to prove a point. Inordinately pleased with his selection he spread them on his desk: a wooden spinning top, a wooden doll on a platform, both made in Yugoslavia, a box of coloured pencils, a tiny weaving loom and strands of yarn, a bag of marbles, and two Irish-language picture books.

"I knew it, I knew it," said Maggie as she arrived

to check James's appointment book with him. "A second childhood. And you never got over your first."

"Ha ha," said James flatly. "Really, what do you think?" he asked, knowing Maggie had numerous nieces and nephews.

"I think you're like the rich bachelor uncle. They'd probably rather have video games and a few busty dolls, but these will impress the parents."

"One parent, at least for now," said James, chagrined.

Maggie saw his face. "Listen, James. They are beautiful and show that real thought went into them. You'll be fine. Who is it, by the way? You Prods aren't usually that fertile . . ."

"Maggie!" James was shocked.

"Sorry. Listen, I've rescheduled your day. Your clerk is calling on Mrs. Hanlon to check the inventory of her jewellery, bringing your very personal apologies. And Mrs. Cullen is coming tomorrow instead of today, to talk to you about a codicil, she says, a bequest to her niece who will look after her cat. So . . . as of right now," she looked at her watch dramatically, "you're free to go and play house, wherever that is . . ."

"Carrigbawn, and you've reminded me. Get the bank manager again, will you please?"

"Sorry, Mr. Fleming, but the news isn't good. For you or for the Whites."

James was standing on the gravelled drive of Oakdale Lodge, thunderstruck at this obstacle suddenly thrown in his path.

The surveyor, a small grumpy man in a crumpled coat, looked up at him.

"I can't believe it!" exclaimed James. "They only bought the house last year!"

"So they say. Perhaps it was financed from England, I don't know. But I can tell you, no lending institution here will pass this house until the roof is done. Very poor condition. Over a third of the slates missing on the right wing. Letting in rain. Several of the joists are already rotted. It's only a matter of time till more damage is done. The good news is everything else is in order. But until the roof . . ."

"Right, right. I get the picture." James scuffed his toe in the gravel.

"You know, it's usually the seller who takes responsibility. No other institution will approve a loan without repairs as part of the preconditions. Talk to the owners." He tilted his head. "They're anxious to leave, I can tell."

James shrugged, looking up at the expanse of roof yet again.

"As soon as the work is done, the bank can move along the mortgage. Or they can grant you a temporary mortgage subject to the work being completed within a three-month period. So either you or the vendor will need to get estimates for the work. Until then . . ."

"I know, I know." James was curt with disappointment.

James entered Fred's house as the surveyor drove off.

Fred was waiting, already shaking his head.

"I can't believe this," he was saying. James followed him into the sitting room and was startled to see that the room had been stripped of all but the largest pieces of furniture. The sofa and wing chairs stood naked in the empty room.

"What . . . I didn't . . ."

"Didn't you know?" said Fred smoothly.

"Frankly, no."

"Elsie's youngest doesn't like her summer school.

Can't blame her. Boarding school all year and then summer school. Acting up. Smoking," he dropped his voice. "There's a boyfriend. Anyway, Elsie wants to get back, settle in the bungalow and have Barbara stay with us for the rest of the summer." At this he rolled his eyes to the ceiling.

Was all this really true? wondered James as he followed Fred into the now empty hall.

"Well, what do you think about the roof?" he said disconsolately.

"Can't say, Fleming, can't say. This move now. Costly. And we've already bought the bungalow." James realized they'd been able to finance the house in England without selling Oakdale.

"Don't have the money now, Fleming, to roof a house we're not living in . . ."

James was riled. He felt he'd been set up, by Fred, by Eustace, by Lamia—all urging him on. But why?

"I don't see that the buyer should be responsible for the roof!" he said quietly.

"No doubt, no doubt."

"I'll get back to you," said James, at a loss.

He pulled the Citroën out of the drive and proceeded slowly on the winding roads to O'Brien's house, pondering his next step. Although Duggan was on his mind, he was distracted by his disappointment over the house.

To make the cheese more binding, as the saying goes, James discovered that O'Brien was not at home.

"Jesus," said James under his breath as he stood at the door, suitcase in hand, confronted by Maria's blank face.

"Not to worry, Mr. Fleming. He didn't tell me, but that's not unusual. I've no doubt he's expecting you. He's hopeless about time. Kevin," she called, her soft voice carrying through the house and cluttered yard.

A thin red-headed boy of ten appeared at Maria's elbow.

"Listen, pet, take Mr. Fleming here over to the wood. I think your Da's gone out there, hmmm?" She ruffled the boy's hair and he looked at her with adoration in his eyes.

Without a word he walked off determinedly, James following behind.

Finding it was impossible to get the little boy to talk, James left himself to his fate. They walked for about ten minutes through a flourishing wooded area with no discernible paths. The bright July afternoon sun filtered through the leaves throwing bars of light and shadow onto the soft spongy ground. James surrendered himself to the moment, letting the peace of the scene erase the disappointment of the past few hours.

Eventually Kevin stopped, listening. The sounds of snapping branches reached them and he turned to the left. Mystified, James followed. Somehow he'd imagined O'Brien tooting about the forest with a sketchbook in hand. What confronted him was O'Brien chopping the large dead branches that littered the forest floor and piling them on an already laden handcart.

O'Brien looked up suddenly as Kevin approached wordlessly.

"Bejaysus, laddie, you put my heart crossways in my chest, creepin' up on me!" O'Brien stopped as he saw Fleming following on.

"Fleming, it's like a ghost of yourself. Come here to me and put your back into this."

Together they loaded the wood, then moved the handcart further into the forest.

"I imagine this is a bit new for you, growing up in Dublin as you did," O'Brien said at last, his strong muscled forearms bulging as he hacked with the ax, the branches yielding to him like twigs.

"Well, yes . . ."

"It makes great fuel. And it's free. Lamia lets me take whatever windfalls I want. She just acquired this parcel of land a few months ago. A strange business. The farmer who owned it—every one of his dairy cows died. It's not the first weird happening around here. The last few years, there's been a poisoned well on one of the farms. And another parcel of land turned up poisoned a couple of months later. There's been people here from the AAB, the agricultural advisory board, scouring the land for the last six years or so and with no result. It's a mystery, Fleming, and no mistake! But this farmer now, he was lucky in one way. Lamia bought him out at a good price."

He moved toward what seemed to be a clearing and gestured to the clear rolling lawns that bordered the wood.

"Do you know where we are?"

James glanced up, seeing in the distance some outbuildings, and shook his head.

"That's the Desmonds' house, Monks Hall. All this great leafy wood too." O'Brien's voice began to intone: " 'And now I wander in the woods, When summer gluts the golden bees, Or in autumnal solitudes, Arise the leopard-coloured trees . . . They will not hush, the leaves a-flutter round me, the beech leaves old.' Ah, Yeats is the man for the telling phrase, don't you think?" He didn't wait for James's answer. "Yes, she lets me take up the windfalls. Not that she'd have need of them herself."

James sensed O'Brien's gratitude was a grudging one.

"Perhaps Yeats was right," he offered.

"He was right about some things anyway," said O'Brien, smiling.

"When he said that artists needed patrons?" said James.

"I can't yet tell with you, Fleming, if you are astute, or just an innocent. If you're talking about patrons, open your eyes. After you've been here a while, you'll judge for yourself." With that, he continued Yeats's poem about King Goll in his booming voice and they moved along the fringe of the wood. They soon came upon a boarded-up cottage that sat on an overgrown path.

"Wow!" exclaimed James.

"Like a kid's fairy tale, am I right?" laughed O'Brien.

They skirted the solid little cottage as O'Brien towed the handcart and James kept the pile of branches balanced precariously.

"It's Lamia's. Well, rather she owns it, and it's on her original property. Not that she's ever used it herself. It was poor Duggan's for a long time. She let him stay there for years, once she adopted him, as we say around here. And he was happy in it." O'Brien's face clouded over.

"You knew him? The potter?"

"Knew him as well as one man might know another." O'Brien stood and looked frankly at James.

"You know, Fleming, you're a puzzle. I think to myself when Eustace rang me, what's this young Dublin fella up to? You're like a ship blown off its course and you've come afoundering up on these strange shores. Maybe, Fleming, the natives aren't so friendly . . . mmm?" He looked intently, though in a kindly way, at James's reddening face.

When James didn't answer, O'Brien merely tugged at the cart. By a circuitous route they meandered back to the front yard of O'Brien's house.

"We're neighbours, you see, the fair Lamia and I. But my property's my own, I can tell you. She'd have trouble shifting me out of here, if that was her intention."

James was puzzled as to why this thought would even arise and said as much.

"Forget it, Fleming, I was just blathering."

"Lamia's an unusual name, isn't it?" asked James. "It's Irish?"

O'Brien was starting to unload the cart. "No, it's not Irish. It's Greek. Her mother must have had a fair love of Keats, I used to think . . ."

"What do you mean?" James interrupted.

"Lamia was the name of a temptress in Greek legend, a sensuous, sinuous, shimmering creature, a mythical charmer of men. Keats wrote a helluva poem about her, even managed to make you feel sorry for her at the end . . ."

"How so?" James paused in his efforts to pile the logs and branches on the ground.

"Her chameleon-like nature, her true identity is revealed by a cold-hearted magician cum philosopher at the end of the poem. And when that happens Lamia is forced to return to her original form—that of a snake! Wonderful imagery, you know, Fleming! Ach, people don't read Keats the way they used to. I tell you, I came to know old Mrs. D'Arcy. And she'd no time for poetry. Or for her dear daughter Lamia when it came to that. Or the daughter for her. You know, Fleming . . ." O'Brien stood back from his work, wiping his brow. "Lamia only came back here from London to bury her and to take possession of her great inheritance." Again the bitter tone, noted James. "Makes you wonder, doesn't it?"

James stripped off his shirt as they worked together stacking the branches and logs under a lean-to made of corrugated metal supported on posts against the back of the house. Once finished, O'Brien next turned to the turf.

"You'll earn your keep today, Fleming."

"I'm only too glad to, since I'm your unexpected guest," James said genuinely. He liked O'Brien more and more but could hardly tell if O'Brien liked him.

"I've got some rough-cut turf here." He waved at a huge pile of bulky burlap bags. "Since I've got you to help me, I'll ask you to take these with me and we'll tip them into the coal bunker."

This structure, also near the house, was a simple concrete box with a well-fitting lid. The turf on the bottom was dry and soon they'd added the contents of the bags. Perspiration poured off James, but O'Brien hardly broke a sweat.

As they finished he looked at the pale blue sky streaked with faint pink-orange strands, a mackerel sky. "Ah, the light's failing but that's a good evening work's done, bedad! And I thank you. You've earned your drink."

James felt a sudden chill in the air and wiping himself with his handkerchief, he pulled on his rugby jersey and followed O'Brien into the house, curious as to where the flock of children had been.

He said as much as he heard the faint sounds of classical music coming from some distant room.

"Toys is it?" O'Brien said in answer to James's query. "They'll be your friends if you want to buy their affection." He laughed at James's insulted face. "Come on with ye then . . ."

James followed O'Brien down a longish passage and into a large cheery room with a picture window facing onto the wood they'd visited earlier. Darkness had fallen here and Maria had made up a small turf fire in the grate. She sat on a low stool surrounded by the flock, each of them with a child-size fiddle in hand.

"You see, Fleming," boomed O'Brien, waving his large hands, "my own version of Suzuki! How's about a tune then?"

Six faces turned to him, smiling, six little bodies clad in all manner of nightwear, scrubbed faces shining.

"I'll start them off," said Maria mildly, not the least ruffled by an audience. "But I should say it's an air. No jigs or reels tonight." She glanced at O'Brien pointedly as she drew her bow across her fiddle and the first notes of "Slievenamon" hummed in the room. The children joined willingly enough, concentrated attention on their faces.

"A ballad, bedad," cried O'Brien, beginning to sing: " 'I shall never forget the sweet maiden I met, la la la, in the valley of Slievenamon . . .' " Humming happily he beamed at James. But when they played the tune again, O'Brien listened silently, leaning his weight on his elbow on the narrow mantel. With his florid face, his huge head of auburn hair, and his flowing beard, he looked down upon his offspring with pride and grace. The brood finished and sweetly smiled—at Maria.

"That was grand, grand. You're a grand bunch of fiddlers and no mistake." He swung the littlest girl of three into the air and kissed her cherub cheeks.

"Now, you remember I'm sure, this fine man from Dublin, Mr. Fleming. He's brought you presents . . ."

With one accord they swarmed to James's feet as he sat on the chair nearest the fire, feeling like Santa Claus.

He dispensed the gifts quickly, thankful that Maggie had had the sense to wrap them, for it would never have occurred to him, as she had pointed out, that half the fun of presents was the unwrapping, the sweet anticipation. All the children seemed pleased, and each shook his hand one by one. How stupid not to have brought Maria something, but he said nothing and O'Brien roared out: "It's gone half-ten, now it's to bed, you pack of varmints, and no mistake." He bent down and kissed and hugged each of his children with enormous affection in his face. James wondered how their mother could have left them even for a day.

Feeling at ease as he followed O'Brien back through the passage, he wanted to ask him, but at the same time had no desire to open old wounds.

They entered a small snug room and James was yet again amazed at the sprawling, comfortable nature of this house. The room had a small black iron fireplace, a few old easy chairs, stacks of papers, a fender, and not much else.

"This is my snug," he said. "It's not so easy to get to the pub nowadays." He nodded in the direction they'd come. "So I brought the pub here. Now sit yourself down and tell me your pleasure."

They both decided on Guinness, whereupon O'Brien lifted the lid of the turf box and revealed a good two dozen pint bottles of beer.

"Just enough I'd say, and there's whiskey if we need it." James realized it was to be a night of serious drinking, as O'Brien sung to himself the words: " 'Day is done, gone the sun . . .' "

"Ah, God, it's great to know the fuel is in, the kids are in, I'd a grand day at my studio, as Malachy would call it. Time to put up the feet and bend the elbow."

He handed James an expertly poured pint glass of Guinness.

"Here's to my host," said James.

"And here's to good conversation and perhaps, new friends," he roared at this. "Now, Mr. Fleming, sir, tell me the real reason you're here in bloody Carrigbawn . . ."

The flat, relatively new graveyard outside Carlow town was not to Tom's liking. As he stood bareheaded in the light rain the numbness he'd felt for the last three weeks slowly started to ebb. John was home, in Ireland at last. And he wouldn't have minded the new cemetery. He had paid no heed to such petty things. If it was what his sister had chosen for him, then he would have said it was good enough. The family had talked a lot about a headstone, its style and the wording, and Tom had tried very hard to be helpful. It didn't matter. Their grief was assuaged by their planning and frantic activity. Their comings and goings, the arrivals of relatives, the wake, even their questions had all seemed hectic, disjointed somehow. He was relieved, for he had no real answers. They hadn't pressed for answers.

He took the small spade from the brother-in-law and shoveled the dirt onto the plain pine coffin. He didn't hear the thud. John didn't either. He was gone, long gone from this terrible world.

The family had had weeks to get used to the idea John was dead, but only now, at the burial, had his death become real. One by one they took their turns at the shovelling, the gravediggers standing at a respectful distance. John's sister, Mary, sobbed and Tom moved to her side. But there was nothing to say.

John was dead. He'd brought his body home in its sealed, lead-lined coffin.

Officials had wanted to open the coffin at Dublin airport, some rule coming into play. But the Church in its power prevailed. It was to be taken on faith this was John's body. God, Tom trembled violently, it had to be. At least he'd seen the body himself, he could swear that John was dead. Don't ask him to swear this was his body. He wiped the perspiration from his brow and declined the invitation to return with the family to Mary's house.

"What can I say then, Father," she said simply, "but thank you for taking care of John." She wiped the tears from her swollen eyes. "I'll pray for your work out there in that dreadful country. He's a saint now, I know it." She too trembled in the rain.

"He's with God, Mary. John's with God. He's happy now and nothing can hurt him again."

"A saint in heaven, Father Tom, and he'll watch over you . . ."

"Like a mother, he'll watch over me, and you, Mary, and you." They'd reached the funeral car. "He was my brother too, and I'm sorry . . ." Haggard and exhausted he gratefully turned to go.

"Tell me, Father, wait, tell me just one more time. They didn't torture him, did they?"

"No, Mary."

"I know you'd not lie to me." She stared into his face, every muscle straining as if she'd leap inside his head and hear his thoughts, see what he had seen in Peru that terrible day.

"No, Mary, he died immediately. There was one shot, and it killed him instantly. Right before our eyes. No," he whispered intensely as he grasped her arm, "he was not tortured and for that we thank Almighty God, am I right?" His dark eyes were alight with a strange look. And his thin strong fingers pressed into her flesh. She shuddered and took a breath.

"Then it's done," she said composed, truly composed for the first time since he'd met her. "He'd no time then to despair,'' she said simply and walked to the car without a backward glance.

No, Mary, that's left to the living, Tom almost called out, but with an act of will he instead got in his rental car and sat, waiting, waiting until the cemetery was empty but for him and the gravediggers and the rooks in the trees.

# 13

"TELL ME WHY YOU'RE SO INTERESTED IN DUGGAN."

James was completely taken off guard and to cover his surprise, made much of settling at the fire and sipping his pint.

"Sorry, Fleming," said O'Brien quickly. "I offer you hospitality and then I manage to offend you. But I'll tell you this, I'm a plain-spoken man, not an easy thing here in Carrigbawn I might add. I'm not in the inner circle . . ."

James looked at him boldly, saying nothing.

"You're a shrewd character, Fleming. I think you've picked up on the atmosphere around here. As I say, I'm not part of the clique, but I watch it pretty carefully. It doesn't pay to be on the outs with the likes of Lamia and her lapdog, Eustace. When he phoned, he asked me to find out why you're so keen on Duggan."

James didn't now which question to ask first, enraged as he was at the tenor of the conversation. He took a breath.

"Since we're being so frank here, O'Brien, maybe I should ask if you are acting as Eustace's messenger boy?"

His barb hit home as O'Brien's face hardened. But he chose to answer.

"I see why you might think that, the way I've ap-

proached you. No, I don't think I am. I am curious
myself . . ."

"All right, then why do you or any of the others
think I'm interested in Duggan?"

"Fleming, you've been asking questions about him
since you've arrived. That might have been okay, but
he's the only one you've ever inquired about. I suppose it stood out. These people are very suspicious
of outsiders."

"For God's sake, why?" James exploded.

"That's a big question. You'll have to figure it out.
The evidence is all there before you. I'll tell you one
thing, though. Lamia knows you've investigated
other cases in the past. Eustace told me that."

James nodded.

"She's wary that you are here on a formal investigation into Duggan's death."

"But what if I was, what's that to her?"

"Are you?" O'Brien said simply.

"Look, O'Brien," James paused, wondering if he
should take him in to his confidence, since he liked
the man. "From the first time I came here to Carrigbawn, when Reverend Desmond mentioned him in
his homily . . ."

"I wouldn't know about that," said O'Brien, point-
ing out he was a Catholic who barely made it to Mass
on Christmas.

"Well I'm telling you, Desmond mentioned Duggan
that day, and naturally I was curious. Then Eustace
himself told me Duggan was murdered in Dublin. Of
course I'd seen it in the papers at the time. I quoted
this back to Mrs. Desmond when she spoke with me
in Dublin. And just today you yourself showed me
his cottage. Desmond said in his sermon he wants the
community to remember Duggan and yet when I did
ask the simplest of questions about Duggan and his
work, I was met with evasion. Oh, not a stony silence

but a lack of information. As I understand it, he'd only been gone from Carrigbawn six months or so, yet people seem to be very vague about him!"

"But you just said he's been mentioned . . ."

"Yes, but not in the normal way. You know: 'I remember Duggan and he did such and so . . .' Normal chat, normal gossip. No, people are not talking, O'Brien."

"You're reading too much into this, Fleming. Duggan was killed, remember. The fact he was killed stands out larger in our minds than his life. Can't you accept that it's human nature to focus on that?"

"I'd agree, if they at least talked about his murder! But they don't."

"Perhaps because it is you who are of a suspicious nature, you see things that aren't there."

"Perhaps that's true." Privately James thought the opposite. It was because of his experience he sensed, if not a conspiracy, then a strangeness in the village's attitude. "Look, O'Brien. Naturally I'm curious. It's my line of work. I don't expect artists and musicians and sculptors such as yourself to be as intrigued by a murder as I am."

"And you're going to solve this case?" said O'Brien, turning to get two more bottles of stout.

"If I can."

"For your own purposes?" said O'Brien, pouring the beer.

"Who else's?" said James, immediately regretting it.

"That is exactly the question I think Eustace wants answered. Are you working for someone else?"

James blustered, seeming offended. "I came down here on spec to look for a house, for Chrissakes. I stumble on a story about Duggan. I remember the case from the papers of some months ago. And I'm curious. Tell Eustace to put that in his pipe and smoke it!" James was feeling the effects of the beer.

"I doubt I'll say anything to Malachy, Fleming. Personally, I'd like to know what happened to Duggan. But I have to tell you this. All of us accepted the report in the papers. The police said a robber hit him, maybe accidentally too hard. A tragic death, but not a mysterious one."

James was somehow disappointed in O'Brien. He'd expected more. But what? What O'Brien said was perfectly logical. Hardly designing. And yet . . .

"Do you believe that, O'Brien? In your heart?" James faced O'Brien with a pointed stare.

In response, O'Brien poked the fire with the heel of his heavy boot and stirred up the embers to a red flare. James waited.

"All right. I'll tell you why I am uneasy in my mind about Duggan. This is only my reason. I can't tell you why the others seem agitated, each of them may have his or her own reasons and you'll have to discover those for yourself. But myself, now . . . I knew Duggan pretty well. Not at first. He was a quiet, skinny youth when he came here. He rented a cheap room over the old pub in the town. On a weekly basis, from Mrs. Molloy. He'd done a course in one of the commercial colleges, I forget where now. He became friendly with a retired couple who did some pottery in a small way and they let him use their studio for his work. He worked as a barman to support himself, at that same pub, Molloy's. I didn't pay much attention to him then but he had a small showing at the gallery and I was impressed. Mrs. Desmond was too. She thought he had potential," he stressed the word almost sarcastically. "So he'd been here about two years when she offered him the cottage I showed you, at a nominal rent. He invested in some excellent equipment, his own kiln of course, and a new wheel. He kept on at the pub until about a year ago, until his work began to bring in some money. And he was making out all right. He'd come up with a very nice line of covered earthenware jars. He was supplying the shops in the town, a few in Dublin, another in Oughterard and elsewhere around the country. You know the type, they appeal to the tourists, foreign and Irish alike."

"What were these jars?"

"They were a little series for flour, sugar, tea, and so forth, graduated in size. Good little sellers they were. And he was trying some new stuff, too. Animals, small animals on little patches of grass at first . . ."

"Dogs?" said James. "Yellow dogs . . ."

O'Brien looked blank. "No, no. He had a series of sheep. He'd got an idea of building them up from inside and then making a rough surface. It resembled the sheep's or donkey's shaggy coat for example. I took a great liking to these and at that time we became friends."

"Did he confide in you?"

"How do you mean?"

"I'll get to the point. What you are describing sounds idyllic, at least to me. What I want to know is why he left Carrigbawn when he did."

"Ah, I've racked my brain over that, Fleming, and no mistake. I thought he was on the pig's back. I know when he got the grant he was over the moon. Planted it in the bank he did, and said he would be happy just to see it grow. But he used some of it to buy supplies. He was set up in his cottage cum studio. I saw no reason for him to up and leave for Dublin."

"Perhaps Lamia wanted to charge him more than a nominal rent for using the cottage? And he objected?"

"I doubt that. I think he would have told me. But more than that, he and Desmond were great friends. I don't think Lamia would have been so mercenary as to raise the rent to the point he'd leave. And if she had, I think Desmond himself would have objected. I know those two were friends."

"So that accounts for the mention of Duggan in church?" James mused aloud.

"As I say, I didn't hear all that, but I've no doubt. They were of an age. In fact Desmond might be a little younger. Desmond doesn't drink in the pubs, naturally. But I suppose he'd have clerical friends and Lamia's social life is pretty hectic. Every weekend it's a showing or party of some kind. She's a prime mover in people's success here. But that's off the point.

"Desmond and Duggan were friends, used to go walking together. I can hardly say hiking, since Desmond is none too healthy and never was. Duggan and I were mates all right, but if you're serious about finding out why he left, perhaps Desmond's your man."

O'Brien left the room indicating the child's crying that had been steadily building in the background.

"It's Caitlinn, she's the four year old. She cries most nights at this time. Wakes up lookin' for the Mammy. And then she only wants me . . ." O'Brien looked at the ceiling and shrugged his huge shoulders. "A right bitch. The Mammy, I mean," he added as he left the room.

As James repositioned himself in the rickety chair, he reflected on O'Brien's difficult position raising six very young children without their mother. He felt the evidence of the man's integrity was vouched for by his affectionate children. Thirsty and content James fished two bottles from the coalbox and set one at

O'Brien's place. He'd done right. O'Brien was soon back settling down again pleasantly.

"Well, I hope that was a help to you," he said bluntly.

"How so?" said James, surprised.

"I'd like to know why he left Carrigbawn. It was sudden. One day he was here, the next he was gone. No goodbye drink. No letter from Dublin. Nothing. I tell you this, it wasn't like Duggan to act so. Granted he was a quiet chap, didn't talk about himself. But who does in this country? But leaving without a word was not in character. Makes him sound like some kind of strange one, but he wasn't." O'Brien shook his head sadly.

James did not feel obliged to answer and they sat in silence for some while, fatigue creeping in on the foot of the drink.

"So, Fleming, you think you'd like to live here," O'Brien said tiredly.

"That I can't say. I know I've fallen in love with Fred White's house! It's a wonderful house. Do you know it?"

"I knew the family before the Whites. Not a house to my taste, but I see its appeal. Too dark for an artist, I can tell you that. Not enough natural light, but great grounds. They run along my own, you know."

James laughed. "Perhaps we'll be neighbours then?"

"Perhaps that may be up to other people, Fleming. Tell me this, does Miss Gallagher love the house as much as you?"

James was startled at the mention of her name, she was so far from his thoughts at that moment.

"I hope so."

"And if she doesn't, may I ask. Are you still going forward with your plans?"

James didn't answer what seemed an open-ended question. The fire was dying and they finished their stout in a not entirely comfortable silence. That night James's dreams were filled with the crying of motherless children, real or imaginary he never knew.

James discovered early in his weekend visit that although O'Brien asked the most personal of questions, he was inclined to leave James to his own devices.

The house was deserted when he rose late and found a cold breakfast laid for him on the table. It was eerily quiet. The children, Maria, even O'Brien, had all gone off. As James quickly ate, he formulated a plan that he was anxious to put into action.

Later that day he approached the gallery during its most crowded point. After a quick roam around the large crowded room, he ascertained that Eustace and all of the usual gang were present including Lamia, the centre of the attentions of a group who, by their dress and demeanor, represented prosperous pickings. He watched her from afar, overhearing snatches of conversation in plummy London accents. These, James concluded, were the dealers and afficionados whom Eustace had mentioned.

Mingling with the thickening crowd, James drifted unobserved from the gallery, and almost surreptitiously he gained his car and drove quickly back to town. Leaving his car at the inn he walked in a seemingly casual fashion until he reached the grounds of St. Killian's. After a quick visit to the church itself to establish his cover, he turned his steps to the small office at the side of the church. Knocking on the wood and wrought-iron door, he waited with anticipation, marshalling his thoughts.

The Reverend Desmond opened the inner door and peered through the grillwork.

"Hello," he said, not immediately recognizing James.

"My name is James Fleming, Reverend Desmond. We met a couple of weeks ago when I was visiting Carrigbawn."

"Yes, indeed, step in, will you? I remember now. I think you came by for coffee?"

"Yes, at your beautiful home."

"My wife's home," Desmond said simply.

James stepped into a small square room, lined on two walls with oak shelving, crammed hodge-podge with books. The far corner of the room was in complete shadow and James realized there was only one window through which light came slanting feebly. A strong light illuminated the desk. As Desmond moved around the room switching on additional lamps, James glanced at the titles of the texts on the desk. He glanced up guiltily as Desmond spoke.

"Please sit down, Mr. Fleming." Desmond indicated a chair across from his desk. "How can I help you?" he said, looking James in the face, kindness and concern showing there. He leaned forward, folding his long thin hands on the book in front of him.

James came straight to the point.

"O'Brien, with whom I am staying this weekend, has told me that you were a good friend of Patrick Duggan?"

Desmond reacted violently, sitting straight back in the chair, dropping his hands to his sides. His pale face grew even paler in the yellow light from the desk lamp.

James waited, letting the silence grow uncomfortable if that was to be.

Desmond at last leaned forward once again.

"Yes, I was his good friend," he said. "Why do you come to me?"

"Reverend Desmond, I want to speak in confidence. This is to be strictly between ourselves. Can I rely on you?''

Desmond hesitated again. James didn't know if this manner was habitual or whether the man was wrestling with some hidden problem.

''I don't know with whom I might discuss this. Go on, please.''

''I am a solicitor in Dublin, as I told you. And I sometimes undertake extraordinary cases. I have a client whom I cannot name at this time, a man whom you would find in sympathy with you in many ways. He, too, was a friend of Patrick Duggan. I know that Duggan was killed. There have been some details, albeit small, that trouble me about his death. And so I am making some very simple inquiries about his life.''

''In Dublin?''

''Yes, but I am also anxious to know about his life in Carrigbawn. I think that you might be able to help me.''

Desmond stood up, surprising James, who thought he was going to be asked to leave. He watched as Desmond distractedly turned off each of the lights he had previously switched on. Walking slowly back to the desk, he spoke.

''It's a beautiful day, Mr. Fleming, a day that Patrick would have enjoyed. Perhaps you'd like to go for a walk?''

James agreed with alacrity, relieved that Desmond seemed more relaxed. They stepped from the dark into the bright light. Walking to the rear of the church, they turned across a small field and came to a simple stile. They crossed into a larger field, where wheat waved back and forth in the light breeze. They spoke of the weather, of James's college background. He sensed that Desmond was sounding him out, perhaps ascertaining his sincerity.

"So," he said finally, "you yourself did not know Patrick?"

"No, I had read of the case in the papers, and subsequently a third party approached me. I can't yet tell you the circumstances, but I can assure you this third party is as reputable as yourself in every way." How much simpler it would be if he could reveal Father Tom's identity. He knew these two men could share much besides their association with Duggan.

"I believe you," said Desmond. "What can I tell you that might be of help?"

"Do you know why Duggan left Carrigbawn?" Suddenly the question seemed too bald, but time was short.

Desmond thought for a while. James began to get used to the slow rhythm of his conversation. And he waited.

"No," he said at last, "and it troubled me then and since. We were friends. I don't have many friends here in Carrigbawn, personal friends I mean. I met Duggan quite by chance, maybe two years ago. He liked to walk, ramble, as I do, nothing dramatic," he laughed. "Just long walks in this beautiful countryside, in all weathers I might add. He was a quiet man, much like myself. Not taciturn. We talked but not overmuch. I found him to be an extremely sympathetic sort. I imagine it looks as though we'd little in common and it's true our callings were very different. But he enjoyed speculating on life, if that doesn't sound too pompous. He was religious in his own way. And was a keen observer of nature. He had a wonderful eye."

They walked up the side of a sloping field and James began to understand the appeal of Desmond's personality. Hard to characterize, Desmond's manner was comforting. With him, there was an absence of challenge, of the need to be witty or profound. Makes him sound bovine, James commented mentally. And yet that was far from true. It was as though Desmond was much older, as though he were wise beyond his years, that perhaps he'd found some secret, a wisdom whose existence others weren't aware of.

At the top of the field Desmond spoke again. "I could confide in Duggan, you see. I had a few things troubling me, of a complex nature. He was more worldly, if I can use an old-fashioned phrase. I came to rely on him in a way, I'm afraid. And now I miss him, and I miss his advice."

"I suppose you had things in common?"

"In a way. As it happens, there aren't many men locally who are without family commitments of one kind or another. I used to say Duggan was free as a bird. And so he was. He took flight."

"Had you any indication of this before he left?"

"He had seemed a little troubled. I wonder now if I, my problems, could have contributed to his sense of uneasiness. Just prior to his leaving he'd cancelled a number of our rambles."

"So you didn't have a specific disagreement?"

"No, but, well . . ." Desmond seemed to hesitate longer than usual. "This is completely confidential, between us?"

"Of course," James said simply. Straight talking was all that Desmond ever seemed to require.

"My wife is a powerful person in the artistic community here. I keep out of all of that. I know little of such things. But because of her substantial wealth and interest, she wields considerable influence. She seemed to want him to alter course."

"In what way?"

"She had for a while taken an interest in pottery. I met him through her, actually. She let the cottage to him and liked a lot of his commercial stuff as she called it. But it seems she wanted him . . ."

"To develop new lines?"

"I don't think so. I'd say she didn't think highly of pottery after a while. Too simplistic I guess, for her personal taste."

"Are you saying her letting the cottage to him made him dependent on her favour?"

"Oh, it sounds very grand. This patroness of the arts thing. To an outsider it might look that way. It was simpler I think. She indicated to me that she'd lost interest. Subsequently, they had an argument . . ."

James's ears pricked up at what he saw to be at last something tangible.

"An argument," he repeated neutrally.

"I walked in on it. She was rather cutting."

"About his pottery."

"Well, she told him if he weren't sensible about things he'd end up in a potter's field, or a potter's grave. I can't be sure. She said he'd become an outcast like the potters of Biblical times."

"I don't understand."

"Neither did I." Desmond stopped walking to catch his breath and James wondered at this frailty in a man so young. He remembered Eustace's comment about Desmond's health but felt he could not yet ask Desmond what was wrong. They sat for a while on a dry-stone wall, watching a flock of ducks spreading their triangle low across the sky. The fields beneath and around them were burgeoning green and James marvelled at the lushness of this splendid area of Wicklow: the patchwork of many shades of green, broken only by low walls and tiny winding streams.

"What a beautiful day," he said.

"Yes, but I think we should turn back." Desmond rose slowly. "I'll tell you now what I learned about the potters. I knew that phrase from Matthew 27, where the Pharisees took up the thirty pieces of silver

Judas had thrown to the floor. Because it was blood money they couldn't use it for their own benefit, so instead they purchased the potter's field, to 'bury strangers in' as the passage says. And after that the field was known as the field of blood.'' He fell silent, looking around the fields that surrounded them now, as though he were looking at that Biblical field.

"What do you think your wife meant then? I always thought the phrase referred to a place where people were buried who couldn't afford the price of a grave.''

"Yes, sort of a pauper's grave. I knew that reference as well. I kept looking and found one older reference, that the ancient Hebrews thought very little of potters, held them in low esteem on account of their work. These potters were buried apart from the community in a so-called potter's field. In other words they were outcasts, at least in death.''

Privately James thought Lamia's comment to be threatening, and he wondered if Desmond did not think so too, given the fact he and Duggan were friends.

He wanted to lead him to reveal more, but Desmond was already turning the conversation.

"I find that common in Scripture, these exclusionary situations. Indeed right through to Revelations. People were marked in many ways . . .''

"And it has followed through history, hasn't it? I remember first reading *The Scarlet Letter*. How the young woman wore the *A* to proclaim her adultery.''

"Indeed, and how in that case it transformed her, or the experience of wearing it changed her, into a virtual saint.''

"Things have changed,'' said James. "Times have changed.''

"Yes, but you've given me food for thought. I see the germ of a sermon here.'' Desmond laughed heartily, for him. A man at ease again, happy on his own territory. "I tell you, James, I have to find them where I can. I'm intrigued with this idea: wearing some emblem of one's primary failing, let's say, admitting publicly our folly. Have you ever visited St. Michan's?"

"Often." James expanded. "My granny used to take me faithfully to shake the crusader's hand for luck. Since the legend says each handshake lasts seven years I should be set for life."

"Well, in that church there's an interesting antique, the confessing chair. Such a chair, or sometimes a kneeler, was used in our faith in earlier centuries. A member of the congregation would make a public confession, on the direction of his confessor."

James was interested. "Was this routine?"

"No, it was used very selectively. Remember this was at a time when the concept of the communal church was very strong. Perhaps a merchant in the parish had charged unfair prices. Or, more seriously, a moneylender had charged usurious interest. Or someone had committed adultery. He would admit this sin in front of the congregation, publicly, because it was a sin against the communal bonds, against actual people, his neighbours."

"Wow!" James whistled low.

"I know, I know." Desmond was growing animated as they approached the level field behind the church. "Can you imagine standing up on Sunday and confessing your most private sin?"

James jumped, face to face unexpectedly with the state of his conscience.

"I'm sorry," said Desmond, placing his hand on James's arm. "I didn't mean you in particular."

"Glad to hear it!" He was wry.

"I've got to get back to work, though I enjoyed our walk. I'll tell you now, it broke a spell, let's call it. I hadn't rambled those fields since I heard of Duggan's death.''

"Perhaps we can do it again then," said James impulsively, feeling sorry for Desmond, but also admitting a growing affection for the man.

"I'd like that."

"And could we talk more about Duggan? I still have a few questions.''

"Of course. If you're not trustworthy I can always brand you in front of the congregation.''

"That is the most unusual threat I've ever had.''

On Sunday morning James felt anxious. Time was running out and he'd not yet accomplished what he'd charged himself with that weekend. Desmond had unknowingly given him some leads. It had become imperative to pursue some of those leads with Lamia, even more so since he'd called his phone service and received Father Tom's message. The priest would call by James's office on Monday. If he hadn't been pressed for time before, thought James, he certainly was now.

As he listened to Desmond's sermon on Sunday, James smiled to himself. Desmond had developed the theme of public confession and it was a strenuous, uncompromising sermon. In his robes, the man seemed larger than life. The congregation was uneasy, unused to even this mild version of fire and brimstone. James had gone to the service in order to attend the subsequent morning coffee hour at Lamia's, and even this slight dishonesty stung his newly awakened conscience.

I'll be glad to escape all this religion, he thought as he fled the church and attached himself to Eustace in an obvious way.

"Need a lift?" asked Eustace, surprised.

"Sure," said James amicably, but he got little more from Eustace as they walked to the car.

"Enjoying your stay at O'Brien's then?" he said sullenly as they drove off.

"Yes indeed, although he went out last night. I ate at the inn and when I arrived back at O'Brien's he invited me to babysit so he could take Maria somewhere. It was all very chaotic, but the kids were great, slept like logs . . ."

"So he drew you in?" said Eustace, still distant.

"How so?" said James, at last picking up on his mood.

"Everyone falls for that act he pulls."

"What act?"

"The mastiff with his pups at his feet, the last bohemian, the only one of us living the true romantic life of the artist. All that hogwash."

"Whoa! Hold on there!" said James, taking offense for the first time.

"I'm telling you, Fleming, I've not a doubt that he and Maria were off in the county somewhere, dining *intime*." He stressed the word.

"What are you, jealous?"

"Hah! It's not me that is jealous. When Tessie, O'Brien's wife, had the last child there, whatever its name is, she needed some help in the house. O'Brien literally installed Maria under the same roof. Taking over from Tessie, in every way, we have no doubt. Tessie couldn't stand it. She was replaced by Maria right in her own home. It's no wonder she fled."

"To Paris, with the artist? He told me that." James was defensive.

"For heaven's sake, her brother's an accountant there. She'd no family. When she left O'Brien she had to go somewhere and she went there. I imagine she thought O'Brien would come to his senses. That was two years ago."

Christ, was nothing what it seemed in this crazy place? James almost spoke aloud, but then he thought better of it. For after all, why believe Eustace over O'Brien? Or O'Brien over Eustace? Why believe anyone?

As they parked the car at Lamia's, he imagined his proposed conversation with her and became glum. How would he know if Lamia was telling him the truth either? There seemed to be no benchmark for the truth, for establishing what was fact. He looked again at Eustace who seemed very much the worse for wear.

"Hard night last night?" asked James, to restore equanimity.

"The party at the gallery went on quite late, actually, and I'm still feeling the effects of the wine. I thought I'd see you there."

"Oh, I saw you when I dropped by," said James truthfully. "You were talking with the London crowd."

Eustace eyed him for a long minute and then let it go.

The sitting room was, as usual, crowded. James, taking note of her shimmering green dress, walked purposefully towards Lamia. She stood at the urn pouring the coffee.

"James, how convenient," she said, signalling to Goretti to take over. "Come, I have to talk with you."

Yet again James had lost the initiative.

"It's about the house," she said as she indicated to him to sit beside her in the alcove.

"I was hoping to see Fred this morning. I rang him yesterday but there was no reply."

"That's because they're gone."

"Gone?"

"To England."

"What!"

Lamia waited.

"I spoke to him about the roofing. He never said that . . ." Words failed again.

"I see this is a shock, and that's why I wanted to speak with you. Given Fred's problems, he came to me. They were truly anxious to move, and to accommodate him I've arranged to purchase . . ."

"You bought my house?" James squawked.

"But James, I believed that we could come to an arrangement. It would be a simple matter for me to rent the house to you . . ."

"But that's not quite the same thing, Mrs. Desmond," said James stiffly as he recovered his demeanor.

"I realize that, of course. What I would propose is that you rent with the option to buy."

"But that hardly solves the problem of the roof. I'll never get the mortgage loan without the new roof."

"It's the best I can do for you, James." Lamia's voice was businesslike, and James saw her form the words through her rows of small teeth.

He was stumped. She had no intention of fixing the roof. It would be up to him and him alone to foot the bill, on top of all the other expenses he'd foreseen in the renovating of the old house. But damn it, it was his house, and he knew it. He showed his hand.

"It's a possibility. I'll have to think it over of course, Mrs. Desmond. Let me just say this, I'm still interested."

"I knew you would be, James."

She started to stand up.

"Pardon me, but I have a few questions."

"About the house?" She sat again, smiling triumphantly he thought.

"No, actually. About Duggan." A surprise attack was best.

"Duggan who?" She was up to it.

"Patrick Duggan."

She waited, unsmiling.

"I understand that you rented him a cottage. I also understand that you had a falling out of some kind. What I want to know is if your disagreement might have contributed to his leaving Carrigbawn so abruptly?"

"Ah, but who said he left abruptly, James?" Her tone was level. She had deflected the question.

"I believe it is common knowledge in the *community*." He stressed her word ironically.

"Then it must be so. But I don't know if it needs to be so characterized. He came one day to me, paid his rent, and I believe he said he'd be gone the next. That was all."

"He gave no reason?"

"No, nor did I ask for one."

"You weren't curious?" James was led off his path by his own curiosity about this woman.

"His life was his own, to lead as he wished. We had a business relationship, not, I might add, a personal one. I help many artists, James. He was one."

"Did you argue?"

"About what?"

So she didn't deny it. At last a chink in the armor, thought James. He paused, desperate for a brilliant answer.

Then he bluffed. "Perhaps we shouldn't discuss it here?" He glanced knowingly around the room.

She hesitated. "Yes, you're right. This is inappropriate. I'll be free after the guests leave." With that she stood up and mingled elegantly back into the crowd.

An hour later she stood in the foyer of her massive home, alone with James. But since they were standing, he felt pressured into rushing, into leaving.

He looked for Desmond, who was nowhere to be found.

"I've been talking with my husband," she began directly. "It seems you've had a chat. I hardly think I can add to what he's already told you. However, I do have something for you." She dangled a set of old-fashioned keys on a wire ring. "These are your house keys. My lawyer will send you the necessary papers during the week. But as of now, James," she paused for effect, "you have my permission to take over Oakdale Lodge. The rent is quite reasonable, in view of your intention to buy the house."

A vision of himself as lord of his own manor took sudden possession of James. "Thank you," he murmured, and as he grasped the keys a thrill coursed through him. He moved dumbly through the double doors, listening to Lamia's chatter with half an ear.

"One more thing," he heard her say. "I imagine you'll be staying out at the house on weekends. Come next Sunday. I'm having a party. Bring a guest. Say two o'clock?"

And before he knew it, James was standing alone on the wide granite porch, his questions about Duggan left unasked and unanswered. Beaten at his own game.

**14**

JAMES WAS SHOCKED TO SEE HOW THIN AND EVEN more gaunt Father Tom appeared as he sat wearily in the office chair. He languidly sipped on the mug of tea Maggie had brought in, leaving her offering of biscuits on the tray.

He had let James finish his condolences and his description of his own last day in Peru, when he'd learned of John's death from the papers.

"I know," Tom said at last. "It was to be expected, I suppose, that the papers assumed many things."

"Such as?" said James gently.

"As you saw yourself, the papers said John was tortured. They implied he had been captured. But that was not the case, thank God. You see, I had got sick quite suddenly. My old malaria had returned. By the time I arrived at the bus station I felt I was dying. One of my parishioners had come to meet me with a horse and cart and John then decided to come with me. I was due to say a scheduled Mass and do a number of long-planned baptisms. You see these people must travel days, in some cases, to reach my little church. John of course knew that, and agreed to stay on in my parish, to say Mass and perform the sacraments for the people who were coming. I felt bad about delaying his return to his own village, but accepted his Christian charity. I now wish to God I

hadn't." He paused, wiping his face, sweating pro-
fusely as he spoke.

"What really happened then?" said James.

"Much of the congregation had arrived the night
before, and that morning they were still arriving.
Mass was fixed for noon. I had hoped to attend, at
the very least, but I was still none too steady on my
feet. But Father John was in great form. He'd put on
his vestments in the house and said he'd see me after
saying Mass. I walked to the open door and looked
across the little dry clearing, just to see all the people
and their babies. They were standing a little way from
the front of the church, talking and laughing, waiting
for Father John, forming a little alleyway really. John
walked straight towards the open door. It was that
quick! There were three cracks of a rifle from across
the clearing. He fell at the first sound. But they were
so rapid. It all happened so fast! And yet, James, it
was also like slow motion. I saw him falling slowly.
I turned towards the clearing even as I started to
move but I saw nothing in the wood. Strength came
from God then, and I ran to John. Gave him the
last rites, but I could see he was dead. It was surely
instantaneous. He was gone. After that, *ach* . . ." He
wiped his face again. "It was bedlam. People screaming, running, hiding, covering their children with their
bodies. All of us were waiting for the full attack but
nothing came . . ."

James was silent, trying to imagine the horror and
the fear.

Tom put the empty mug on the tray and looked up
at last from his private vision.

"Throughout all that followed, I tried to tell the
authorities that I believed it was a hit, as they say in
the films. I believed, I still believe, that it was di-
rected only at the priest who was saying Mass."

"Surely it was a terrorist act then?" said James, sensing something else was bothering Tom.

"Possibly, but it was not like other incidents. The terrorists attack the church surely, but we, as Irish for example, are perceived as outsiders. We priests are often victims but the terrorists usually attack Peruvians, the people they see who have actually adopted Christianity. You see," he looked imploringly at James, "they attack their own people, to use them, to use their torture, their deaths, as a warning to the local population. Killing a priest is effective because in a sense it kills the head, but they also attack the body, the people."

"And that didn't happen on this occasion?"

"No, and yet we were helpless, totally vulnerable to the attack, at the mercy of whoever it was in the wood, whoever it was who shot John.

"And the rifle. That was different too: shooting from a distance, not being seen. That, plus the fact that there was no message, no warning that more killings would follow, no calling card so to speak. As I told the police, the whole incident was anonymous. But they couldn't or wouldn't make the distinction. A priest was dead, shot, and so it must be a terrorist act."

"A fair assumption."

"Oh, yes, I can see it from their point of view. That doesn't change the fact that I know in my gut the priest was the target that day and . . ."

"Yes?"

"And I should have been that priest!"

"You think . . ."

"Yes! That bullet was meant for me, James, not for John."

James sat in silence for some time, choosing his words carefully.

"Tom, don't take this up wrong, now. But do you

think," he hesitated, "do you think that perhaps you feel guilty? That if you hadn't been ill, John would have gone on to his own village. He would not have been there that day. In that sense you might feel, deeply feel, that he took the bullet meant for you. But they had only one aim that day. To kill a priest. Any priest."

He let the statement hang, but Tom was already shaking his head.

"No, James. You see, after it was all over, I remembered what I'd heard. A voice had called out. It called out 'Father Tom,' " he repeated it in Spanish. "John turned his head at that. That was natural. All the parishioners knew me, they wouldn't have confused me with him. I knew them all personally. Only a stranger would have called out."

"And John turned at your name?"

"Yes. He might have thought someone perhaps had arrived, someone who'd been told to ask for me, by name, you see, not knowing me by sight. He would have wanted to tell them where I was, or who he was. He turned, James, at my name! And I swear that was when I heard the crack from the rifle."

James had to accept the story from an eyewitness. He set aside his own doubts. He knew from long experience as a lawyer that the emotional turmoil surrounding an event such as this did not in the end obscure the true reactions of the witnesses. His reading of events, his gut reactions, would be true.

"I believe you." He watched as Tom sagged in the chair.

"Thank you," he said simply. "I couldn't make myself clear to the police nor the church. A priest was dead, *ergo,* a terrorist did it. It almost looked like vanity on my part, as one priest put it, that it was I who wanted to be martyred." His tone was of restrained anger.

"So I'm still alive, and John is gone. I have got to know why."

James was unsure how to proceed when Tom took the initiative.

"Listen, I'm to go to Rome tomorrow for a retreat. Not by choice, but it's customary under the circumstances. But I should be back the end of next week. Perhaps we could talk again then? I know I'm asking a lot, what with this and Patrick's death. And it doesn't end there." He shrugged. "Poor Patrick left nearly everything to me in his will. He'd no family left and he indicated he thought, given my vocation, that I could use it. I've all the letters here from the solicitors but I'm at a loss as to what to do. There was a life insurance policy. I'll leave all this with you, if I may?"

James nodded.

"Of course this time I can pay you, out of the estate, right?"

James agreed, glad that there was something concrete that he could do for Tom.

"Would it be possible then, for me to see where Patrick lived before I leave?"

"I'm sure we can arrange it. Just let me make a few calls."

Within the hour, James admitted Tom to the small house in the Liberties.

He waited in the living room as Tom walked through it, doing much the same as James had a few weeks before.

"I think he was happy here," Tom said at last, absently fingering the series of small animals that James had admired.

James agreed. "I think he was."

"It's snug, as he said in his letter. By the way, you do still have that letter, don't you? I'd like it back eventually. It was his last. In fact, I sent a few to him over the years. I suppose it would be all right to have those back too.''

"If the will is all in order, Tom, then probably everything here is yours," James said gently.

Tom's shoulders drooped further. "I don't know how to manage all this. You know, it's so unexpected . . ." He spread his hands wide.

"Do you want me to tell you what I've learned, about Patrick?" James said at last.

"I suppose so . . ." Tom looked increasingly weary.

They sat in the small sitting room, uneasy, yet having no feeling that Patrick's presence was with them.

"I've been spending quite a lot of time in Carrigbawn."

"Yes?"

"In sum, I sense that there is an unnatural silence surrounding events that led to Patrick's leaving Carrigbawn. His letter to you sent me down there. And the behaviour of the people I have spoken to thus far can be characterized as vague, if not evasive. If we had more time, I could describe to you my sense, hard to prove at this point, that I am being manipulated.''

"Really?"

"That is my sense. As I've been told *ad nauseum,* it is a tightly knit community, with a patroness of the arts at its centre. A clique. However, the good news is I've met a man, Reverend Desmond, who knew Patrick well, as a friend. Like yourself," he added.

Tom smiled wanly.

"I think I have his confidence. And more to the point, he is not a part of the artistic clique, as I see it. Surprisingly so, since he is married to the woman who holds the most influence there. I hope to learn more from him, but I haven't been able yet to speak freely. I'd like your permission to tell Reverend Desmond that you are my client. I believe it would make

a difference. Two clerics sharing a common goal—
and I'm in the middle.''

"By all means, do whatever you think is best. I
imagine if Patrick liked this man I would find a common bond with him.'' He stopped as if remembering
something. "I want to look through Patrick's letters
before I leave. I sent him some old photos of ourselves when we were kids. I'd like to have them.''

James agreed, knowing technically they would be
breaking the law.

"Why don't I drop the solicitors a note that you've
done so?'' he suggested.

Tom looked through the stack of correspondence
in Patrick's bedroom and returned, puzzled, to the
sitting room where James had remained waiting.

"Do you know if everything is here? Would there
be anything still down in Carrigbawn?''

"I haven't checked, to be honest,'' said James,
thinking of the boarded-up cottage.

"I'm just surprised, that's all.''

"By what?''

"I'd sent Patrick some pamphlets about the politics
in Peru. Along with some snaps and some letters. I'd
clipped them together. The pamphlets are there, but
not the letters or snaps.''

Together James and Tom searched the photo album
for the snaps but found nothing.

"It's a small thing, but it troubles me. Patrick kept
everything. Do you think there's a connection?''
Tom's eyes looked haunted.

"With Duggan's death?'' James was startled.

"No, to John's. These letters and the snaps—they
connected me to Patrick, and they're missing.''

"Tom, they could be anywhere. I'll make a thorough search for them in Carrigbawn.'' He wanted to
calm the man. He was obviously distraught, agitated.

James wondered if perhaps Tom's fearful imagination might be due to his malarial condition.

Tom rubbed his face with long strong hands, then shook himself like a dog after a long sleep.

"I'm sorry, I must seem paranoid. But I can't shake this feeling that I was the target of John's murderer. And it occurred to me during many sleepless nights in Peru that the person who killed Patrick also wanted me dead. Why? Because I was his friend? And remember how Patrick implied there was a secret, but he couldn't discuss it? Perhaps those people think I know something. But I don't. I don't know anything . . . except that two people I loved are dead."

As James pulled the Citroën onto the gravelled drive of Oakdale Lodge late Friday night, he wondered what had possessed him to invite his mother to come down Saturday morning for the weekend. Had it been just perversity, since Sarah had turned down his offer? He thought glumly of the now thwarted romantic evening he'd planned for her, and of the fun he imagined they'd have working on the house as a team.

As he let himself in, he heard the phone ringing somewhere in the house. Fumbling in the dark he discovered the blasted thing at last on the staircase.

"James, is it you?" A faint voice spoke.

"Yes, who is that?"

"Sarah, James. Look, the reporter from the *Observer* can't make it over this weekend, so I'm free to come."

James sat heavily on the stair.

"James? Are you there? It's a dreadful line."

"Yes, I'm here." And I wish I weren't, he added silently, trying to visualize his mother and Sarah as his house guests. "Yes," he said weakly. "By all means, do come. When?"

"I'll drive down tomorrow evening, all right?" She seemed to be calling from a mountaintop.

"Right, right!" James raised his voice. "Go straight to the inn. I've reservations there."

"No need to shout, James. See you around eight then. Cheerio!" The faint voice faded away with no resounding click.

James tapped the button. No dial tone. He hung his head, his surprise subsiding into intense frustration.

"No need to shout," he muttered. "She sounds just like my mother, for God's sake!"

Shaking himself into action, James felt his way to the door and shut it, plunging himself into total darkness. His fingers traced the surround of the door and met a switch. A feeble light fell from a naked bulb overhead.

"God, they even took the lampshade!"

Leaving his coat on against the chill of the closed-up house, he walked from room to room, immeasurably relieved to see light bulbs coming to life in each, including the bathrooms.

It was nearly midnight when he fetched his blankets and bag from the boot of his car and returned to the house. Suddenly aware of the cavernous emptiness, he decided to make up his bed in the sitting room on the one hideous piece of furniture the Whites had left behind: an execrable sofa unworthy of even their taste. He fell fully clothed onto the makeshift bed and, beneath the blankets, huddled against the chilly night air. And deciding to let the problem of Sarah and his mother look after itself, he dropped into a deep and troubled sleep.

Saturday morning found James approaching Monks Hall with some real trepidation. His apprehension was unnecessary, however, as Lamia was not at home. He hadn't wanted to involve Desmond, but when Desmond answered the door himself it couldn't be helped. James, standing on the step, briefly explained his mission, and Desmond, seeing no reason not to oblige him, found the keys to the cottage and they both set off walking.

"So you're still at it then?" said Desmond with more enthusiasm than James expected.

"Yes, and I can tell you who my client is."

After some time, Desmond said, "Go on."

"His name is Father Thomas Mullen. He's a missionary priest in Peru and he was a childhood friend of Duggan's. They corresponded right up to Duggan's death."

"I see the connection . . . a childhood friend," mused Desmond.

"And a cleric like yourself," emphasized James, again struck by Duggan's choice of friends.

"Yes."

They walked briskly this time, across a level wooded area. Desmond seemed more energetic than previously. The air was bright and clear, and the woods were quiet but for the sound of some distant chopping.

"O'Brien's hard at work, I hear," James smiled.

"How do you mean?"

Surprised at how little Desmond seemed to be involved in day-to-day matters at his home, he explained about O'Brien.

"I see," he said simply. "To backtrack, James, what is it you hope to find at the cottage?"

"Primarily letters. Father Tom was concerned that some of his letters to Duggan are missing. We thought he might have left them behind when he moved."

When they reached the cottage Desmond waved

James on in. He stiffly explained that he chose to remain outside.

Well maintained, the cottage was sparsely furnished with good sturdy fundamental pieces: chairs, a bed, a few tables. James began a quick search in the bright light, though he knew at a glance the cottage had been swept clean. There were no letters nor any other items that would have belonged to Duggan. Relieved to be quit of the place, James rejoined Desmond, who was now sitting on a fallen log reading a breviary in the bright morning sunlight. James thought him the picture of a young graduate student.

"Nothing here," he reported and returned the keys to Desmond. "You didn't want to look 'round yourself?"

"No!" said Desmond with some ferocity. He turned his back on the small house. Recovering his mild tone he added, "I'm sorry your client is worried." James could detect curiosity in his voice.

"Oh, he's not so much worried. It's just that he'd sent Duggan some snaps of when they were both lads, and he'd like them back. In view of Duggan's . . ." he hesitated.

"Death. Of course. And he sent them from Peru, you said. I seem to remember some mention of Peru. I imagine Patrick told Lamia at some stage about his friend, because I have a recollection of Peru in some conversation with her. I'm surprised he never mentioned Father Tom to me, though."

So am I, thought James, but he didn't comment. "He would have in time, I imagine," he said.

"Yes, I suppose we were just catching up on each other's lives. We were of an age you see. Well actually he was a little older than I. He was a solitary sort of character. By choice. Now, don't mistake me. And I . . . I suppose I'm a solitary type too. We were misfits here in a sense, not really a part of the social scene."

James remained silent, encouraging Desmond's reflections, those of a man, he suspected, who rarely talked about himself.

Desmond continued as they walked. "I often wondered why Patrick hadn't yet married. He'd laugh and say he could barely support himself, let alone a wife and family. And he was curious as to how I'd married so, um, so young." Desmond stumbled shyly over the subject of marriage and James caught it.

"How did you meet Lamia?" he asked, suppressing the many other questions on his mind.

"My first job was as a locum in Wexford, a summer replacement for a rector who was studying abroad. Lamia was visiting friends in Wexford and heard me preach one weekend. After the service we met at the social hour. It happened that Lamia returned a number of times that same summer and we met briefly on each occasion. Then when a post became vacant here, I was appointed. So simple, and yet I imagine that Lamia had some influence in the situation."

"You don't know?" James was amazed.

"No, no," he said slowly. "We've never discussed it. Anyway I came and resided in the parish rectory. It's a fine house. Small and very comfortable. I was fond of it. Lamia hosted the morning coffees in the church hall. I would see her frequently. She generously supported many of the church's activities and was very effective in persuading, shall I say, the wealthier members of the parish to contribute to the stewardship appeals and so forth. Many of the parishioners were a bit antagonistic to me here at first. Lamia told me to ignore it, but it was difficult. She was, of course, well established here and I came to rely on her. We were often together. Actually we saw more of each other then than we do now," he laughed ruefully.

"It seemed somehow logical, natural, to be in her company. And somehow friendship and courtship merged very gently into the one thing. I realized I had strong feelings for her, and she said as much to me. I think we mutually proposed." He laughed again, more genuinely. "Those early days of getting to know her, they were special days. I imagine you've experienced much the same yourself, James."

"Yes, well . . . Yes, some years ago I hoped to marry a girl who has since married someone else. She was my first real love, and I think, although I have loved since, that was the most special time. With Teresa."

"What happened?" Desmond's curiosity was not pastoral.

"A misunderstanding. I'd wanted her to come to Russia with me, on a train trek. Oh, I don't know now. She didn't come to the station. It was some kind of stand she was taking. I went anyway, taking my own stand. When I returned I found she'd met someone else, someone she eventually married."

"And so do you feel that marriage, your marriage, was somehow not meant to be?"

James thought for a while as they walked aimlessly through the wood to a wide field.

"For a couple of years I did feel that way. That, as you say, it wasn't meant to happen. To be frank, I still wonder if she was the one. My subsequent relationships have been more tumultuous. Perhaps as a result . . ." James hadn't thought of Teresa in a long time and now he realized he'd nearly forgotten her.

"Then he was the right one for her . . ." suggested Desmond.

"Ah, but what if she weren't the right woman for

him? They've two or three children now," added James as if to confuse the issue. "We're talking as though certain marriages are predetermined. I admit there is a unique feeling when one is in love. That special sense that you are meant to be together—by fate or divine plan or whatever. It's tempting to think so, surely. The love is so strong, so exclusionary. Those early days when you believe that only you two together can fulfill your mutual destiny. Yes, that's the word. Destiny . . ."

"And you don't believe that now?" Desmond remained serious, almost pushy.

"I can't tell anymore. Let me say I haven't felt that unique sentiment with anyone else since. And yet, I can't quite remember Teresa. I wonder now, as we are talking, what I loved so madly in her. . . ." He paused.

"And now you also wonder when you stopped—when and why you stopped loving her?" Desmond completed the idea.

"Yes, exactly. I loved her, and then at some indeterminate point I stopped. But if I still loved her, surely that wouldn't be right?"

"Because she's married to another? What you're questioning is: what if she were the one for you, and what if he were the right one for her, then how can that be?"

"Yes, the whole experience has led me to think that there is no divine plan—with no disrespect to your vocation, Desmond." James smiled lightly. "But then at other times I also doubt that very conclusion. When I see people whose paths have crossed thousands of miles from where they live, or chance meetings that lead on to a series of events, which then seem somehow preordained. I'm not sure that's the right word."

"You feel some events seem meant to be, in their inevitability?"

"Yes, but I only see this in retrospect. For example, a fellow goes to a dance in college—believe me, this happened to many of my friends. Perhaps for lack of something else to do, they go along in a group. That group meets another group, that fellow meets a girl. They fall in love, marry, buy a house, have a family. Just because he went to the dance that night and not to a film or a pub."

"Dances are out of my league," Desmond laughed. "But you seem surprised by this?"

"No, not surprised. But would those two people have met under a different set of circumstances? If they had met others and married others, then their children would not exist?"

"I sense you'd like to be married, James," Desmond said suddenly.

"I guess that's true. When I see my friends from that period in my life all married now, I think somehow I missed the boat." James paused as Desmond stopped to lean against a cow gate leading into a muddier field.

"Marriage is a wonderful sacrament," said Desmond a bit sadly. "It's a worrying one at times, too." He smiled wryly. "I find myself talking to you as I did to Duggan. Can I speak in confidence, James?"

"Of course."

"When you were talking just now I was reminded of my early courtship with Lamia. One thinks that quality of happiness will last throughout the marriage. And yet . . ."

"And yet . . . it doesn't," said James. And, uncomfortable giving advice on love and marriage, he changed the subject. "What about Duggan, now? Despite his finances, did he want to marry?"

"I think so. There was a local girl he was very

fond of, but she met another fellow, a farmer here, and they married. Duggan was not heartbroken however. He told me he was 'between women,' as he used to put it. But there was no one special to keep him here obviously, since he chose to move away.''

"I think you said he didn't tell you he was planning to move?"

"Did I? Well, that's correct. He didn't tell me. I'd seen him perhaps a day or two before he left."

"What was his mood?"

"He'd called 'round to the vestry to cancel out a walk we'd planned. I remember it well. He was so agitated. Very unlike him. Stood hopping, literally hopping from one foot to another, he seemed so anxious to be away. I have to admit, James, that his behaviour was so strange that it crossed my mind that," he paused, obviously embarrassed, obviously struggling, "that perhaps he and Lamia were involved in some way. In those last few days before he left, I had begun to wonder. They were so at odds with one another, as I mentioned. And less than frank about each other. Well, Duggan was, when I tried to mention what I had noticed. I actually believed for a while," he paused again, "that they were having an affair."

James was struck by this idea, recalling Desmond's unwillingness even to look at the cottage.

"Michael, I'll be blunt with you. The only cause I've discovered for Duggan leaving Carrigbawn is the one you've given me, and that is the argument you overheard between Lamia and Duggan. I spoke to her about it. . . ."

Desmond looked at him nervously. "I didn't realize that you had talked with her. Did she deny it—the argument I mean?"

"No, she didn't deny it. What was interesting is that she put no weight at all on it. What she said was basically that she'd lost interest, or had no interest in Duggan. He was just one of many artists. He'd decided to move on and that was that.''

"I see. Or rather, I don't see. I told you what I heard.'' Desmond started to walk again, musing. "The argument I heard came at the end of a period when Lamia seemed, as she told you, to be losing interest in Duggan. I thought, briefly, that it was a deception on her part, to cover a deeper involvement with him. Her loss of interest seemed to coincide with the time when he and I became friends. But I'm not sure why.''

Suddenly the pieces fell into place for James and he was amazed at Desmond's naiveté. But unfortunately they had arrived back at Monks Hall and as they stood talking, James watched Lamia glance from the doorway and then walk commandingly across to them. Her well cut Norfolk jacket and riding boots made her a picture of the mistress of the manor.

"Michael, here you are!'' The tone was icy and it was as though she meant to confirm James's sudden insight: that Lamia wished to control her husband's life, as she wished to control everyone's around her, including his own. She quickly changed her tone and laughed. "How dare you scamper off without letting me know? I was worried sick.'' But her tone belied her words.

"Lamia, don't be daft,'' said Desmond, nearly blushing.

"James, James, if you insist on leading my husband astray on these foolish woodland rambles,'' she waved her hand petulantly, "you should know about his condition. I'm sure he hasn't told you.''

James almost blurted "Naughty boy,'' but bit his tongue.

"Lamia,'' Desmond interrupted, but he didn't mention their walk to the cottage and neither did James.

"Poor Michael has diabetes, James," Lamia continued as though he weren't standing there. "A very serious condition. We must be so careful. So it's important, you see, that I know where he is at all times. He's apt to collapse. He could suffer a hypoglycemic reaction brought on by unplanned exertion."

"Lamia, I do not drop to the ground at a moment's notice."

She ignored the interruption. "And if I'm not there, then his companions need to know exactly what to do." She made no offer to tell him what this was, nor did James ask.

Desmond shook his head gently. "I'm perfectly able to manage on my own, James. I always carry my glucose tablets with me. Lamia takes it all too seriously."

"Hardly," said Lamia stingingly.

"I'd best be going . . ." said James gracefully.

"By all means, James, I . . ." Desmond started.

Lamia interrupted in an entirely different tone, light and pleasant. "I know you must be enjoying Oakdale, James. We'll see you tomorrow, then. So glad Sarah can make it," she added as she took Desmond's arm.

"How did you know that?" blurted James.

"She phoned me this morning. Cheerio then," she called over her shoulder as she walked away, in command, as ever.

# 15

"IT'S HALF-NINE," SHE ANSWERED TO JAMES'S GREET-
ings. Sarah was sitting alone in the lounge bar of the
Carrigbawn, which was packed with the Saturday-
night crowd. Her glass of wine stood untouched, her
features frozen with irritation.

"Right, early still," James countered.

"I've been sitting here since nine," she replied.

Ignoring her tone, he barrelled on. "How's your
room?" He remembered his own cozy room at the
top of the stairs and smiled.

"It's all right, a bit cold. And the bed is lumpy.
Honestly, James, you'd think they'd provide some
newer bed coverings. Mine is decrepit."

"What room is it again?" James asked uneasily.

"Number five, the room you booked."

James was about to say that that had been his
room, that he'd had loving fantasies of her in that
very room, and had slept the sleep of the just, of the
hopeful, in that same bed. All this passed through his
mind and his face fell.

"I suppose this place can't compete with the Berkeley Court," her hotel of choice in Dublin. She merely
shrugged.

Hollow with hunger James changed tack, ordering
for both of them, although Sarah claimed she couldn't
eat. She did of course, when the delicious simple fare

arrived. And as they ate their mood lightened. But James had still one irritant to assuage.

"I understand that you phoned Lamia?" he said conversationally.

"Mm, yes. She was very gracious."

"I thought you didn't like her?"

"I don't particularly like her, James. But I thought it was polite to accept her invitation."

"But you're coming as *my* companion."

"Listen, James. She's a very powerful woman, a manipulative woman. I thought . . ."

"That you'd play right into her hands?"

"No, that I would take the initiative, that I would take the upper hand."

"I don't see it. I don't see it that way at all. I suspect you're currying favour."

As soon as he said it he knew he'd made a mistake.

"It's better than pussyfooting around her the way you do."

James was stung. "It may seem that way, Sarah, but you forget I am working on a case here, and I need to learn a few things from Lamia."

"James, you want to buy that house, and you don't want to put a foot wrong with her." Sarah threw down her napkin on the table in disgust. "Perhaps I was just trying to cement you with her. It's obvious to me that she considers me a catch for her 'little community.' " Sarah was sarcastic now. "She'd be only too happy to tell her wide social circle that along with the other celebs she has here at her feet in Carrigbawn, she also has Sarah Gallagher, the violinist. Can't you see her telling her London friends, 'Oh, and by the way, she has some solicitor friend, Fleming, I think his name is.' "

James was appalled. "Is that how you read this situation?" But it was already painfully obvious to him that it was.

"Of course it is. You were of mild interest to the people here, but I think you'll admit that interest and even approval increased when I arrived on the scene."

Was he naive to be so stunned at Sarah's game-playing? Perhaps he should take it as a compliment that she would further his goals in this way, but somehow the whole scenario rang false. He didn't, in fact, believe that Sarah's goal had been to help him procure a house, and that worried him mightily.

"You'd like me to get this house then?"

"Of course, if you want it, which you certainly seem to. All I've heard from you is how much you love it. You've said you've agreed to this mad idea, of renting with an option to buy, haven't you?"

James watched as if from a distance as Sarah attacked her salad with gusto. He left his untouched, drinking the wine instead.

Sarah continued, not noticing his silence. "I should tell you, James, she does think it's very useful that you are a solicitor. She's already spoken to some 'dear friends' as she puts it. Throwing business your way."

"You're joking," exploded James, thinking back on his last tension-filled meeting with Lamia.

"I seldom joke, James. You have no idea what you're dealing with. Oh, she admits these people have their own lawyers and it might take a bit of doing to pry them away. But she's obviously very sure of herself and her influence. And she says your reputation for handling wills and estate planning is very sound."

"How would she know?" his tone was bitter.

"Oh, James, come on. Don't be naive. It doesn't become you." Sarah assessed him over her bread roll, and he returned her gaze. James wasn't sure if he appreciated this worldly and, it seemed to him at least, different side to Sarah.

"You know, Sarah," he spoke slowly, finding his way, "I came here to work on a case. In the course of that, I saw Oakdale Lodge and I fell in love with it. It seemed to me at the time a simple enough situation. I wanted the house. I think I still do. I did *not* think it was anyone's concern but my own, and, I hoped, yours."

He stopped, shifting tack when she didn't answer. He had wanted her to say she loved the house as much as he did. He saw it as a future home. But did she?

"Listen, I'm closing in on something here. If I resolve this case over the next few days, I'll be free to concentrate on the house . . ."

"Whatever you say, James." Her indifference stung him. Matt would have shown more interest, he brooded. And she refused to inquire after his case, denying it even existed. She looked up from her meal, aware at last that he was silent.

"Are we going back to the house tonight?" she asked.

Was it an innocent question, he wondered, dismayed. Why hadn't she asked if he was staying at the inn with her?

He cleared his throat. "I think I neglected to mention that my mother decided to come down for the weekend, as well. She's there now."

"Signs of the future, James?" snapped Sarah.

"You should talk . . ."

He was never to know what she would have replied, since at that unpropitious moment Malachy Eustace arrived at their table, drunk as a skunk, and accompanied by his ever attendant crowd of younger friends.

Without leave they pulled their chairs up to

James's table and began to order. Within seconds Eustace had James's ear, and James watched Sarah's face freezing into disdain.

"Margaret's away," Eustace blurted, "the cat will play. Like you, James?" Eustace leered, lifting his whiskey glass and leaning confidentially on James's arm. "Lucky bastard, you have your pick, don't you?"

"Keep your voice down, man," James snapped, trying to end the unwelcome confidences.

"Ah sure, who's to hear?" Eustace was nearly resting on James's shoulder. "It's hard, I tell you, when you want it and you can't get it."

James was disgusted. He ordered coffee but, when it arrived, Eustace let it stand untouched.

"I wasn't always like this, man. It was only a fling, I thought. But she's slipping away from me. I thought it wouldn't matter, but by God it does. An hour here, an hour there, it's not enough. Maybe there've been others. I don't even know that."

James tried to imagine Margaret Eustace having a series of affairs and it boggled his mind.

"You said she was away," murmured James.

"Who?" Eustace said, stupefied.

"Your wife."

"It's not the wife, you fool! Maybe it's you. Maybe she wants *you* now. Another conquest."

"Margaret?" James was stunned.

"Don't act smart with me, Fleming. Lamia is on to you. Wanted me to befriend you, can you credit that! She's coveting you, I told her. I've lost her . . ." Eustace was becoming maudlin.

"Looks like you've lost your Ms. Gallagher for tonight, Fleming." He threw a heavy arm across James's shoulders, pinning him to the chair just as James realized Sarah was in fact leaving. He watched helplessly as she hurried from the room without a backwards glance. As the group erupted in laughter at some joke, James stood up to leave.

"Can you drive me home, Fleming?" Eustace waylaid him. "This bloody lot are too drunk." His eyes swam in his head.

"Right, let's go. Now, Eustace!" James said angrily and he pushed the limp Eustace to his unsteady feet. In the parking lot, the fresh air seemed to revive him a bit as he staggered towards the Citroën.

"I think I've said too much," Eustace mumbled as they drove with the windows wide open. "I can trust you, can't I, Fleming?"

"After that disgusting performance?" cried James, simmering with rage.

Eustace didn't heed him. "You know I was just blathering. . . . I don't really believe that you and Lamia . . ."

"Me and Lamia? What's wrong with you, man!"

"I'm in love with her, Fleming. I didn't intend any of this. It was just a thing that happened. She's not the first. Being alone with someone, you know, painting is such an intimate thing. I've had other women, but it didn't mean much. A bit of fun," his voice was slurred and weary. "But she was different. I can't get enough of her. She's . . . she's . . . enthralling, yes. It was like being hypnotized, Fleming. Drugged, maybe. I didn't think ahead. I didn't think. I finished her portrait tonight. She came by the studio to collect it . . ." Eustace paused to burp. James pulled the car in front of Eustace's dark house and sat silently, eyes straight ahead, boiling with anger.

"Go to bed, Eustace!" James commanded, stretching across him and pushing open the passenger door.

"No, listen to me. It's over. She told me it was over . . ." Disbelief filled his voice.

At this, James shoved him out of the car, pulled the door shut, and sped off back to the inn.

# 16

THE "INTIMATE" LUNCHEON PARTY AT THE DES-
monds was enormous. Lamia had hired the village
gourmet shop to do the catering, and numerous
white-coated young men and women moved about the
crowded ground-floor rooms bearing trays. The number of guests was far too great to be seated, and small
groups formed randomly. Somehow, although the setting was the same, the mood did not resemble that
of the coffee hours and James realized that for this
party Lamia had drawn on a much wider circle of
friends. As he chatted amiably he discovered many
of Lamia's connections from London, stockbrokers
from Dublin, the assistant director of the National
Gallery, and other luminaries of the art world.

Lamia, as always, was brilliant, glittering, animated. She moved from guest to guest as if in accord
with some secret protocol. James realized that he was
way down on the list for her attention but he waited
patiently as he studied Lamia. She wore a densely
sequined royal blue dress, more suitable for evening
wear but somehow underscoring Lamia's signature
style. She drew Sarah into one small group, and then
moved with her to another. Watching from what
seemed a great distance, James saw Sarah chatting
more engagingly with others than she ever did with
him.

Through that morning's church service and since

their arrival, Sarah and Mrs. Fleming had studiously avoided each other. James was anxious both to free himself of his mother and at the same time to ensure she was entertained. He now gratefully introduced her to O'Brien, who immediately engaged her in some enthusiastic and bombastic conversation regarding, of all things, lilac bushes.

James moved quickly among the three connecting rooms looking for Desmond, hoping that this social obligation would bring him out. He finally found him in the study, which was, like the other rooms, open to all the guests. But the cleric was deeply involved in a conversation about euthanasia with an elderly gentleman and James saw no way to break in. He wandered back to the main room, where he found his mother, leaning dramatically on the grand piano.

Her face was cross and James sensed boredom brewing.

"Where's O'Brien then?" he asked, unused to his mother in the role of clinging vine.

"Demolishing the refreshments like a savage," said his mother, holding a full plate herself. "The house is impressive, James, but I really hoped to meet the Desmonds in person." She indicated the photographs on the piano and on the wall behind it.

The numerous framed photographs dating from the twenties and onward showed Lamia's mother and father in wedding dress, a fat baby, a family christening photo, a young attractive schoolgirl, a stunning young woman still in school garb. There were pictures of Lamia in formal studio poses. All but one were in black and white; a color photo of the house and grounds somehow spoiled the artistic arrangement. James looked for pictures of Desmond, but there was only one: his commencement photo from Trinity College. James was struck by the absence of a wedding photo. His mother, too, noted this.

"He's a striking man, the Reverend Desmond," said Mrs. Fleming. "Very impressive in his appearance. His sermon, however, was quite beyond me. And a little too much emphasis on the sins of the flesh. However," she continued, "I'm pleased to witness this return to the fold, James. I've never known you to attend church so regularly."

James nearly blushed, unwilling to confess his motives. He glanced around hoping to see Desmond emerge from the study. Instead he saw Malachy Eustace making an entrance, looking fresh faced and ebullient.

"Confession must be good for the soul," he said aloud, amazed at Eustace's effrontery after the events of the previous night. And yet, he would have been more conspicuous by his absence. James could barely look at him, now that he knew about his affair. But human nature being human he looked to see if he could catch Lamia's reaction to Eustace. Eustace lounged towards her and she kissed the air on either side of his face, much as usual.

At that moment James spotted Desmond at the study door. Like a ship with a tender, James and his mother moved across the room to Desmond's side.

Unfortunately, Lamia had also spotted Desmond's entrance and she swooped like a hawk on three hypnotized pigeons.

"Michael, you're here at last." Her mouth was smiling but her eyes were not. Her small teeth seemed bared. "Our guests are longing to talk with you," she added, including Mrs. Fleming in her sweeping glance.

"I somehow doubt that, Lamia." Desmond's voice was quiet but not self-effacing. He glanced beyond them at the crowded scene.

"But darling, they are! Clamouring for you."

James was struck by the false note in her voice, even her diction was unfamiliar and strained.

"You know I'd rather stay behind the scenes, Lamia." Again Desmond's tone was forceful and James grew uncomfortable.

"I for one would like to chat," said James.

Desmond ignored him.

"The refreshments are outstanding," added Mrs. Fleming, aware of the tension too. "I must compliment you on your selection."

But it was as though the Flemings were not there.

"Indeed," Lamia said automatically, still watching her husband. "Michael, you haven't eaten." Lamia reached for a plate on a nearby table.

"No, thank you, Lamia." A social stalemate was reached.

James opened his mouth to speak but stopped.

"You're just like your father," he heard Lamia mutter, but then turning suddenly to Mrs. Fleming, she regained her composure.

"Come with me, Mrs, Fleming. I've a friend here who spoke of you, a great supporter of the Adelaide Hospital." The rest was lost as Lamia steered a newly charmed Mrs. Fleming away to a tidy little group of well-dressed older men and women.

James stood, ill at ease with the morosely silent Desmond.

"If you'd like to take a walk I'd be only too glad to escape," said James quickly, indicating the crowded room. But he was again derailed by the sudden summoning sound of a knife against a glass. Waiters arrived bearing ice buckets and positioned themselves around the room.

Lamia spoke, standing near an easel holding a covered object. "Ladies and gentlemen. What you don't realize—" Lamia began, her strong clear voice carrying throughout the rooms. She paused until the crowd was appropriately hushed. "What you didn't realize is that I had an ulterior motive, as they say in the mystery stories, in arranging this party today."

She indicated the object on the easel covered with a red cloth.

"As some of you might recall, Michael, the Reverend Desmond, and I were married just over a year ago. To celebrate that anniversary I commissioned a portrait from our own highly regarded Malachy Eustace . . ."

At this point Eustace moved near her and grasped the cloth.

Lamia continued. "I would like to present this portrait to my dear husband on the occasion of our first anniversary."

As Malachy swept the cloth away, a dozen champagne bottles were uncorked. The fizzing and the popping accompanied the clapping and the murmurings of the crowd: an orchestrated manoeuvre that had its full effect.

But the murmurs and mutterings were of surprise. In the few seconds when thought and anticipation had formed in the collective mind of those gathered, they had somehow assumed that what they would see was a portrait of Desmond himself. James sensed that the crowd had seen, for just this once, a lapse in Lamia's usually perfect taste.

Desmond, beckoned by Lamia, moved reluctantly towards her. And James, thunderstruck by the woman's gall or nerve or bravado—he didn't know which—stood rooted to the spot.

Desmond thanked his wife formally for her gift and without looking at the portrait moved with her to take up a glass of champagne. Her animated face and manner were the picture of innocent pleasure. James, fascinated by her conduct, moved closer, craning his neck over the crowd to see if Eustace's portrait was equally innocent.

"It's his best work, at least that I've seen," said O'Brien at his elbow. "I hate to admit it, of course." O'Brien laughed but he was not his usual self. "This is different . . . striking. . . ." There was a question in his voice.

"Striking—I'm not sure that's the word." The portrait made James uneasy.

"Speak up, man."

"I'd rather hear your more astute opinion," James countered.

"I think," O'Brien hesitated uncharacteristically, "I think he's seen something in Lamia that the rest of us only suspected."

"Yes?"

"It's . . . the portrait is cold and seductive at the same time. The angle of the head, and the suggestion of a lithe, sensuous, sensual body. It's daring and yet conventional. The face is hers, no mistake. But then it's not. It's as though he's captured another self, a shadow self. Look at the passion there, the suggestion of lust?" O'Brien dropped his voice. "We might have suspected it, but we've never seen it. I never knew Malachy to have such insight before. It's a triumph for him surely."

"But she seems to like it," said James wondering, amazed that Lamia would allow something so revealing to be seen. Lamia the arch-manipulator letting down her guard. He was puzzled.

"It's this mirror of the soul stuff, Fleming! Of course she'd like it: she's not seeing it as we do. She's seeing herself as she knows herself. She's consumed by her own power, besotted with herself." O'Brien suddenly resumed his habitual boisterous tone. "It's a good picture. Just like you, Lamia," he said pointedly.

James turned, warned by O'Brien's sudden change.

"Congratulations are in order," he said as Lamia stood silently near them.

"Malachy did well," she agreed, but her usual confident manner was missing, as if giving the lie to O'Brien's assessment of her. She talked with them absently, looking, watching as Desmond stood alone in the crowd. For no one among them commented on this portrait of Lamia to the man who was her husband.

"It's a side of you perhaps we haven't seen," said O'Brien, rather boldly, thought James.

"Perhaps it's my London self," she sighed and the effect of her sigh was startling. James realized that he'd grown used to her forceful manner, accepting her endless dissembling, her continuous facade. This sudden revealing remark had come unexpectedly and it rang true. He looked at her closely. The sigh was of even greater impact than the words. It was the first honest thing he'd ever heard her utter.

But just as quickly the mask was back in place. "Now James, I must talk with your mother."

Disappointed that the charade was to begin again, James walked with her to his mother's side. The Adelaide having been thoroughly discussed, the small group was energetically engaged in reviewing a recent play at the Gate Theatre in Dublin.

Mrs. Fleming turned at their arrival. After the briefest of pleasantries she let fire. "Mrs. Desmond, Oakdale Lodge is an interesting house," she began directly. "Although I have seen much better of its type. And I'd rather *not* see my son, a prominent solicitor in Dublin as you no doubt know . . ." she paused for effect, "reduced to renting. . . ." Mrs. Fleming's voice rose on the last word with withering disdain.

Even the suave Lamia was taken off guard. "But it's . . ."

"James is impulsive, Mrs. Desmond. A failing since he was a child . . ." James blushed to the roots of his hair, but she careened on.

"Surely it would suit you both better if he purchased the house. This roof thing, really, I see it as a roadblock of sorts?" She looked challengingly at Lamia.

"If James wishes to roof the house . . ."

"Nonsense. It's customary for the vendor to do such work. The sooner the better. And the sale can proceed."

Lamia paused, glancing at James. "We'll see," she said, effectively ending the discussion.

James expelled a breath as she walked away.

"Now, James," said his mother as she turned a baleful eye on him, "I want an explanation as to why Miss Gallagher, no doubt your companion of last night, has been so insufferably rude."

"I don't know," he said simply.

James sat at his desk, grateful for the sense of rhythm and harmony that filled his offices, leaving him free to confront his most immediate concern. Tom was due back in a matter of days and he was resolved to conclude his investigation by then. He looked again at the open folder on his desk.

Simple notes and his own speculations filled the pages. The argument between Lamia and Duggan. Her references to potters. Her implied threat. His sudden leaving of Carrigbawn. His return visit later, on the bus, which Miss Conly had mentioned.

James mulled Duggan's return over in his mind. Wasn't it possible that Duggan and Lamia had had an affair? She'd had a liaison with Eustace, if he could believe Eustace. Did she routinely seduce her artists? Yet, what he knew of Duggan led James to disbelieve this, or to wish to. Duggan had been Desmond's friend. Or had he? Only Desmond could say. Duggan's voice was silenced. If Duggan had had an affair, it would explain the references to the secret he could not reveal to Father Tom. What had he written: that if he acted he'd cause pain, if he didn't he would cause pain.

He examined Duggan's letter to Tom, the little yellow dog in the corner. Something tugged at James's memory. He thought of Tom's concern over the missing letters. His wild idea that John's and Duggan's deaths were connected. James's own visit to the cottage with Desmond. Desmond's reluctance to go in—suspecting an affair had taken place there with his wife. Eustace's drunken state. And then the portrait.

Pictures, portraits, snaps, photos . . . that was what had tugged at his memory. James opened his locked desk drawer and withdrew the black-and-white photo he'd purloined from Duggan's ledger. He studied it again and came to the same conclusion: this was no picture of Duggan. He turned it over, noting for the first time the small series of words, printed in red and forming a small oval. It was a simple stamp, a logo made of an oval with a lens in the middle, made to resemble an eye. The legend read: Donnely's Photographic Studio.

Quickly James snatched up the phone book and within seconds had found the name and address of Donnely's on Dame Street Court.

Waving blithely to Maggie he raced from his office, across Stephen's Green, down Grafton Street, cutting up Andrew Street and thirty minutes later he was at Donnely's. Fully expecting to find a dingy little studio, he was surprised to enter the modern glossy premises presided over by a young, black-haired man in his late twenties.

Quickly explaining he'd found the picture in Duggan's studio he was met with a mild response.

"Ah, it's Duggan is it?"

"Yes . . ."

"And you are?"

"I'm James Fleming and I'm a solicitor dealing with Duggan's estate. I'm doing an inventory for the probate." Not far off the truth, thought James, since he'd need to start work on the estate in the near future.

"Well, I'll tell you. Duggan and I were at art college together. We kept in touch—maybe once a year. You know the way." Donnely smiled sadly. "Poor old Duggan. He came to me, let me see, he came to me with a snapshot several months ago now. A bit worn. He asked me to enlarge it for him, make a better copy, and so I did."

"This one?" James showed him the print again.

"Yes."

"Did he say why?"

"No. He came by to pick it up and mentioned in passing he was thinking of coming up to Dublin for good."

"But he was still in Carrigbawn at this time?" James was excited and insistent.

"Oh, yes, he'd come up in his bockety old car. We went for a pub lunch out at the Beggars, on the Canal. You know it? It was the last time I saw him. Terrible sad thing. I read it in the paper and I couldn't believe it."

"Were you able to tell the age of the original snap?" asked James.

"I still have it here in my files. From the paper and processing, I'd say that it's about twenty-five years old."

"And it's not a picture of Duggan as a boy?"

"Not at all. Though to tell the truth, I did ask him and he said it wasn't."

"But he didn't say who it was?"

"No, I assumed it was family. Isn't it? What's the mystery here?"

"No, no mystery," said James mildly.

"Well sure, you're a thorough man to be running around trying to find out who might want old photographs. Give lawyers a good name, if you're not careful."

James bid the amiable young man goodbye and returned to his office. He studied the enlarged photo with a magnifying glass.

He decided conclusively that it was taken near Stephen's Green. The old boathouse on the pond stood in the background, glimpsed through the railings, hazy because of the enlargement, but the railings were definitely recognizable. He knew the place, passed it almost daily. The gate in the railings behind the child was open. In the background was a large, expensive-looking car with its driver's door open wide. Probably a Wolsey. Or an Austin.

The startled child on the pavement, the concerned nurse. What did it mean? What did it mean to Duggan, to take such time and effort to enlarge the picture. Was it meant as a gift? Perhaps in the move he had forgotten all about it, sticking it in his ledger to be taken care of later. This didn't seem likely either. The man had been too organized. He looked again. Had it been for some artistic purpose, James wondered. Had he thought to make a painting, a sculpture perhaps? But of what?

James continued to scan the picture but no sudden insight came to him. He glanced at his watch.

Within the hour he was seated comfortably in the formal dining room of the Shelbourne Hotel. Opposite him sat Desmond, weary and silent. He'd phoned

James that morning and asked to meet for lunch. But now it seemed he had nothing to say.

James ordered two neat whiskies and sipped his, wondering how to facilitate the conversation.

"How was the drive up?" he asked. "The traffic last night was heavy." James thought ruefully of his mother's complaints as she'd left Oakdale Lodge. "Too far from Dublin," had been her parting shot. Not far enough, he'd wanted to reply.

"Not bad," he heard Desmond say at last, again falling silent.

"It was a large party. I take it the portrait was a bit of a shock then?" said James, taking the bull by the horns.

Desmond looked up at last, waving his hand. "That isn't why I wanted to talk to you, James. . . . I've an appointment this afternoon. One which I dread. . . ." He pushed his whiskey aside. "Thanks for the drink, but the diabetes, you know . . . Sorry."

"Not to worry."

"And I need a clear head today. It's a relief to talk to you, James. A relief to get away from Carrigbawn, where they view me only as their minister. Rightly so, I might add. Or as Lamia's husband. I'm not so sure they're right there."

James's heart sank. He waited in silence.

Desmond spoke confidentially. "You see, it's good for me to talk to someone who sees me differently. As Duggan did. As I think you do?"

"That's correct, Michael," urged James. "I know you as a friend, a new one, but still . . ."

"I appreciate this more than you realize, James. You see . . ."

Unfortunately, at this moment the waiter arrived. James quickly ordered the recommended special for both of them, sliced roast beef, mashed potatoes, buttered Brussels sprouts, a traditional Irish lunch. But

Desmond seemed to lose the thread of the conversation.

"You know, Michael, it helps to talk. For some people it's very difficult to talk about themselves. . . ."

"Yes, I'm not used to doing that."

"Is it about Lamia?"

"Yes. Please never repeat this." Desmond looked seriously at James, peering through the heavy glasses.

"All of this is confidential, Michael, of course. Solicitors are accustomed to that, much as clergymen are." His voice was reassuring, although he privately dreaded what was coming.

"I'm thinking of seeking an annulment."

James was stunned. So Desmond knew what was going on with Eustace.

"Have you spoken to Lamia?"

"No, it's too soon. You see, it's all my fault."

James wanted to shake the man for his misplaced guilt, his passive humility. Lamia was surely to blame.

"Whatever Lamia might have done," he continued as if reading James's mind, "is only on account of my failings."

"Can you say . . . ?"

"Please. Now I've started, I need to finish. You see, I am not a husband to her in the physical sense of that word . . ."

"I don't think I understand," said James, still assuming they were discussing Lamia's infidelity.

"I tried to talk to Duggan but I could never bring myself to tell him. I hinted of course, perhaps he guessed. I don't know. Perhaps my feebleness in this matter disgusted him. But you are older, James, than Duggan was." This seemed important to him.

James nodded but he was truly lost now.

"You see, we have not consummated our marriage.

191

There, I've said it. And today I'm going to discuss this with the counselor in the church who handles such delicate matters. I need his advice. I want to know if I can obtain an annulment and still remain as a priest of the church." Recklessly he took a sip of his whiskey, and then took up his fork. He put it down again.

"Sometimes I wish I were Catholic," he smiled slightly, "so I could enter a monastery. But that would be an escape, a running away, not a hurrying to. But it's a relief certainly to talk about it to someone who is not a cleric, nor a parishioner."

"But have you talked to Lamia?" James asked again.

"No, no."

"Why not?"

"At first it was because it didn't seem to matter. I know that sounds ludicrous. But when we married we were in no hurry to . . . It had never been a big part of our courtship, you see. Talking, working, traveling a bit. Just being together was so satisfying. There were times after that when I knew I should take some initiative, but those feelings made me uncomfortable."

He continued with obvious difficulty, his words coming even more slowly than usual. "Nonetheless, I did try my best, whatever that is. I would make overtures to her, if you take my meaning. . . ." He looked at James squarely.

"Yes, I think so."

"Perhaps it was my inexperience, but Lamia, well, she rebuffed my attempts. After that things became more . . . well . . . difficult. To be rejected by a woman in that way . . . You see, I never had a girlfriend, even as a teenager. My life was very . . . restricted, let's say."

"Maybe that's where the problem lies?" said James. "Tell me about that time in your life."

"My parents are both dead."

"I'm sorry."

"No, it's all right. My mother died when I was born, so I had no sense of loss you see. My father was in his fifties, a very successful man, and a very distant man. We lived here in Dublin in a lovely Georgian building that now houses offices."

"Too bad."

"Indeed. But I had no great fondness for it. I had a series of nurses and nannies as a child. And the diabetes was very bad then, when I was very young. I was sickly as a child. But strong enough to attend boarding school later. My father travelled a great deal. He was a cloth and fabric broker. But I know nothing of his business. When I was seventeen I was expected to go to college. He wanted me to do business studies and then join him in his firm."

Desmond paused to eat some of the beef and take a swig of water. James ate without appetite, troubled and wary of what was to come.

"I wanted to do social studies. You see, I'd had it in mind to become a social worker of some kind. He was furious. I cannot tell you how furious." Desmond paused and pushed his heavy glasses up on the bridge of his nose.

"Did you win the argument?"

"In the worst possible way." Desmond pushed his food away. "We had a terrible row, yelling, screaming. He was in his seventies then. I should have known better, but I was totally selfish . . ."

"It was your life, though, your career."

"But was it worth it? I didn't take note of his red face, the sweat pouring down. I was too caught up in my own anger, and he in his. We had never been close. It was the first argument we'd ever had. I had been a docile son, a withdrawn teenager at the boarding school. I knew the housekeeper better than I knew my father. I always believed it was because my mother died when I was born. He refused to speak of her, and never once allowed me to ask him about her.''

"What finally happened? Did you do social studies?''

"What happened? What happened was moments later when I had stormed out of the house to wander aimlessly around the streets, he keeled over with a massive heart attack. When I arrived home the doctor was with him, right there on the parquet floor of the hall. The housekeeper had found him when she'd come in to do the evening meal.''

"Oh God!''

"Yes, indeed, oh God. He died on the floor. A big man he was too. Very formidable. So much so I'd never ever thought of him as old, let alone of his dying.''

"The shock must have been terrible.''

"Yes. I was very ill for some time after that, in a private rest home for weeks. I was suddenly entirely alone in the world, but more than that . . .'' Desmond's eyes were glassy, as if staring into the past.

"More than what?''

"You see, I killed my father, James. I've lived with that now for years. I killed him just as if I'd shot him, all through my own selfishness.''

James wanted to disagree, but realized that many others must already have done so. Obviously Desmond still carried his huge burden of guilt, and apparently he had let it prevent him from getting close to another human being.

"I was never sure I had a vocation, James, a true calling. But I wanted to do something to atone for what I had done to my father.''

"So you entered the church?" James fairly shrieked.

"Yes, it wasn't a far cry from social work. And until recently I believed I'd found my calling. I was fairly content. But my marriage has somehow disrupted that sense of peace. Who knows?" he sighed. "Perhaps the church will tell me to leave, to work on my marriage rather than my vocation."

"Which would please you more?"

"To be honest, the pressure I feel in the marriage is agony. Not to be able to love Lamia as a husband . . ."

"But you do love her?"

"Oh yes, immeasurably. I crave her company. I've been so well since she's been monitoring my diabetes. I've felt loved, James. And succoured. I found that with Lamia, not in the church."

"Then why take such a step?"

"Because . . . because I am a fraud." The effort to say it cost him mightily and he sagged back in his chair looking years older.

"The longer it goes on, the worse it gets. I can barely stand up in front of the congregation. Who am I to preach to them when I myself am unclean? Instead of Hawthorne's *A*, I should be branded with an *F*. For fraud. My life is a lie, James . . ."

"Please, don't say anymore, Michael." James was alarmed at his appearance. "I think . . . do you feel all right?"

"No, actually, James, I don't. God, what a useless man . . ." With this Desmond's eyes seemed to James to become fixed, his jaw slackening. He started to rise in an ungainly way and then fell back awkwardly in his chair.

James quickly called for a cola and in the fuss of diners standing, sitting, craning, and generally being alarmed, he forced the liquid into Desmond's mouth.

The maitre d' summoned help and within minutes an ambulance had arrived. Desmond, now conscious, was able to tell them to take him to Blackrock Clinic. Waving James's offers of help aside, he revived enough to further instruct him not to ring Lamia. He would do that himself, he grimaced, and was gone.

After settling the bill James walked slowly back to the office, his mind swirling with the unwelcome confidences Desmond had shared. How quickly he seemed to have become involved with this couple, he mused. How much about their secret lives he now knew. He thought, then, of Oakdale Lodge, so inextricably tied up with Lamia. He thought of Lamia and Eustace, of Lamia and Desmond, of Lamia and Sarah. And of Sarah and his mother. And then again of Oakdale Lodge. The bloom was off the rose.

# 17

ON SATURDAY EVENING OF THE FOLLOWING WEEK-
end James knocked on the door of the lattice-
windowed office beside the darkened church. He felt
glad that Desmond had at least this much privacy in
his life, a place to work away from the tension that
must surely fill Monks Hall.

Desmond, looking pale but better than he had on
Monday, welcomed James into the room.

"How are you managing at your new house?" he
inquired.

"Not bad at all, but there's a lot to do. I've been
working on the grounds. Foolish I know, but this
summer weather has been so spectacular I couldn't
resist."

"I asked you here to thank you for helping me
last Monday. It was an embarrassing episode for me.
Lamia was furious of course, but she never did realize I had been with you . . ."

James wondered why this was important. Did she
restrict all of his movements, all of his friendships in
this way?

"Have you spoken to her yet?"

"Not yet."

"I think you should."

"I intend to, tonight. I supposed I wanted to tell
you that myself, since I've told you so much already.
I also wanted to make it clear that I don't believe

Duggan and Lamia had an affair. I've been so depressed lately I believe I was reading far too much into a few disconnected events. I knew Duggan, and he was honourable. Whatever their quarrel I don't think it had anything to do with affairs of the heart . . .''

"That is my sense too, although I didn't know Duggan, obviously. But I do have one last question I think you might be able to help me with." James withdrew the photograph. "Duggan had this in his possession when he died. In his ledger. He'd taken pains to have it enlarged. But I haven't a clue as to what it is or why. I'm certain though that it is not a photo of Duggan himself."

He laid the picture on the table and Desmond bent over it, studying it through his glasses. Suddenly he jumped as if stung. "Where? What?" He looked up at James.

"Do you know it?"

"Yes, I do. I gave it, not this, but a small snapshot, to Duggan." Desmond was plainly surprised and confused.

"It's *yours* then?"

"No, no, I can't say that. I found it quite by accident. At Monks Hall. Lamia's mother kept a large collection of framed photographs . . .''

"Yes, on your piano. I noticed them."

"Well, when Lamia inherited the Hall she occasionally added to the collection, as she came across other old photos. She calls it her family gallery. I had disputed her using the color photo . . .''

"Of Monks Hall?"

"Yes, that one. It seemed jarring to me, but she liked it and it's the only one she had of the house. There were none taken of the house in the past." He paused, looking into the distance. "Idle hands are the devil's workshop, as they say . . .

"One day I was in the sitting room listening to some music. Lamia was out at a showing. Again the photo struck me as jarring and, suspecting that she'd merely used an old frame to house the newer photo, I wondered if an old photo lay beneath it that might be more in keeping with the artistic arrangement she'd created.

"Idle hands, as I say . . . What I found beneath the coloured photo was a snapshot, matted wide to make it fit the frame. It was the original of that picture there." He pointed to the photo on the desk, genuinely puzzled.

"I don't understand," James interjected.

"I still don't. What I know is the longer I studied the snap, the more familiar it seemed, and yet I knew it was not mine. I'd never seen the picture before. I would swear to that. . . ." He was vehement, as though James had questioned the accuracy of his memory.

"I still don't understand."

"I'd never seen it before, James, and yet I remembered when it was taken. That was the horrible part. The longer I looked, the more fragments of memory were stirred. You see," he hesitated again, "I remembered how I felt when it was taken."

"Then you were there, obviously," said James, wondering why this was so disturbing to Desmond.

"Oh yes, I was there all right," said Desmond almost bitterly.

"Well then, there is no real mystery."

"But there is. I remembered how I felt because the picture was taken of me!"

"What?"

"I am that wretched child, James."

"Then it's your photograph."

"No, that's just it. It wasn't mine. I removed the snapshot from the frame and I kept it. I pored over it here in this study. Why would Lamia's mother have had a snapshot of me as a child? I remembered when it was taken because I had been frightened. My father didn't even own a camera. I'd hardly ever seen one. This was taken in the Green where I used to walk with the nurse when I could, or was allowed, I should say. Someone, a woman I think, came upon us suddenly. And just as suddenly she pointed a camera at me and I heard it click. The abruptness of it upset me and I cried. When the nurse looked up to admonish the stranger, she was gone. I can tell you all this as a narrative now, but these memories only came disjointedly as I strained to remember. But I do remember.''

"Did you mention it to Lamia?''

"Yes, and she was as puzzled as I was. Although I don't think she believed me, that it was a photo of me, or that I could remember it being taken. She claimed it must have been a cousin, a niece, some relative of her mother's who must have taken it, but with her mother dead we'd never know.''

"But you're sure that this boy is you?''

For the first time James saw Desmond angry. "Yes,'' he shouted. "I grow tired of not being believed. It's a small thing I know, when we have so many other problems. But it bothered me at the time. So much so that I showed the photo to Duggan. He said he knew a photographer who could enlarge it and perhaps then I'd remember more. So I gave it to him. That was shortly before he moved away. When he grew so distant, as I've told you, I thought better of raising the subject again. I thought I'd get it back from him one day.''

"And then he died.''

"Yes, and I forgot about it. It was no longer important to me. I wouldn't have remembered it now but for your showing it to me this way.''

"It's part of the estate, Michael, otherwise I'd give it to you now."

"No hurry, James. It's not a picture I would frame anyway. It reminded me that I was more lonely than I even remembered being." He handed the picture back with something like disgust. "And it caused trouble between me and Lamia, which I don't need to be reminded of. . . ." He glanced at his watch.

"You're going then, to tell her now? Will you tell her you want an annulment?"

"I think so," Desmond said uncertainly. "I don't know if that is possible. I never did speak to the church counselor. I had to reschedule the appointment for next week. But it's more honest this way. I think that's what you've been trying to tell me, isn't it?"

"Mmmm."

"But it's a hard thing, James. A hard thing to deal with . . ." He shook his head sadly and stood up, concluding the conversation. "I'll pray a while before I go home. There's no knowing if she's there anyway. . . ." He looked at James squarely. "Eustace phoned at tea time, something about yet another exhibition. . . ." His voice was flat and he watched James as if to see what James might know. But James was neutral, merely nodding, as they shook hands goodbye.

On entering the vestibule of St. Killian's, James immediately noticed that the congregation that Sunday morning was sparse. A few familiar young faces and some of the older population sat scattered around the dim interior. James felt a sense of sadness, a sympathy for Desmond whom he hoped would not take this small turnout personally.

James wondered if Desmond's recent sermons

were discouraging attendance. Perhaps realizing this, Lamia was seated prominently in the front pew, the first time James had seen her in church since he'd come to Carrigbawn.

Eustace had come too, with Margaret for once. Seated beside them was the film producer James had met at his very first gallery showing. He nodded to the Eustaces as he passed down the side aisle and took up his seat, not too close but in a place where Desmond could see him. He hoped his presence would offer some kind of support.

As it transpired, Desmond spoke simply about a coming fund-raising drive to answer a current urgent need in East Africa. He admonished his few listeners that part of their duty to Christian values was to share their wealth. James noticed that despite his mild demeanor, Desmond was markedly drawn in the face and he seemed unsteady on his feet as he returned to the altar. The simple hymns chosen for the service seemed to reflect a move by Desmond towards the comfortable and familiar. The whole service brought James a sense of intimacy and peace he now realized had been missing on the other Sundays he'd attended. He relaxed, believing that Desmond had somehow come to a good decision, one that was reflected in the mood of the day.

Desmond, too, was different. He moved through the ceremonial gestures and delivered the prayers with a dignity even more solemn than before. The time for the consecration, the blessing of the bread and water, approached and the parishioners knelt. James bent his head, leaning an elbow on the back of the pew, shielding his eyes and praying sincerely, undistracted for once by questions about Desmond or Lamia or Duggan or anybody else.

James did not know what made him look up. He

watched as Desmond lifted the cup of wine above his head and then lowered it, taking the first sip. He replaced it carefully on the altar cloth, closing his eyes as he did so. There was a pause, too long a pause. The congregation began to look up expectantly, waiting for Desmond's signal to approach the altar rail. Desmond was now kneeling. James felt something was wrong; the minister's head leaned in a grotesque mimicking of prayer. He seemed then to brace his hands on the altar itself.

Lamia leapt immediately to her feet. James and Eustace and others of the congregation who knew of Desmond's diabetic condition began to stand in their pews, hovering, unsure whether to interfere.

Desmond dropped, and was now lying on the altar step. Lamia knelt, desperately fumbling in her handbag. James quit his pew and went to her side. Kneeling, he lifted Desmond's head off the thick carpet and watched as Lamia forced a glucose tablet between his lips. James felt the slackness of Desmond's muscles and he held his mouth closed tight, willing the tablet to do its work swiftly. Desmond's pallor was dreadful, and the look of death passed over his features. The muscles in his upper body stiffened in a spasm and then subsided. James called out to the congregation to fetch help.

Voices were now raised and someone rushed into the vestry to find the phone. Lamia knelt clasping Desmond, leaning her face to his, whispering and muttering endearments and encouragement in a wild flow of words. James, desperate with helplessness, debated whether he should chance moving Desmond from the altar to the robing room. In his confusion, he saw two elderly women kneel down and begin to pray.

"No! No! No!" Lamia cried out suddenly and the shriek that followed rang through him.

Desperate grief overtook her as she attempted to lift her husband's body into her arms. Tugging and dragging in a frenzy, she pulled him onto her lap as she rolled back onto her heels. His weight and his height were unwieldy. She dragged at his shoulders as his head lolled sideways, and James, appalled, supported it. He looked at the stricken face, the eyes suddenly staring behind the spectacles, the lopsided mouth, and he saw again the young boy in the photograph, the face of a frightened child. He turned away from the sight of Desmond's mouth dropping open, away from the intimacy of Lamia's grief as she kissed, a hundred times over, the mouth and face and lips and eyes of her dead husband.

Trapped by his position with the body, James experienced a terrible confusion. He sensed, rather than knew, that tears were pouring down his face. He sensed that people had moved closer, that people were talking to him, to Lamia. Two women had knelt beside her and were now supporting her back and shoulders as she rocked Desmond's body back and forth in her arms as though it were some great child.

"No . . . o . . . o . . . o . . ." A long wail came from Lamia, and she called her husband's name. Over and over the same word in a keen that went back generations to the dark distant days of Ireland.

It was with relief that James felt a strong hand on his shoulder, and another strong hand pull his own arm away from the dead man's neck. A local doctor had sped over from the Catholic church and now took charge. Slowly the scene dissipated in intensity as James stood up, straightening his aching legs and arms. He watched, stupefied, as a group of parishioners awkwardly bore the body of their young rector into the robing room and laid him on a couch. Lamia, stricken to silence, followed with two women supporting her.

James sat in the front pew as the congregation slowly dispersed, talking amongst themselves. He sat as he heard them reassemble outside the church's open double doors, their voices carrying down the aisle in agitated gossip. He sat on, until the ambulance arrived and the body was taken past on a stretcher, Lamia and the doctor following behind.

Unexpectedly the doctor paused by James. "Are you all right, son?" he asked. While he awaited an answer, he took James's pulse.

James glanced up at the kind pale face of the tall older man.

"I wish I could have helped him," he said simply.

"I know, I know. Dunphy's the name. Dr. Joseph Dunphy. And you are?"

"Fleming, James Fleming."

"If it's a consolation, you did all you could, Fleming."

"I did nothing though. The diabetes. If I'd known more what to do. Mrs. Desmond had the tablet, but it didn't seem to help . . ."

"Were you his friend?" Dunphy bent low to whisper.

"A friend? Yes. I'm a solicitor, though. I know nothing of diabetes . . ."

"A solicitor, good. I can rely on your observations. Fleming, between you and me this was no diabetic coma. There'll have to be an autopsy, but the wife is so hysterical I've not yet told her. I'll get back to you."

Stunned, James allowed the doctor to rush on without further question. If not diabetic coma, then what?

\* \* \*

*Ann C. Fallon*

That afternoon a loose queue of people stood restlessly outside the church office door. A few stiff bran-
dies at the Inn had done little to dull James's shock.
Avoiding Eustace and Margaret, he sat, leaning his
back against the rough bark of a tree, glancing at the
door of Desmond's office, which now housed the police investigating team.

Everyone who had been present at the service was
to be interviewed. Cooperatively, or out of curiosity,
members of the small congregation had been returning to the church all afternoon.

James wondered where Lamia was. Much as he
had disliked her manner and behaviour in recent
weeks, he felt nothing but sympathy for her. Whatever wrongs she'd done Desmond they were beyond
redemption now. Guilt over their troubled marriage
and her affairs, guilt over the fact that she'd driven
Desmond to seek an annulment—even to consider
leaving his calling—would walk hand in hand with
her grief now and forever.

Desmond was gone. What had the doctor meant?
James wondered gloomily. He knew nothing about
his disease. Had years of diabetes affected his heart?
Desmond's father had died of a coronary during their
dreadful quarrel. He should have told Dunphy this.
Perhaps even Lamia had not known of that family
history. Surely his doctors in the clinic had been contacted by now. Surely they would have his family's
medical history.

"Hello!"

He glanced up as one of the other men waiting
beckoned him. "You're next."

James nodded as he walked wearily into Desmond's small dark study. It was no longer attractive
to him.

Inspector Dorsey was soft-spoken and shy. He let

James tell him how he had attended the service, the
little help he'd rendered, his recent rental of Oakdale
Lodge. It was obvious he was not under suspicion
and he chose not to volunteer any of the private information he had regarding Desmond or his wife. Until
he knew more, he decided to keep his peace.

# 18

IN THE ENSUING DAYS JAMES'S CALLS TO EUSTACE and O'Brien revealed that they knew as little as he did. Dr. Dunphy hadn't contacted him and Lamia had closed herself off in the manor house, refusing visitors and phone calls.

When James took courage and went to Monks Hall he was met with a nearly exhausted Goretti. James took advantage of her youthful indiscretion. He led her on, not unkindly, to tell him what she knew.

"This must be hard for you, Goretti." Did this child have a surname? he wondered.

She stepped onto the granite porch and closed the door behind her. She shredded a crumpled tissue in her hands.

"You must be very sad . . ." he added sympathetically.

At this she started to cry. "Oh, Mr. Fleming, there's been hundreds of callers here, hundreds I tell you, and you're the first to say anything to me. It's so awful. He was very kind to me, very polite, always asking after me and my mother. I shall miss him so." She lowered her voice. "I've made up me mind. This house is like a prison to me now. I'd never let Mrs. Desmond down, but when this is all over and she's herself again, I'm leaving here."

"That's too bad."

"No it's not," she said, asserting herself. "She's

run me ragged. The cards, now, of sympathy, and people bringing food and cakes in the old way. I'm ashamed to be turning everyone away, turning kindness from the door. And me ma can't use all the food I'm sent home with. She won't answer the phone, you see, and I don't like talking to all these people. And being rude to them."

"Has she taken to her bed?" James was discouraged by this picture of a demoralized Lamia.

"Not at all. She's up and around. She's on the phone half the day herself, making calls. It's just that she won't see or talk to anyone not of her choosing. She didn't eat for a day or so but this morning she had her French coffee as usual, horrible stuff. Instead of a nice cup of strong tea. And she wanted me to be making an omelette, for a treat, she says."

"A treat?"

"Oh yes, she said she needed her strength, needed to tempt her appetite. You see, she's much the same only she's all dressed in black, so much black. I'd no idea she owned so much black. Listen, Mr. Fleming, I've got to get back inside before she misses me. I'll tell her you called by with your condolences."

"Right, then. Just one more thing. No one seems to know about the funeral?"

"Oh, it's all set for Friday. It'll be in the Irish and the English papers. She told me this morning and I'm to tell everybody."

It was now Tuesday morning. James had remained in Carrigbawn, taking advantage of the inevitable summer slack at his office. There was enough work to go around, as Maggie had crisply informed him, but not so much that demanded his return. However, she did imply that Mr. O'Connor of the two wives had driven her crazy with requests for legal texts that he wished to read himself. She advised James in no uncertain terms to bring Mr. O'Connor into line.

As he walked to his car, James realized he missed Maggie and his office more than he cared to admit. He drove back to the bright, clean, and empty village. Neither marketers nor tourists drifted around the square. Having entered the deserted French bakery, he sat disconsolate, lonely, in fact. He began to get a sense of Carrigbawn on an ordinary weekday, when weekenders and visitors had returned whence they came.

He didn't like the silence, the absence of activity in what he'd seen before as a bustling mini-metropolis. Country music blared from a radio somewhere in the back as the esrtwhile bakers sat and chatted in the kitchen. The taped classical music was apparently reserved for the tweedy weekend types who crowded the place on a Saturday, displaying their riding boots and sporting horseboxes attached to their inevitable Rovers parked outside.

James glanced idly out the window and watched as the Dublin bus drew up at the patriot's statue. Only two locals got off and the bus driver, switching off the engine and leaving his door open, seated himself in a front seat for a doze in the sun.

Seizing opportunity when it presented itself James quickly scoffed his currant bun and, carrying a paper cup of tea, he entered the bus, waking the young man.

"Thought you'd like some tea," he said.

"That's a kind thought," said the driver warily, suspicious at this kindness. "Going up to Dublin?"

"Not today. But I do live in Dublin. I'm down here investigating a case." At this the driver's eyes widened.

"A detective?" he said dubiously.

"Not a police detective though," said James confidentially.

"Sure to God you're not from CIE?"

"No," said James, calming the fears of the young

man who suspected him of being an inspector for the bus company. "Listen, do you remember several months ago a young man was killed in the Liberties, in his house?"

"I remember something of the kind. There's not that many murders that I'd forget it. A drug addict, am I right?"

"Well, the police think it was drug related. But that poor fella, Duggan, he was no drug addict. They think he was murdered by a robber stealing to buy drugs. The thing is, I'm told he, Duggan, took the bus from Dublin to Carrigbawn a few times, maybe just before he died. I know it's a long time, but do you think you'd remember?"

"Hardly."

"Well, let's say it was February, for example." James took out the passport shot of Duggan that he'd found in the house and he showed it to the driver.

"Aye, I remember *him*."

"Why?" James was excited but wary.

"Because it was a weekday much like this. And I'd no fares from after Roundwood. It's boring, you know, if the bus is empty. A few oul' wans with their market baskets and that's it. But this fella, he was going all the way. He moved to the front of the bus when he saw no one on it. He was bored too. So we passed the time . . ." He paused as if only now putting the pieces together. "Are you telling me he's the one killed?"

"Yes, I'm afraid so. Do you think you might remember what he spoke of?"

"Oh God, I think we talked sports, he favoured Donegal, can you credit it that? I'm for Cork meself. After that I think I asked him what he did, was he on the dole or what. He said it might seem he didn't work for a living. Nice fella he was. He said he was a potter. Well now, I know nothing of that carry on, what's a potter, says I. And he told me. I liked the sound of it. Making bowls and jugs and jars out of his house, he said. And little creatures. I said I'd look out for his stuff in the shops, and o' course I forgot all about it and now you're tellin' me he's dead and gone?"

"Yes, he's gone."

The driver was visibly shocked. "I never knew anyone who was murdered," he said at last. "He was a decent sort."

"Yes he was and that's why I'm working on this case. I'm curious why he came down here . . ."

"I can tell you that at least. He got off the bus and crossed over to Molloy's there, the pub and the shop. He said did I know it and I said I'd taken a leak there many a time. He said he used to live there. I just assumed he was going in to see the family. . . ."

A small queue was forming at the open door. The driver gulped down the tea and stood up.

"You'll let me know if you get the murderer?" he said.

"Yes, I'll find you as I did today," agreed James and then he hurried from the bus across the square and entered Molloy's pub.

Early as it was, there were a number of patrons sheltering from the glorious summer day in the permanent darkness of the spit-and-sawdust bar. Here the local farmers congregated, eschewing the bright clean premises of the other modern pubs and eateries. They were already eating their lunch and James joined them, ordering a plate of ham and bread and cheese, washing it down with a pint of stout. He sat at the bar and, after a suitable interval during which he'd been silently scrutinized, he asked if the barman was in fact Molloy.

"And who might you be?"

"My name's James Fleming. I'm a solicitor in Dublin. I'm investigating a case and I think you can help me.''

"Not the diabetic Desmond thing, is it?" The man looked hard at him. "I'm not Protestant, and he never drank here . . ."

"No, no. I'm helping a friend of a friend. A friend of Patrick Duggan's."

"Duggan!" The man's look showed both surprise and recognition. "You knew Duggan?"

"No, but I know a friend of his, a priest out in Peru." This was enough of a bona fide to gain the man's confidence.

"Well, I knew Duggan too. Very well. He lived here above in the room. Was a damn good barman, too, after I trained him. Honest. I can tell. Honest as you could want. We couldn't believe it when he died. Couldn't take it in. And we'd seen it in the papers too late. Couldn't get to Roscommon for the funeral. But we had three Masses said for him. God help him, he was little more than a lad.''

James listened while the publican reminisced about the three years Duggan had worked with him and lived above. His mother had taken to him. He was like a grandson to her. Never forgot her birthday and so on. And they'd missed him when he'd moved to the little cottage but they were happy for him, too.

"Should never have gone to Dublin," Molloy said sadly. "If he'd stayed here he'd still be alive, wouldn't he?" he added challengingly, as if James, being from Dublin, was responsible for its collective crime and violence.

"That's what I'll find out. But perhaps it made no difference.''

"What are you saying? That if he'd stayed here he'd still have been killed?"

"Perhaps."

"Are you saying whoever killed him knew him?"

"That's what I think. I know the police don't, but I've my own theories. Do you know if he had any enemies?"

It was so refreshing, thought James, to speak plainly at last, not to dissemble with Carrigbawn's other population. For now he saw that alongside the glittering bohemians, there was the familiar population that inhabited every Irish village from here to Galway Bay and back.

"Your own theories, is it?" Molloy pondered as he washed the scarred surface of the wooden bar. "I can tell you he had no enemies that I knew of. He was well liked by all who came in here. I know when he moved to the cottage he'd come back and drink here. He kept himself separate from the arty-farty crowd."

James laughed at this apt characterization.

"And Patrick was a quiet lad, liked to walk and to work. Had a fine young woman for a while but she saw better in that hulkin' farmer over there." Molloy indicated a handsome, strong man packing away an enormous plate of ham. "But no one was bitter. Och, he was an easygoing boyo and that says it all. No enemies."

"I understand he came back to Carrigbawn at least once after he'd moved away."

"He did indeed. He came on the bus. He said he'd sold his car up in Dublin and was waiting on a van. He was going to start up deliverin' his own pots when he got going. He'd great plans. A good head on his shoulders for business in a plain way. I saw it when he worked here."

"So he came to see you?" James did not know whether to be glad or not.

"Aye, he called in off the bus. Had a whiskey with me and then went on up to the see the Ma. He always called her the Ma."

"Do you think I could speak with her?"

"Don't see why not. I'll bring you up."

James followed him into the back of the pub through a narrow passage lined with heavy beer barrels from various breweries, past stacks of wooden pallets piled high with beer bottles, to a back staircase equally narrow.

At the top they faced a bright small kitchen all yellows, blues, and whites, curtains and crockery and gleaming delft.

"Ma, Ma! She naps, you know," Molloy said, turning to James. He went ahead into a sitting room. "Ma!" He shook her awake as she dozed by an electric fire, the morning paper still in her hand.

"Is it sleeping I am?" she said, lifting a small pink and white face quizzically to her son's. "I'm a disgrace, sleeping away the morning. Who's this then?" She smiled at James and he saw where her son had got his amiable nature. After quick introductions, Molloy hurried back to the pub.

Mrs. Molloy roused herself and made a pot of tea and brought out fresh scones. Already fit to burst from his big breakfast and his early lunch downstairs, James still managed to demolish a half dozen with butter.

"Nothing like a good appetite and regular bowels," said Mrs. Molloy, patting his hand across the kitchen table.

James smiled. He wanted to sit there all day and swap stories. He leaned back lazily in his chair and let Mrs. Molloy talk, hoping he would learn all he'd come for.

And talk she did—about Patrick, her son, her husband, the pub. Her only regret was that there were no grandchildren, since her oaf of a son hadn't married. Yet. Since he was now in his fifties James wondered when, but this didn't trouble her. Gradually

James brought the conversation around to Duggan's last visit. She grew sadder and cried a little. She then recovered herself and went into the sitting room to fetch a small statue.

"He gave me this when he came by." She held out the little item that sat in her hand, perhaps four-by-two inches, a perfect rendering of the yellow dog asleep in the sun on Duggan's quiet Dublin street. James admired it, telling her of the smaller version he'd seen at Duggan's house.

"Yes, he said as much, but this was the only one he'd made of this size. He'd made it just for me." She stroked the yellow dog. "There's great peace in it, don't you think?"

"Yes. I think so." There was something so ineffably sad in her stroking of the dog that James felt a lump rise to his throat.

"Poor Patrick," she said, tears dropping one by one onto her arm and sleeve. She sniffed and put the dog away. James was glad.

"I'll tell you, Mr. Fleming, Patrick was troubled when he came here. He said he had an errand but that he'd wanted to see us all the same."

"What was the trouble?"

"He said it was something that he couldn't rightly talk about. He said he'd been thinking things over. That he loved Dublin now and his wee house. He was going to bring me up to see it when he bought his new van. My son can't ever leave the pub—you know the way. But Patrick said he'd bring me up even with these old legs. No steps, he said, I'd have no trouble. And then he said he had to resolve something. Some unfinished business here. It was weighing on his mind and getting in the way of his new life. He even told me, and he said not to let on to anyone in Carrigbawn, that this was why he'd left. But moving away hadn't helped him after all."

"But what did he mean?" James fairly shouted.

"I don't know. But I do know his own conscience was clean. He was honest and straight, was Patrick. Never liked shadows, as he used to call them. Couldn't stand pretending. That's why he kept to himself. He'd a good thing going here with the cottage and his pots and the grand countryside. And he kept himself clean and straight and out of the click—that's what he called it."

"Ah, the click. I know exactly what he meant," murmured James.

"Then he left, kissed me, and said he was going up to the big house. Oh, he didn't call it that. I do. And he said there might be talk, nasty talk about his friend Desmond, but that I was to take it from him that Desmond was a fine and good man and to pay no attention to the gossip I'd be hearing. Then he gave me the dog in wrapping paper and was gone."

James let her draw breath as they finished their tea. She looked at him expectantly.

"And was there any gossip?"

"No, nothing. The next thing was we heard Patrick was dead."

There it was again, thought James. Duggan had come to Carrigbawn and then he was dead. As simple as Mrs. Molloy had put it.

Full to bursting, James chose to leave his car behind in the the deserted village and walk by a circuitous route back to Oakdale Lodge. He let Mrs. Molloy's information simmer as he began the arduous but satisfying task of washing down all the woodwork of the large hall and central staircase with oil soap. The physical exertion was welcome. As he laboured, he imagined his house fully furnished, clean and decorated, with fires in every grate. He imagined the Christmas tree he would cut on his own property, the holly and the ivy that he'd hang. He imagined coming in from the Christmas midnight service cold and excited, bringing in friends to share a wassail, pouring out mulled wine and . . . He sat heavily on the middle stair.

"What service? What friends?" he said aloud. Who were these friends who'd come bustling in, full of Christmas cheer? And what service would he be attending? What would it be like, he thought for the first time, to attend church in Carrigbawn without Desmond? Would there be a new curate, a temporary rector? Someone who would come from another parish and fill in? And what of morning coffee now? Would Lamia sit in the front pew? Would Eustace and the others even attend?

For the first time since he'd come to Carrigbawn, he saw clearly that it was Lamia, not Desmond, who'd formed the focal point of the parish. At least as he'd known it. With Desmond gone, Lamia's role became ambiguous, outside the functioning of the church. Would the clique still attend if they were not also going on to her house for their weekly ritual of gossip and intrigue, socializing and wheeling and dealing? The charmed circle had been broken.

What friends would he have here? He enjoyed the company of Mrs. Molloy and the environs of the old pub far better than anyone or anything else he'd encountered in the village. And would his Dublin friends be bothered to come so far? Country weekends, maybe. But not on Christmas Eve surely. He looked around the bare cold walls, the cold stone-flagged hall. He would be cut off in Carrigbawn, as alone in his big fine house as he'd been in his bachelor flat.

Sarah was off on her third tour of the year, to the Vienna, Salzburg, and Freiburg summer music festivals. When he'd phoned her in Vienna to tell her about Desmond, she'd been so excited about her success at the first concert that he hadn't the heart to tell her. Either Vienna seemed light-years away from Carrigbawn to him, or Carrigbawn light-years away from Vienna to her, he wasn't sure which. He let it go. She'd been friendly and that had been nice. No recriminations, nor family questions, and no inquiry as to how Oakdale Lodge was shaping up.

If this was to work, he thought, then we both should be doing it. Making this her home as well as mine. Not as discouraged as he might have expected, he turned again to his task of scrubbing the stairs on his hands and knees.

James was not surprised to see the tremendous crowd at St. Killian's as he reached the churchyard. Cars had been pouring through the village for hours before the scheduled service and every available parking spot was filled. The whole of the parish was there, virtually the whole of the Catholic parish as well. Every shop in the town was closed, including the bars. The Dublin bus couldn't make the turn in the square and had to drive south for a mile out of town to turn and come back. Dignified emissaries of the hierarchy of the church were present, as were many of Lamia's Dublin and London friends. Cars with English registrations were well represented, many left parked in front of the Inn. Others were trailing slowly down from the direction of Monks Hall where, James guessed, they had stayed the night. He was impressed. To come from London on the car ferry was no quick journey. He wondered, however, why the car license plates so caught his eye and he tried to drag back an image from the fringes of his memory.

At that moment the threatened break in the two-week spell of fine weather finally came. Black-bottomed clouds tumbled menacingly over the hills and a stiff breeze blew in. Within seconds the sky was darkened and, as the downpour came, black umbrellas sprung up like ominous mushrooms in a cursed field. James plonked his hat on his wavy black hair and stood cow-like, remembering that he'd left his umbrella in the hallstand he'd recently purchased.

"So be it," he said grumpily to no one in particular.

"It's called rain, Fleming," boomed O'Brien as he moved to James's side and opened his own tattered umbrella. Tall as James was, O'Brien was taller, and from the resulting height of his umbrella a stream of water fell onto James's neck and down his collar.

"Glad to see a familiar face," said O'Brien, scanning the crowd. "What a turnout. Desmond would be mortified."

James agreed. The shy, retiring cleric would not have relished this display.

"They've heard, of course," said O'Brien with disdain in his voice.

"Heard what?" snapped James, sodden and irritable.

The line moved forward. He only hoped now that they'd get inside the church.

"That it was poison."

"What?"

"There was poison in the altar wine, man. Surely you of all people heard this."

"No I did not. I don't believe it," James snapped again.

"Don't bite my head off, Fleming. You're not in the loop, I guess you'd say. I would have called you meself but I didn't think you'd got the phone reconnected in that lodge of yours."

"Well for your information I did." James was sour, but on reflection wondered who would have called him and when. When he hadn't heard from Dr. Dunphy, James had assumed Desmond's death was from the diabetes after all. And if Dunphy had phoned him, he could easily have missed him. Over the past few days he'd run up to Dublin twice, once to oversee his clerk on some research for a forthcoming probate, and once to calm the agitated Mr. O'Connor, who claimed he'd felt death approaching in the midst of a game of golf and that his affairs were not yet in order.

"Tell me, please, what you've heard," James said more pleasantly, sticking to the important issue.

"The wine was poisoned. The amazing thing, the truly amazing thing is it might never have been found out but for Joseph."

"The doctor?"

"Yes. Whoever did the deed would never have known this. But our Dr. Dunphy has a hobby. He's a medical man all right. Retired. But he's a great gardener. Well known here, has open house in the spring . . ."

"O'Brien!" James was stern.

"Sorry. The thing is, when he saw Desmond he knew something wasn't right. Everyone, Lamia and everyone else, assumed it was the diabetes. If he hadn't spoken up, the autopsy might have missed it."

"Missed what, for Chrissake?"

"Dunphy guessed it might be poison and he requested that the police lab in Dublin test the altar wine. He'd given them a list, you see. His hobby is researching common natural poisons. Like the flowers of the lily-of-the-valley. You know, the fleur-de-lis the bloody frogs like so much."

"I take it you mean the French," said James wryly, remembering the absent wife in Paris.

"Yes. It wasn't that though. Look man, look at those dripping trees."

James glanced across the grounds at a bank of magnificent Laburnum trees he'd admired before. Their yellow blooms were hanging in profusion, weighted down now with the rainwater pouring on everything.

"Go on," said James, dreading what was coming.

"It seems you can steep those yellow blossoms. Say in wine. The poison leaches out into the liquid. Simple as that. And Dunphy knew it, and anyone else who'd ever gone to his open house in the spring. He has a huge stand of Laburnums and he'd always warn the children visiting about their poisonous properties."

"But who would do such a thing? Such a horrible thing. Why? Anyone at the altar rail that day could have been poisoned, one and all." He shivered at the malignancy behind the deed.

"They don't know. The wine bottle was there, altar wine, half full. Anyone could get into the vestry if they really tried. The church was often open for tourists and the holy alike. They think . . ."

"Who are they?"

"Now I don't know. The police maybe. Word is that perhaps it was vandalism or teenagers pulling a prank, not knowing the consequences."

"Christ, I'm sick of this!" exclaimed James, causing a few heads to turn. "Is no one responsible anymore? The man who killed Duggan, the police think he didn't mean it. The vandals who did this, they are not supposed to know what they were about. What a load of shite!"

O'Brien looked startled. "You don't believe it? You know what you're saying? That if someone did it and knew what they were doing, then it's murder."

"Of course it's murder! The celebrant always drinks the wine first! And whoever did it returned the wine to the bottle and the bottle to its place and Desmond never noticed! You think a couple of wild teenagers pulled that off?"

"Then who?"

"I don't bloody know. But as God is my witness I'll find out."

The crowd had moved into the church and James was separated from O'Brien. There were no seats left and he stood through the long, grim service, preoccupied and damp.

The eulogy was standard, the cleric not having known Desmond personally. It was only at the end that Lamia, heavily veiled, walked with dignity to the communion rail and stepped up onto the wide step of the altar.

She began hesitantly. "I had planned to say my few words at the graveside. But in view of the inclement weather the Bishop"—she nodded infinitely gracefully in his direction—"has given me permission to speak at this point in the service."

James had never seen her look more striking: tall, willowy, the heavy black clothes giving her an ageless aura and elegance. Her face was serene, but her eyes seemed wild and staring. James wondered about her state of mind.

"My husband's untimely death is a great tragedy for me personally . . . the greatest loss I will ever sustain. At first I wondered how I would have the strength to go on. But already I've come to realize that it is not I alone who have suffered this loss. You, his congregation, his flock as he used to say, have also suffered. And I thought of you as a flock without its shepherd. And now I see that his death is larger than all of us. For he was greater than we ever knew. He was unknowable to us and his passing is so disruptive that even nature weeps." She waved a thin strong hand, indicating the rain and wind beating against the stained-glass windows.

James watched as the assembled clergy shifted restively, glancing at one another. Some of the congregation, too, he noted, seemed startled at the strangeness of Lamia's words.

"Yes he is gone. But perhaps that was the intention. For now he will remain amongst us, unchanged by age or illness. Because of the manner of his death—here before you, on the altar—you, we, will never forget him.

"Michael Desmond's death is more than the death of a good man. His death is more than that of a priest. His death is the fabric of myth. And although we grieve, as nature grieves around us now, nature will restore itself. As it always does. And we too will restore ourselves."

She finished so abruptly that no one knew quite what to do. She stared for a moment at the assembled faces and they looked back, shock and confusion mingled in their expressions.

The pallbearers quickly moved to the coffin and the impasse was over.

James walked with the dispersing crowd preparing to follow the hearse to the nearby cemetery. Among the mourners, he spotted Inspector Dorsey, who'd interviewed him earlier in the week. Throughout the large crowd James saw, not only reporters he knew by sight, but other policemen studying the behaviour of the mourners. He approached the Inspector.

"I've just heard that Desmond was poisoned. Is that rumor or fact?"

"You're Fleming, the solicitor, right?" The man's eyes continued to rove over the throng.

James nodded.

"Yes, it's true. It was Dr. Dunphy and the lab who found it. Have you something to tell me?" The man looked at James shrewdly.

"Yes. Do you remember Patrick Duggan, who was murdered in Dublin some months ago? In the Liberties?"

"Yes, I remember the case."

"Did you also know that Duggan and the Reverend Desmond . . ." He paused while the policeman blessed himself as the coffin was loaded into the hearse. "Did you also know that they were friends?"

The man studied James for a full minute, expressionless. "No, I did not. But I'd like to know a lot more." He placed a hand on James's arm but James shook it off.

"Perhaps later, Dorsey. I'm going to a funeral." With that, James put his damp hat on his head and caught up with O'Brien—he did not want to be alone as he stood at the foot of the grave.

FOR SOME HOURS JAMES SAT UNOBSERVED IN HIS CAR in the circular drive outside Monks Hall. He watched as mourners of all descriptions came and went. He watched which cars remained, Eustace's among them. The time passed quickly enough though, for he used the hours to assemble his thoughts, dreadful as they were. Periodically he smoked a Gauloise, and then opened his window to let the acrid smoke out and into the endlessly drizzling rain. It had rained continuously for hours and there was no end in sight. The heavy clouds lay over the area like a pall but the air was warm and heavy. James, although stiff, was not chilled.

After dropping O'Brien at his home after the graveside service, James had driven aimlessly for some time. At the beautiful local reservoir, he looked out over the lead-gray, rain-dimpled water. Making his mind blank he allowed images to form there, and connections to be made. He'd come to an inescapable conclusion and now it remained to ask the final questions of Lamia. Her answers would complete the series of images, which had formed a narrative in his mind. It was a familiar one, he'd realized. So familiar he could have written the ending, but for Desmond's death.

He had returned home to change. There, he had telephoned a man in Dublin, a man James had paid handsomely over the years for his help and discretion. He could find out in minutes information it would take James days of going through the usual channels to locate.

But James merely needed his suspicions confirmed. When he'd got the answer back, there was no alternative but to speak with Lamia. After two more essential calls, he had headed for Monks Hall.

He fingered the folder on the front seat for the hundredth time, assuring himself it was there, touching it like a talisman.

As the last group of callers emerged in the darkening evening and went to their cars, he sat up and started his own motor. No one heeded yet another car in the dark drive, seeming to start up to leave with all the others. He hung back, allowing the others to pass him. Grateful he'd not caught Eustace's attention, he waited until every car had departed, then shut off his engine.

Taking his folder in his hand he approached the house. A weary Goretti opened the door and, recognizing him, allowed him in.

"You're the last, sir."

"I won't be long." He strode ahead into the familiar sitting room.

Lamia jumped up from her seat at the fire when she saw him.

"James, it's so late." He could see fatigue in every line of her face and body. She'd let down her guard and relaxed when everyone left and was looking haggard and worn and more than her age.

James had ordered wreaths to be sent in his name and in Sarah's and she thanked him dutifully. He waved away her comments.

She then offered him a drink and poured it herself, telling Goretti she was free to leave for home as long as she came early in the morning to clean up.

"Well, James?" She stood near the fire.

"It's all over, Lamia."

"Indeed, it was a long day."

"Yes, an endless day."

She sipped her drink, standing at the fire, but James sat down and she winced ever so slightly.

"I'm a little tired, James." The hint was obvious, but he ignored it. "Well," she said resignedly, "the service was well attended, don't you think?"

"Everything you organize is well attended, Lamia."

She stared at him, trying to see if his rudeness was deliberate. "Is there something else?"

"I want to know why you murdered your husband," he said forcefully.

Lamia moved back in surprise but instantly regained her composure. Her hand trembled only slightly as she took another sip of her brandy.

"I think you should leave, Mr. Fleming. Perhaps you are drunk, but that is no excuse for harassing a helpless woman alone in her own home."

James stood up. Angry as he was, he was still aware that he was intimidating a woman. Her black dress had drained every bit of colour from her face. Her skin looked papery and brittle.

He spoke calmly, evenly. "You know, if you hadn't given that eulogy this morning in church, I'm not sure all the pieces would have fallen into place for me."

She didn't answer, but at the change in his voice she sat down on a leather ottoman and stared into the fire.

"It was your mention of myth, you see. That single word got me going. Shall I tell you the Greek myth I have in mind?"

She shrugged, not looking at him.

"It's the famous one, Lamia, about the young man who kills his father and sleeps with his mother."

"I've read *Oedipus Rex,* Mr. Fleming. Is this a test?" Her voice was scornful.

"Ah, but you changed the ending, didn't you, Lamia? In the myth, in the play, Oedipus was allowed to live. Blinded by his own hand, he remained alive with at least the faint hope of atoning for his deed!" James was yelling now, no longer able to contain his anger. "But you couldn't allow Desmond to live, could you? I want to know why. Why, Lamia?"

"This is madness, Mr. Fleming. I ask you again to leave my house."

"All in due course, Lamia. Perhaps you'd like me to recount your revised version of the myth?" He moved around in front of her, menace in every muscle and in his tone. She didn't answer.

"Once there was an elderly rich man and a young ambitious girl. How they met I do not know, but soon there was a child. This man perhaps had not loved the ambitious girl. He did not want to live with her as his wife. But he wanted his child. He wanted a legitimate heir who could inherit his name and fortune. So he married her, and the child was born. The father would raise the son but on the condition she never see him again. The girl went away to make her own fortune, a considerable one, in London. But that wasn't enough. She wanted her son. And years later they did meet, and the woman, no longer young, lured him to her.

"That wasn't too difficult, was it, Lamia? Desmond was young, sickly, half blind, and alone in the world but for his vocation, which in itself had set him apart from the everyday world. You set your trap."

Lamia failed to react and James resumed his narrative.

"She wanted to possess him, to own him, to bind

him to her. What better way than to bind him in marriage? It all worked for a while. He had no idea the kind of woman she was. A woman of means, and a woman obsessed. In her obsession to extend her property as far as the eye could see, she poisoned the land she coveted. She manipulated all around her. And then she spread her wings into good works and philanthropy. What better way to establish her power in a country place. But bored with that in time, she had a brilliant idea, a stroke of genius. She would use her husband and his church as an attraction and make herself the centre of that circle. Aware of the artists already living in the village, but not an artist herself, she gathered them to her, working with them as she would manipulate clay. Her money, her influence, her connections, her generosity, her very personality drew them to her.

"Innocent as her child-husband was, sheltered as he was, he never thought to look around him, to see what was happening. In that, he was truly blind. He followed her lead, doing what she bid. That is, until he began to make friends of his own.

"He was lonely, and he hardly knew why. He loved his wife. She was his security, his haven. And yet the marriage was never consummated. That didn't worry her. She could find gratification elsewhere, whenever she chose it seems."

James watched Lamia but she didn't move from her seat.

"But it wasn't enough for Michael. He believed the marriage should be whole and complete and sacramental. He began to fret, his loneliness within the marriage wearing on him. He began to worry. Worry that his wife was having affairs, worry that he was not fulfilling his vows in marriage, or his role as a clergyman. Perhaps he had doubts, questions. Was he going to get an annulment, Lamia? Was that what he told you the night before he died?"

She refused to answer.

"I know he did. He talked with me last week in Dublin."

At this her head snapped up. "Dublin?"

"Yes. He was on his way to discuss an annulment with an advisor in the church hierarchy. He was quite plain with me."

"Where was this?"

"At the Shelbourne."

"I don't believe you," she began to laugh.

"Where he collapsed. The ambulance took him to Blackrock."

Lamia hesitated. "What did he tell you?"

"Enough that I am here tonight."

"And why exactly are you here, Mr. Fleming?" Her confidence was returning.

"To accuse you of the murder of your husband and the murder of Patrick Duggan."

"Mr. Fleming, you are mad. Ever since you've come here to Carrigbawn you've tried to involve us all in Duggan's death. Duggan was killed by an intruder as the police have said. There is nothing to tie me to that man since he left Carrigbawn. As to my husband, some horrible evil prank was played. Some vandals tampered with the wine. Poisoned the wine. Perhaps they had no idea how powerful a poison it was, but there it is. Another horrible accident, but accident nonetheless. This other myth, as you call it, is just that, a myth. You saw some parallels in an old story and you've drawn wild conclusions. You see some significance in my name and, presto, I am a seductress. This has nothing to do with reality." She put down her glass. "Your stupidity is even more inexcusable than your callousness. In the future, if you wish to deal with me regarding Oakdale, you will contact my solicitor." She stood up.

James had expected her to crumble under the shock of his attack. Now he tried desperately to find a chink in her armor. He thought back to the last time they'd spoken, kneeling together on the altar over Desmond's body. For a moment he was assailed by doubts. Her grief had been genuine, hardly that of a murderer. But he spoke again.

"I watched you, Lamia, on that awful morning. When you held Michael in your arms, like a pietà. You kissed him, you held him, you keened for him . . . as a mother for a child."

At this she turned away, trying to stem the flood of sobs that came quickly and as quickly subsided.

"He was my husband," she murmured through the hands that covered her mouth.

"He was your reason for living, Lamia. And now he's gone . . ."

"Enough!" she cried.

"Yes, it is enough. Why not admit it? Your life can never again return to what it was before. Do you really believe that you can pick up and go on, running the gallery, holding coffee hours? Holding parties and showings? Sleeping with Eustace?"

"Stop it! It will take time, but I can get it all back . . ."

"No. No you won't. Because every day of the rest of your life you will see Michael's face, feel the weight of his body in your arms. Do you think you can make love without remembering that? Do you think that you can step foot in that church one more time and not remember what you caused to happen there . . . ?"

"I did it today," she said triumphantly.

"Ah, yes, but Michael was still there. His presence filled that church today. It won't ever again."

"I can go back to London . . ."

"To what? You never married all these years. Why not? There was a reason. And you have no family. You have no children! Any longer."

It was his best shot. James knew that he was dealing with a woman who had killed at least twice. Yet she showed no remorse. He knew how well she'd carried on her life after killing Duggan. His only hope was to reach her through Desmond.

"But you had a child, didn't you? And you watched that child grow over the years, without a mother, alone, sick. You never had another child. You wanted that child, you wanted Michael!"

"All right, all right." She raised her voice, close to hysteria in her obvious fatigue. "It's true. Part of what you say is true. I wanted Michael, for years and years and years. When I found out I was pregnant and still not married, my own mother disowned me. Banned me from this very house. She had no other family except me, and yet she cut me off as though I were dead. It didn't matter when I did get married. She said the neighbours would talk when they saw the baby was born only a couple of months later. In all those years we never spoke. She was dead to me, as I to her. Michael's father wanted no part of me. He said I had trapped him for his money with the baby, and he'd show me. I wouldn't get the money or the baby. He swore I could never have the baby. My mother would give me nothing. My husband would give me nothing. But I had a plan.

"So I went to London, where the economy was booming. I got a position in an old firm of stockbrokers and I worked hard. I knew nobody and work became my life. And I had ability. Before long I was bonded, and in time I became a broker in my own right. The client list I built then I still manage. I went from forty pounds a paycheck to four hundred to thousands. Not overnight, mind you. I worked long and hard and I loved it." Her eyes shone at the memory of her success. "But always it was to have enough money to go back, back to Dublin and get Michael. Money would make that happen. . . ."

"You had to prove something to his father?"

"I had to show him I had more money than he did, that I was his equal, if not his superior. I would prove I could take care of Michael and hold my head up. But he wouldn't listen. We spoke on the phone when he'd take my calls. He said he'd told Michael I was dead. That the child was frail and sickly, that the shock of learning about me would kill him. He wanted to know then how a sick, frail child would fit in with my wonderful new life in London.

"And I listened. I had always listened to him, I have to admit. But this time I listened because it suited me. I had a gorgeous flat, men when I wanted them, holidays abroad, nightlife. At that time a whining child did not suit me. But . . ."

"But . . ."

"I still worked with him as my goal. Perhaps I thought he'd come to me when he was older, stronger, whatever. Years passed and I was more settled. Men kept pestering me to marry, not knowing of course that I already was. Not that I was interested in marriage. I'd enough of that. No man would control me the way Michael's father had! But I'd suddenly long to see Michael. I'd come over secretly and watch and wait. I used to see him when his nanny took him for walks on good days. And then he went away to school. Twice I managed to visit that school, on parents' night. What a joke! I saw him once in a play. He was twelve or fourteen, just on the threshold of becoming a man. It thrilled me to see him so tall and handsome despite the glasses. You know, when we married I had him checked to see if he could wear contacts but his disability was too great . . ."

She fingered the ornaments on the mantel, lost in thought, as James shook his head, amazed at her calm demeanor.

"Then my mother died. When the dust settled I came back here to Carrigbawn to take what was rightfully mine. All those years in exile I had pictured that triumphant day. To come back here and show Carrigbawn what I could do, what I was capable of. So many nights I had lain in bed in London, planning how I'd put paid to those neighbours my mother had been so worried about. And over the years I've managed to buy nearly every piece of land that abuts this property, and more. So much for neighbours." She thrust back her narrow shoulders in a gesture of pride.

"It kept me busy. And I'd kept track of Michael. It was easy once I was back in Ireland. I did it through lawyers mostly. Of course I knew when his father died, from the financial pages. And that very weekend I held my first soiree here in the house. I'd decided to put Carrigbawn on the map. Take what was here and mold it into something unique, a rival for the Left Bank or Greenwich Village, an artists' colony with one great advantage . . ."

"Which was?"

"Me!" She laughed as she faced him.

"Behind the scenes?"

"Exactly. Only six years and look what I've set in motion. There's life here, and art . . ."

James couldn't take it. "Your little community? Right? Your favourite word. You wanted to control it all," shouted James. "Even down to who was accepted or not. Like Fred . . ."

"Fred was a mistake, but the owners were elderly and refused my offer to buy Oakdale. They knew my mother, you see. Thought I was a bad seed. That's a direct quote I might add."

How right they were, thought James.

"But it wasn't enough?"

"No, I enjoyed the power my money bestowed, but I was still not accepted. They'd take my money, they'd eat my food, but I wasn't a part of things. By then I knew Michael was finished with his theological studies. It was so easy, a call here and there, a generous donation now and then, and I was kept informed of his career . . ."

"That's when you went to hear him preach?"

"Yes, and I was struck by his intelligence. It made me proud to think he'd inherited my native intelligence, if not my ambition. We'd had a long series of temporary rectors here at St. Killian's and so the idea presented itself to me. Michael could come here and forever . . ."

"Stay under your watchful eye! My God, Lamia, why didn't you leave it at that?" That would have been bizarre enough, he wanted to add.

"I did initially." She paused, for once seeming reflective. "It was so simple. He was so simple. So trusting. We spent a lot of time together and I wanted more, more . . ." She paused again, for a long time, and James was afraid she'd finished.

"Then why marry him?"

"Because then, don't you see, he would be mine, at last, once and for all. All mine. No other woman could ever have him then. No other wife. And then I could make up for all those lost years, when he had been so alone. He used to speak of those days, of his lonely childhood. The empty holidays, the mean-spirited Christmas days. He had never fit in. He always felt something was missing. And he was a child still, still young enough that I could love him, take care of him, manage his career, mold him . . ."

"Manipulate him, unman him! Lamia, you kept him frozen in an endless adolescence. That's what you did for him. All to serve your own twisted maternal desires. More than that, your own thirst for power!"

"How dare you?"

"You babied him, with his illness, his eyesight, his dependence on you. You used all that to keep him away from his normal parish work. You influenced his sermons, you used him to attract a following—for yourself. You forced him to play a role he didn't even understand. And you prevented him from making friends with men and women his own age. You came between him and Duggan, his only real friend here in Carrigbawn!"

"Duggan! A trumped up little potter. A peasant! What could he offer Michael? He came from nothing. *God,* he lived in a pub and served at the bar! What could he offer someone as pure and rare and special as Michael?"

"Friendship, Lamia. Friendship for a lonely man you claim you cared for."

"He was coming between us, I tell you, deliberately. Taking Michael off on walks, talking of who knows what. I set out to rid Michael of Duggan. He owed me, you see, for the cottage. I'd made a mistake. I'd let him have the cottage because I thought that would keep him busy at his petty little pursuits. But he was too close to the house, to Michael. And then I flirted with him. He was so unsophisticated that he was insulted, can you imagine? Told me he'd never betray Michael. Told me that I was too old . . ."

"Not his type, Lamia?" sneered James.

"A peasant like that could never understand someone like me."

"But he understood Michael. He was his friend, and not yours. So you drove him away."

"It doesn't matter now. He left, and now he's dead."

"Ah, but it does matter. I know why he left."

"No you don't."

"I know this much. I know he discovered your terrible secret. I know he left Carrigbawn because he didn't want to destroy Michael."

"You don't know that . . ." she repeated more loudly.

James withdrew Duggan's letter from the folder and waved it tantalizingly.

"A letter to Peru," he said simply.

Her reaction was electric. She lunged at him, tore the letter from his grasp, and tossed it triumphantly on the fire. Breathless, she turned on him.

"You know nothing."

His suspicions confirmed, James pressed home his point. "I know Duggan came to you here some months after he'd moved to Dublin. He couldn't live with what he knew about you and Michael. I imagine that he pleaded with you, didn't he?" He waited but she only stared, breathing hard. "He pleaded with you to be the one to tell Michael. To leave Michael some dignity. To allow him to start again somewhere else, a new life. A healthy life . . ."

"Why would he? What could he possibly have on me?"

"I tell you, he threatened to go to Michael, Lamia, and tell him what he knew, unless you told him yourself. Duggan was a simple, straightforward man. He wanted no part of Carrigbawn and all its facade, its cliques . . ."

"To which you aspired?" Lamia sneered.

"He wanted to put all that behind him, all the deceit he'd encountered. He wanted to do the right thing for everyone, not least of all, for his own conscience. And it cost him his life!"

"I don't know what you're talking about. Get out, or I'll call the police."

"I doubt that, Lamia. I'm not leaving until this is settled."

"What?"

"You killed Duggan to keep him quiet. You killed him to keep your secret safe. Michael's father, your husband, was dead. Your mother was dead. You were in charge of all you surveyed. Only Duggan had found you out. Duggan would ruin you, your marriage, your standing in this bloody community! But Duggan didn't care about you, Lamia. He cared about his friend who'd confided his marital troubles to him."

"That was a betrayal!" she spat. "How could Michael do such a thing to me? But I hardly killed Duggan to keep that quiet. All married couples have troubles. He could know nothing, surmise nothing."

"You're right there. Until he had proof. He had an artist's eye, and a friend's eye."

"Eyes, eyes! You're raving, Fleming."

"Duggan had a photograph, a photograph of Michael as a young child . . ."

James watched as Lamia grew even paler, her breath coming in short gasps. Her eyes slid to the pictures on the piano and on the wall and back again.

"He had a photo and he realized that it was no accident you had it in your possession. He got the photo enlarged . . ."

Lamia started towards the piano.

"Pity he didn't bring it with him that day . . . to show you. He'd kept it safe from you though . . ."

"He mentioned no picture. He made his wild accusations and I threw him out of the house. He had the grace to go, I might add.''

She moved suddenly, rushing to the framed colour picture on the wall. Smashing the glass on the piano, she tore at the matting, the cardboard surround. She threw the paper to the floor and tore up the colour picture in a wild frenzy.

"Where is it? Where is it? Michael told me he put that photo back!" she screamed at James.

"What are you searching for?" James leaned over the sofa and drew the enlargement from the folder, holding it high. She moved towards him and then stopped.

James watched as she turned away and poured another brandy. She drank it, quietly, assessing her position.

"Show me," she said at last.

James handed her the picture.

"If you're suggesting this is Michael as a child," her voice trembled and with great effort she calmed it, "then it could be so. But to have a photo of one's husband as a child is of no consequence."

"But *you* had it, not Michael."

"You can't prove that. The only one who could is dead."

"Yes. You buried him today. Dead and buried— by your own hand."

James came around and stood in front of her, wanting to see her expression.

"Killed by you, Lamia, his wife . . . his mother . . ." he accused.

She sat back as if struck.

Unlike Lamia, James had heard the car on the gravel drive. He heard, too, the click of the front door.

He lowered his voice.

"It's over, Lamia."

"The picture proves nothing."

"You're wrong. Duggan knew it was a picture of Michael, knew in his heart, knew with his artist's eye, as I said. He had the photo enlarged and he kept it, studying it, I imagine. He chose not to say anything about it to Michael until he'd spoken to you about what he suspected. Until he knew from you the reason why you had that photo. He knew Michael and he knew you, Lamia. And he put the pieces together. But I . . . I needed proof."

"There's nothing there. A child on Stephen's Green? You can prove nothing. You think you can prove something, but there are no witnesses here to repeat what I've admitted to you. I'll deny everything I've said today if you dare to repeat it. An hysterical, grieving widow, intimidated by a shrewd solicitor. Who would believe your story? Who would want to? And Duggan. Why would I kill him, and how?" She laughed, at ease again, and he saw her small white even teeth.

He paused for his final assault. Lamia watched him carefully. "The old woman collecting goods for the poor?" he asked in a knowing voice. "Does that ring a bell? Easy enough for you to take some clothes from your so-called parish charitable work. To dress up as an old woman begging on the streets of Dublin . . ."

"Can you get nothing right? I was no beggar. Far from it." Lamia spoke proudly. "I was a refined round-shouldered old woman, a long-time member of Adam and Eve's parish. Who doesn't know that Catholic church in that part of Dublin! No, I didn't beg for myself. I begged for the poor. And I was convincing. People gave me tins of food, even coins and pound notes from their purses and jars and pockets. Old people who needed it more than I . . ." She laughed strangely. "I was good. Even Duggan didn't know me at first, the fool. He invited me in. And as he shut the door I stood up straight, and he actually jumped back."

"So even Duggan didn't recognize you?" goaded James.

"Oh, I took him off his guard, all right. That was the beauty of it. Once he knew it was I, he asked me to sit down. He thought I'd come to talk about Michael. I let him believe what he wanted. He offered me tea. And I accepted. He turned to go into the kitchen."

"So you had gone to talk . . ."

"Of course not."

"You brought a weapon?" James was noticeably skeptical.

"You simpleton. I'd been in his studio here countless times. I knew he'd be surrounded with his miserable clay jugs and planters and piss pots! He turned away. I caught up one of the largest planters from the floor. It was heavy but I had the strength. There was a terrible shattering sound. I believed then and since it was his skull—shattering."

James recoiled at the image but kept to his purpose. "So when he was dead, you had time to search the little house. Pity you didn't find the photo, wasn't it? But you found letters, letters from Father Tom in Peru. And from those you suspected Duggan had confided in the priest just because he was so far away from Carrigbawn. Duggan had told you about Father Tom, hadn't he, Lamia?"

"Yes. He even thought that priest had something in common with my Michael. But then, when he came here to Monks Hall after he'd moved to Dublin, he told me he'd written to him, told me he needed spiritual guidance." Lamia's sarcasm was scathing.

"You mean," said James carefully, "Duggan wrote to Father Tom, wrote the letter you think you just destroyed. It was a hand-written copy, Lamia. I'd hardly jeopardize the original."

She faced James down. "No matter. And what if he had that photo of Michael? It—it proves nothing!" Lamia's frustration was rising.

"You overlooked something, Lamia, because it was so familiar to you. It was part of your life, like furniture, and so you paid it no heed . . ."

"What are you talking about?"

"It's the car in the background of the photo. Your own car, Lamia. An English car. You brought it over on the ferry when you came to spy on your son. The plate on the rear is plain in the enlargement. The numbers easy to trace if you know how. Even after so many years, your registration was listed on the computer in London, as was a well-established address. Your address, Lamia. It is your car in the photo of that startled sickly little boy, the photo you kept all these years, even after you married that same poor boy, your own son!"

Lamia's brandy glass dropped to the floor. But James would tolerate no interruption now.

"Anyone who knew Michael well, would know that he could not live with the knowledge of what he'd done. He was unworldly, yes. But he was a moral man, conscious of his role as a clergyman in *his* community, not yours. He would have divorced you, Lamia, he would have had this travesty of a marriage annulled. Perhaps, scrupulous as he was, he would have wanted to confess his sins—publicly. You would have been ruined and you knew it. Duggan suspected you'd married your own son, so you killed him. Michael suspected or knew in his last hours—only you can tell us that—and you killed him for it. To keep your secret. You even killed a man thousands of miles away from this miserable place, on the mere suggestion that he might have known something of your secret. Three innocent men, Lamia, three lives!''

At that moment the door opened, revealing Inspector Dorsey standing hesitantly there.

"Come in, Inspector." James stood back.

Lamia whirled around to see the policeman enter her elegant sitting room, followed by a man in priestly clothes, Goretti standing behind both.

"You know Inspector Dorsey," said James. "And this is Father Tom Mullen, Patrick Duggan's friend and the priest you hoped to have murdered in Peru!"

Lamia leapt to her feet. James, expecting her to flee, rushed towards her. But instead she swayed and nearly fainted in his arms. A spasm of hatred crossed her gray, lined face.

He sat her down on the sofa and poured out another brandy, handing it to her.

"It's over, Lamia," he whispered. "Be glad . . ."

"I am glad," she said faintly. "Now I must phone for my lawyer." She looked up at him sharply and studied his face, her own expression changing yet again.

"Lawyers," she said at last, her old manner returning. "I knew you were trouble when you first came here. An outsider, an interloper. I'd thought to bind you to me. It was so obvious you craved a sense of belonging." She sneered at him with disdain. "You wanted to be part of what I had created—yes, a part of my creation. Do you think I would have let you buy Oakdale if Sarah didn't marry you? You had nothing to offer the likes of us!"

She stood up, facing him, oblivious of the others. "But we interested you, didn't we? Our rich, full, rounded lives. You wanted all that. It was obvious.

You wanted it all, the way you want Sarah Gallagher
. . . You even wanted me!"

James felt the blood rush to his head. Was it true?
Hadn't he been attracted to her sinuous beauty, her
charm?

"Never," he breathed at her.

"I should have courted you just a little bit longer.
You were so open to seduction. A little more time
and I would have had you, you would have been part
of my little community . . ." She laughed, her eyes
glittering.

"Never," James repeated.

"Don't be so sure."

She turned to Dorsey, ignoring Tom. "Inspector,"
she smiled. "I'm glad you're here. This man has
made serious unfounded accusations for which he has
no proof. He may well try to tell you that I confessed." Her tone was sarcastic now. She glanced
dismissively at James. "Confessed? Confession, Mr.
Fleming, is for the weak. Proof is needed. And you
have no proof, no witnesses, no fingerprints. Nothing
but isolated deaths, accidents, which you have
strained to link together. Strained, Inspector Dorsey,
to manipulate and confuse a bereaved woman." She
straightened her posture. "I am a woman of means,
with many friends."

"Indeed you are, Mrs. Desmond. But there is the
matter of the photograph . . ." Dorsey began mildly
enough.

"Speak no more to me of photographs. A
coincidence."

"And then there's the matter of a transfer of
funds," said Dorsey. "From one of your London
accounts."

"What of it?" she faltered.

"To a certain bank in Peru?"

"What of it, I asked you? I am in the money business. Transfers of funds are routine to me."

"Yes," Dorsey answered carefully. "They may indeed be routine to you. But are you also in the habit of transferring funds to a man who's been arrested for murder?"

# 20

"WHAT DO YOU THINK, JAMES?" QUERIED MATT as they sat companionably on an old weathered iron bench on the lawn of Oakdale Lodge.

"I think my mind's made up," James said at last, his elbows on his knees, his hands hanging loosely in front of him.

Matt studied the trees above them, in their full summer growth, blue sky and soft mountainy clouds passing overhead.

"It's as beautiful as you described," Matt said softly. "Dorothy and I and the kids have all had a great weekend." He looked at his four young children gambolling on the spacious lawn at the side of Oakdale Lodge. He watched his wife approach in a long flowered cotton dress, bearing a tray set with beer and lemonade, glasses, and fairy cakes. She set the tray and a small wrapped parcel on the grass and sat down.

"It's all like a Renoir painting," Matt murmured. "Nothing can beat Ireland on a sunny day." He laughed, poking James in the ribs.

"This artistic bent is out of character, Matt," said James, groaning theatrically.

"We've had a great visit, James," added Dorothy, aware that for the whole of the long August bank-holiday weekend James had barely spoken about the house. And now the Monday was drawing to its inevitable close. It would be time for all of them to leave, to return to Dublin, to jobs and commitments.

James smiled fondly at Dorothy as he took a glass from her.

"Have you spoken to Sarah, James?" she asked.

"Yes, actually I phoned her at the villa in Italy. She's working with her maestro on some new pieces. I'd like to meet that bastard some day. She tells me he's as old as the hills, but I have me doubts!" He laughed at himself.

"And what did she say?" Dorothy persisted.

"There's to be a tour in the autumn. America, I think she said." He shrugged.

Dorothy and Matt eyed each other.

"What of the house, then?"

"The house? Well . . . I asked her that. She said the house was fine if *I* liked it, and that it's too far from Dublin! I ask you. My mother has said much the same thing."

"Giving you at least one good reason for staying here in Carrigbawn then!" roared Matt, who'd known Mrs. Fleming for years. Dorothy silenced him with a wifely dirty look. Taking up the parcel she'd brought from the house, she handed it to James.

"Why don't you open it, James? It's been on the hall table since Friday and frankly I'm curious."

James undid the brown paper and string, noting as he did so the Dublin postmark. Unfolding the inner wrapping, he whistled softly.

"What is it?" Dorothy asked.

In answer James held out the simple charming figure of the yellow dog.

Looking at the enclosed letter, he spoke quietly. "It's from Father Tom. He posted it from the airport on his way back to Peru. He says the yellow dog speaks for itself, and that he hopes I will accept it as a housewarming present. I will, of course," he said, looking up at last, "but it won't be warming this particular house." He gently wrapped the yellow dog in its paper, thinking as he did so of the many lives Patrick Duggan had touched.

"Oh, James," Dorothy spoke even more softly. "What do you want?"

"I'll tell you what I *wanted,* shall I?" James's tone was suddenly bitter. He drew in his breath. "I wanted to buy this house, do it up, marry Sarah, have my friends to visit. Fill the bedrooms with children as pretty as your own. Give up my law practice, grow potatoes, tend the orchard, make cider, ride steam trains—not necessarily in that order." He sighed. "And when I was old I'd sit and listen to the bees hum among the flowers."

He stood up and stretched restlessly as he saw his mother approaching slowly from the back garden, a gardener's hat planted firmly on her head. He turned back to his oldest friends.

"And now I'll tell you what I'm going to do." He paused again, looking at their expectant faces, a look of fleeting sadness passing across his handsome features.

"I'll break my lease with Lamia, pack up my belongings, and be shut of Carrigbawn forever. And if any one of you mentions Peru or pottery or Keats's poetry to me ever again, there'll be one less Christmas card for you to send."

And escaping the smiles of his triumphant mother bearing slips of plants from Oakdale for reestablishment in her own garden, he ran lightly off to join Matt's pretty babies in a game of toddler catch.